THE SALTERGATE PSALTER

THE SALTERGATE PSALTER

CHRIS NICKSON

3568898

For Shonaleigh and Simon of Dronfield,
the couple who have all the best stories.

Cover photograph: © iStockphoto.com

First published 2015

The Mystery Press is an imprint of The History Press
The Mill, Brimscombe Port
Stroud, Gloucestershire, GL5 2QG
www.thehistorypress.co.uk

British Library Cataloguing in Publication Data.
A catalogue record for this book is available from the British Library.

ISBN 978 0 7509 6485 2

Typesetting and origination by The History Press
Printed in Great Britain

CHAPTER ONE

In the late May light he walked home along the dusty road. The old leather bag of tools slapped against his thigh with every step. His muscles ached from a long day's work, but John the Carpenter felt content.

The job at the farm in Newbold was going well. A barn to complete, another four weeks of steady money, fourpence and a gallon of weak ale each day for his labours. At home his wife, Katherine, was waiting. They'd been wed during the winter, standing in the church porch while the snow fluttered down outside. A few words from the priest and it was done, then they walked back through a white Chesterfield to the house on Saltergate that would be their home.

Now the air was heavy with the smell of wild flowers, their bright colours dotting the copses and the hedgerows. The scent of honeysuckle caught his nostrils. He was happy, he thought. For the first time since he was a child, he believed he had a place where he belonged.

He glanced up and saw the tower of St Mary's, the timbers of the spire rising higher and higher. It would be complete in just a few weeks and visible for miles around. It was work he could do quite easily, but there'd be nothing there for him. Not after last year.

Still, this was better. He took what carpentry work came along, big jobs or small. It was enough to get by. In the autumn of the year before he'd been offered the steward-ship of a manor. A steward. A man of rank and position; how proud his father would have been. And yet … He'd thought long and hard about it, discussed it with Katherine and with Dame Martha, the widow woman who owned the house where he lodged before his marriage. In the end he'd turned it down, with his gratitude to Coroner de Harville for the offer.

In his heart he knew it was the right decision. What did he understand about farms, of crops and cows? He'd spent his whole life working with wood. He could feel the shape in a piece of lumber and bring it out with his hands. It was what he could do well. It was the thing he'd been born to do, his gift from God.

Since his refusal of the steward's position the coroner had barely spoken to him, snubbing him when they passed on the High Street or on Saturdays in the market square. Let him be, John thought. The man had his own troubles, his wife still not recovered after the difficult birth of a son, according to all the gossip of the goodwives.

A cart passed, heading away from the town, and he paused to exchange greetings with the driver, then scooped up water from a stream and drank. It had been a warm, dry spring, and he was grateful: more time to earn money.

Back in March he'd begun cutting and shaping the timbers for the barn, choosing aged, good oak. It was a long, slow task, day after day with the saw and adze. He'd finally drilled and pegged the beams together, then put them up at the end of April, with the help of Katherine's younger brother, Walter.

In the early evening, Chesterfield was quiet. The traffic of the day had passed. A pair of young girls hurried by, heads together as they spoke quickly. Noise came from the houses, but it seemed distant, muted and drowsy. A bee droned close to his head, then hummed away, out of sight.

He stood in front of their house on Saltergate. It still needed a little work, a patch of limewash to be replaced, a shutter to be re-hung in one of the windows. Nothing immediate; there'd be time for that later in the year, after his paid work was finished. Satisfied, he lifted the latch and walked in, past the screens and into the hall. Katherine had put fresh rushes on the floor, sprinkled with thyme that released its smell as he walked over them.

Her young sisters, Janette and Eleanor, were perched on the settle, one on either side of Dame Martha as she told them a story, the tale of an outlaw who only stole from the rich and gave what he took to the poor. They were listening, rapt, not even noticing as he passed.

Martha smiled and winked, never pausing in her words. He grinned at her and walked through to the buttery.

Katherine stood with her back to him, concentrating on stirring something in a bowl. Quietly, he crept up, sliding his arms around her waist and pulling her close to him.

'John,' she warned him with a gasp. But she didn't resist, leaning her head back against his shoulder and giving a small sigh. 'I didn't know when you'd be back.'

It was true enough. As the days lengthened, he often worked until dusk had passed.

'I missed you,' he said, and she turned to kiss him. Sometimes, when he looked into her eyes, it was difficult to believe she was his wife, that this wasn't some long, beautiful dream. Her lips tasted of cream; a tiny spatter of it remained on her cheek.

'Martha came to see the girls so I asked her to stay for supper.'

That was the reason the old woman always gave, but he knew it was really to spend time with all of them. Somehow or other, she'd become a part of their family, welcome and wanted in this house. Katherine's own mother had died the year before, her passing a blessing after her mind had gone. And his parents … his mother buried when he was young, and his father one of so many taken by the Great Pestilence, the leather satchel of tools all he had to leave.

'Where's Walter?'

'He's still out delivering messages.' It was how her brother earned most of his money, delivering things and passing word around the town. She pulled back until he was at arm's length, his hands still on her shoulders.

'What is it?' he asked.

'The coroner was here after dinner. He wants to see you.'

He grimaced; whatever de Harville needed, it wasn't good news. And after dinner? That was more than eight hours ago. The man would be waiting impatiently. The previous autumn John had helped solve a killing. He'd had no choice; he was still new in Chesterfield, a suspect in the murder himself. Finding the murderer had been the only way to clear his name. They'd invited the coroner to witness their marriage. He never came, but his clerk, Brother Robert, had slipped away to say a blessing over them.

And now de Harville was back with his demands.

'Did he say what he needed?' John asked warily.

A strand of dark hair had escaped from her veil. He brushed it back gently with his fingertips.

'Old Master Timothy has died. That was the talk at the market this morning. They've raised the hue and cry for his servant.'

Timothy only lived a hundred yards away, in a grand house at the top end of Saltergate, a beautifully constructed building John admired for its jetting upper storey. But he'd never seen the man who owned it. People said Timothy been on the earth for eighty summers, surviving the plague and the famine many years before. He was supposed to be so frail that he could barely walk around his grand house.

The servant was the only one who ever came out of the front door. He was no young man either, the skin on his hands mottled with the dark spots of age, not a hair left on his head. But he carried himself erect and proud, as if he was happy to serve such a master. Nicholas; he recalled the man's name. He didn't seem the type to kill and run off.

'Don't worry,' he told Katherine. 'It'll be fine. He probably only wants to annoy me.' He didn't believe it, but saying the words lightened his mood. He placed a hand over her belly. A small life was quickening there. She'd told him the week before, when she was far enough along to feel certain that the child wouldn't vanish in a clout of blood. The only other person who knew was Martha, who'd beamed with delight when she was asked to be the baby's godmother. 'I won't let him take all my time. I promise,' he said.

'Make sure he doesn't.' Her eyes flashed. Marriage hadn't dulled her spark, and he was grateful for that. During her mother's illness she'd run the house, fiercely protecting her family. Katherine was no scold, but she expected as much of others as she gave of herself. A few times he'd felt the sharp edge of her tongue when he'd been thoughtless. But making up after had been an even greater pleasure.

'I will.'

'And please, John, keep Walter out of things.'

'If I can.' It was the only answer he could give. Walter had helped him before, and the coroner knew it. If the man expected it … He looked at her helplessly. She smiled and stroked his cheek.

'Try, please.'

He squeezed her hand and put his arms around her. He knew what she meant. He was a man with responsibilities now. And more on the way. He kissed her tenderly.

John placed his bag gently on the floor, out of the way so young feet wouldn't trip over it. Before he'd left the job he'd cleaned and oiled all his tools, the way he did every day. They were a part of him, they'd served his father well, and with God's good grace he'd be able to pass them to his own son, if he had the gift of working with wood.

He kissed his wife again, wiped the smudge of cream from her face, and walked down to the High Street.

The coroner's house faced on to the market square, set at the back of a small yard with a stable to the side. He knocked on the door, waiting until a servant showed him through to where de Harville sat at his table, dictating notes to old Brother Robert, his clerk.

The coroner finished his sentence before looking up. His face had grown leaner and harder in the last few months, leaving him looking careworn and troubled. His fair hair was even more pale, his eyes colder.

'About time, Carpenter. I've been waiting all day. I have a job for you.'

John stared at him.

'I'm sorry, Master. People have ordered my services until the autumn.' Whatever the task, he didn't want it. He had his real work to do. If God smiled, perhaps the coroner would have some pity.

De Harville's expression didn't change. In the heat he'd stripped to his linen shirt, hose and boots, a thin green and yellow surcote tossed carelessly over a stool in the corner.

'If I want you to do something, you'll do it, Carpenter,' he said bluntly. He picked up a knife lying on the table and stabbed the point hard into the wood. 'You understand? I'm the King's Coroner in this town.'

It was a battle he'd never had a hope of winning. He'd put up his small resistance, for whatever it was worth.

'As long as you pay me,' John said.

De Harville put his head back and roared with laughter. It was an ugly scourge of a sound.

'You hear that, Brother? He thinks he can make demands.'

The monk kept his head lowered, his gaze fixed on the parchment in front of him.

'King's Coroner or not, Master, I need fourpence a day and my ale.' If he had to do it, he'd be damned if he was going to lose money on this.

'Done,' de Harville agreed quickly. 'Make a note of that so we can claim it later.' He looked at John and shook his head. 'You should have asked for more. The crown would have paid. Too late now. Be here first thing in the morning. We can let Timothy sit overnight. No one can do him any more harm now, anyway.'

CHAPTER TWO

John was up before first light, slipping out of the room quietly, leaving Katherine and the girls asleep up in the solar. He could hear Walter moving around in the buttery, preparing his food for the day. Bread, some cheese.

'Can I come with you?' he asked as John entered, yawning.

'Not this morning,' he answered kindly. The lad had helped him in the past, and even saved his life once. But he'd do what Katherine wanted, as long as it was in his power.

'Why, John?' Walter was smiling as he asked the question. He'd grown tall during the winter, bigger than his sister now although he was a few years younger. His dark hair was wild, his face so open it showed all his thoughts. The lad was still thin, not much more than a stick, but quick on his feet as he delivered messages around town. No one knew Chesterfield better. People thought the lad had turned simple after a blow on the head when he was young; in truth, he was anything but. Quick to learn and eager to please, he might stumble over words, but there was nothing wrong with his mind.

'De Harville just wants me for now.' He put a hand on the lad's shoulder. 'Don't worry, I'll need you soon enough.' He hoped that wasn't true.

But it was enough to make Walter smile.

'I'm glad, John.'

For some reason the boy looked up to him. He was always eager to help, the way he had on the barn in Newbold and other jobs that needed a second person. John had tried to teach him carpentry and he'd mastered the basics. But no matter how willing, he didn't have the natural feel for it.

He liked Walter's company. On Sunday afternoons, as the church bell faded into memory, they'd often walk in the country, talking, discovering things. The lad had a sharp eye, he could identify the birds and the animals, where to find them and how to watch them unseen.

'Stop,' he whispered when they'd been out one day, halting John with a hand over his chest. 'There.' Slowly, he raised a hand and pointed. It took a while, but after a few moments John had been able to make out the stag in the trees, almost hidden in the branches. Yet Walter had spotted it straight away.

• • •

The coroner led the way through to the top of Saltergate. It was early, the sun barely risen, still a breath of coolness on the land.

John lagged behind, strolling beside Brother Robert. The old monk was limping, a small portable desk with its quills and parchment hanging from a strap on his shoulder.

'How are you, Brother?' He nodded at the coroner. 'He won't let you go back to the monastery yet?'

Robert shook his head. 'He tells me I'm too valuable. I keep saying that he needs someone younger to keep pace with him, but he still won't let me leave. With his wife ill, he's prickly all the time.' He gave a pointed glance. 'I'd advise you not to test him, John.'

'But the other way round …?' He smiled.

'Power does what it likes, you know that.'

'How's the child?'

'Strong and healthy, praise God. He's with the wet nurse.' Robert's eyes twinkled. He paused before adding, 'You'll be a father yourself, I believe.'

'What?' John stared in surprise. 'How did you know?'

'I've seen Dame Katherine,' Robert said gently. 'The glow on her face tells its own story.'

For a moment he was nonplussed, unsure what to say. Finally he just smiled and nodded.

'October, she says. Pray it's a safe birth for mother and child.'

'I will,' the monk assured him. 'Don't you worry about that.'

The coroner was waiting outside the house. The building looked as if it needed some work, as if it has been neglected too long.

'I don't have all day to spend here,' he said sharply. 'Old women move faster than you two.'

De Harville brought out a key and unlocked the door. Inside, the shutters were closed tight, just a little light coming through the gaps. The hall smelt of neglect and the sweet stink of death. John blinked, letting his eyes adjust to the gloom before he moved.

A rich man's house, that was certain. A long table, a settle of good, carved oak, and a pair of fine tapestries hanging on the walls.

'Up in the solar,' the coroner said, and they climbed the stairs.

Here the shutters had been thrown back, showing a man propped up in a bed, a pillow behind him. The smell of putre-faction was stronger in the room; John held his breath and put a hand over his mouth as he approached the corpse. Maggots were already doing their work around the mouth, nose and eyes. Flies buzzed relentlessly. He swept them away, but as soon as his hand passed they returned. Brother Robert stood with his hands together and eyes closed, lips moving as he silently said prayers for the dead.

Timothy's eyes stared sightlessly. Old hands rested on the blanket, the flesh wrinkled, dappled and gnarled by time. A full head of white hair, his linen shirt so ancient it had yellowed.

But there was no sign of violence. He looked as though he'd died in his sleep. John stepped back, still staring at the body. Then he turned to the coroner.

'It looks like he died naturally.'

'I agree,' de Harville nodded. 'But if he did, why would his servant flee? Tell me that, Carpenter.'

All John could do was shake his head. He glanced around the solar. A glazed window, the catch closed. A small chest for clothes stood in the corner, a night pot on the floor, still partly filled.

In spite of the heat, there was a thick cover on the bed, a sheet and heavy, rough blanket. Not too unusual, he thought; old bones loved the warmth and loathed the chill. He approached Timothy's body again. Pulling back the covers revealed little. A man's thin legs, most of the hair gone from them, the flesh very pale. Tenderly, he lifted the head from a pillow made of soft down.

His fingers could feel it immediately. A lump at the back of the skull. John's fingers parted the hair, concentrating as he examined, working his way along slowly. It must have been a heavy blow. The skin wasn't broken, but it had certainly been enough to kill an old man.

He stood back once more, thinking rapidly. The position of the blow … Timothy couldn't have been sitting in bed at the time. Someone had taken the time to arrange him there, to try and make it look as if age had taken him.

'Well?' the coroner demanded.

'Someone murdered him,' John said finally. He began to walk around the solar, searching for the weapon. But there was nothing likely in the sparse room. 'How did you even discover he was dead?' he wondered.

'Timothy owned three houses in Chesterfield,' Robert replied. 'One of his tenants came to see him. When no one answered the door, he tried the handle. It wasn't locked. He came up here. As soon as he saw Timothy he called for the Master–' he nodded at de Harville '–and we arrived and pronounced him dead. When the servant didn't return, we raised the hue and cry.'

Simple enough, John thought, and obvious.

'How long had the servant been with him?'

'Since I was a boy, at least,' de Harville snapped. 'God's balls, Carpenter, the man must have killed him and run off. Anyone can see that.'

'But why now? If he'd been here for years …'

'Who knows?' he said. 'Does it matter? We'll find that out when we catch him. That's what I want you to do.' The coroner walked to the window and stared down at the street. The town was coming alive, the sound of voices, the grate of a cart's wheels as it passed.

'What do you know about the servant?' John asked the monk.

'Very little,' he replied after a moment's reflection. 'Nicholas has worked for Timothy as long as anyone can remember. You must have seen him.'

John nodded. It was hard to imagine him as a killer. Especially one that seemed so calculating. Who could tell what lay deep in another's mind? Maybe Timothy was a bad master and he'd finally had enough. His anger had risen and he'd committed murder. He wouldn't be the first.

Then he stopped and wondered again. If this had been born from years of anger and resentment, would Nicholas have been satisfied with a single blow? And would he have taken the time to arrange Timothy in bed so carefully that it looked as if he'd died while sleeping? That was hard to believe.

'Well, Carpenter?' the corner asked. 'What are you thinking?'

'I don't know yet, Master,' he answered honestly and heard a frustrated sigh.

'No ideas?' he asked mockingly. 'I expected more from you.'

John was about to reply when they heard the tentative footsteps downstairs, moving around slowly then climbing the stairs to the solar. They stood quietly, looking from one to the other.

He knew the face that emerged into the light. He saw it each Sunday, conducting the service at St Mary's Church. Father Geoffrey. A man who spoke his Latin with painful slowness, his voice hardly louder than the mutterings and gossip that formed a constant murmur during the service.

The priest had dark hair that grew wildly from his scalp, streaked with grey here and there, and eyes that seemed to peer like an owl, as if he wasn't quite certain what he was seeing. His surplice was simple, as clean as anything could be in Chesterfield, no more than a few stains on the dark cloth. There was no sense of wealth and riches about him, not like the churchmen John used to see every day when he lived in York.

'God's blessing, Father,' de Harville said, and the priest looked around, taken by surprise.

'God's blessing on you, too, sir,' Geoffrey replied. 'Brother,' he added with a small nod before turning his gaze on John. 'God's grace on you too, my son.'

'Thank you, Father.'

'What brings you here?' the coroner asked.

'When I came home last night, they said that poor Timothy was dead.' He crossed himself as he stared at the body. 'They told me you've raised the hue and cry for Nicholas.' He glanced at the corpse. 'His death looks peaceful enough.'

'Don't believe everything you see,' de Harville said smugly. 'Right, Carpenter?'

'Yes, Master.'

'You mean someone killed him?' Geoffrey sounded shocked.

'The servant. He's run off.'

'Did he …' Geoffrey began, then gave a small, urgent cough. 'Have you seen the psalter?'

'Psalter?' John asked.

'It's a book of psalms,' Brother Robert explained, then looked at Geoffrey. 'I didn't know Timothy owned one.'

'He did,' the priest replied seriously. His eyes seemed to shine. 'He showed it to me. Such beautiful illustrations, and all bound in leather. He promised it to the church when he died. It's been in his family for generations but he had no one to leave it to.'

'Where did he keep it?' John asked.

'In the chest. After he showed it to me, he had me put it back. It caused him so much pain to move.'

John was on his knees, lifting the lid, hands scrambling around inside the chest. A few clothes, all of them old and the worse for wear. Some ancient, cracked rolls of vellum. But no book.

'It's not here.'

'Well, now we know who took it and why he killed his master,' the coroner said triumphantly.

'Nicholas …' Father Geoffrey shook his head. 'I find it hard to believe. He always seemed like such a loyal man.'

'Loyalty's only worth the pennies it's paid,' de Harville told him.

'Did you come to see Timothy often, Father?' John asked.

'Every week. I gave him communion and heard his confession. I doubt he'd been out of the solar in more than a year. He couldn't manage the stairs, you see. His legs weren't strong enough to support him.'

'How was his mind?'

'As clear as ever. It was just his body that betrayed him.' Geoffrey shook his head sadly. 'He was waiting up here for death.'

But not in the way it happened, John thought. Not so violent. He looked around once more. No weapon, not even a sign that there'd been a struggle. Just the corpse in the bed. Someone had taken time here. No fear, no panic. And the psalter missing …

'The psalter?' he asked. 'What does it look like?'

'It's about as big as a man's hand,' the priest said after a moment's thought. 'Easy enough to hide in a scrip or a pack, I suppose.'

'What about money? Did Timothy keep a purse?'

'Under the bed,' the priest told him.

On his hands and knees again, John searched. There was only the dust on the wooden boards.

'Have we finished here?' de Harville interrupted.

'Yes, Master.'

'Good.' The coroner moved to the stairs. Over his shoulder he said, 'Come on, Robert, we have business.' And to the priest: 'I'll leave you to take care of the body.'

There was nothing more to learn in the room. John knew what had killed Timothy and very likely who'd done it. Even why. All that remained was to find Nicholas, and that shouldn't be too difficult. Where would an old man go? With a nod to the priest he made his farewell.

But he didn't leave the house. Not yet. John prowled around the hall, pulling back the shutters to let in the day. A settle, a table and chairs, plate worth good money on display, the expensive tapestries, all of it covered with a layer of dust. And behind the hall, the buttery. Bread, cheese, oats to make oatcakes. Two flagons of ale. Off to the side was Nicholas's room. It was as spare as his master's, nothing more than a bed and a small chest that held a shirt and a pair of well-darned hose. Odd, he thought. If Nicholas had run, he'd surely have taken those. Burrowing further down, he found a small purse of coins. Stranger still. Why would he leave that?

The door at the back of the house was unlocked. He walked out into an ordered garden. Apple trees stood against the back wall, catching the bright morning sun. The soil was well dug and hoed, the first stirrings of plants poking through the soft earth.

The kitchen stood a few yards away, separate from the house in case of fire. Wood was stacked inside, a pan of pottage standing on the table next to a pair of clay bowls.

Against the far wall of the garden, as distant from the house as possible, lay a sprawling midden, flies buzzing noisily around it. John stood, stroking his chin. None of it made sense. Everything pointed to Nicholas as murderer and thief. But why hadn't the man taken his few possessions? They'd be easy enough to carry. And even with Timothy's purse he'd still have use for the coins in his chest.

The hoe was resting against the stone wall of the kitchen. He picked it up and started to poke at the midden, methodically pulling at the waste as he held his breath against the stench. It only took a few moments. The metal struck something and he carefully scraped the pile of refuse away.

He knew the empty face staring up at him. Nicholas the servant.

CHAPTER THREE

De Harville stood a few yards from the body and sighed.

'God's blood, Carpenter. I bring you to help and you turn everything upside down.'

He turned away and strode quickly back towards the house.

'He hoped this would be simple, John,' Brother Robert said sadly, staring at Nicholas. 'What made you look there?'

'The midden seemed too big,' was the only answer he could offer.

'May the Lord rest his soul.' The monk made the sign of the cross. 'Can you see what killed him?'

'No.' He hadn't examined the body yet. Did it even matter how he'd died? Someone had murdered him and tried to hide the corpse. Surely that was enough?

The coroner was in the buttery. He'd poured himself a mug of the ale standing there. Still early and the day was already warm.

'That boy,' he said, 'the one you used before. Your wife's brother.'

'Walter.' It was the first time the man had ever acknowledged that John was now married.

'Have him work with you.'

'He has his own jobs.'

De Harville turned, fire behind his eyes.

'It's not a request, Carpenter,' he roared. 'It's an order.'

He waited before answering. It was the only resistance he could offer. He had no power.

'Yes, Master. But he'll need to be paid.'

The coroner nodded his agreement after a moment. 'Two pence per day. That's as high as I'll go. The crown isn't made of money.' He slammed the mug down on the counter. They could hear the soft voice of Father Geoffrey, still up in the solar as he continued to pray over Timothy's corpse. 'Have him shrive the servant once he's done.' He shook his head in frustration. 'Come along, monk, we have work to do.'

John watched them walk away, the brother limping slowly behind the coroner. Who could have killed Timothy and Nicholas? He had no ideas, nothing to point him in the right direction. What he needed was to learn more about Timothy. What he did, what enemies he might have made during his life.

· · ·

It took a little while for Dame Martha to answer his knock. When she did, her eyes were bright, her veil brilliant white and her gown as fine as ever. But somehow she seemed a little more frail, as if she was slowly fading away. For the first time, he noticed the flesh stretched tighter over her bones and the way her skin seemed more transparent.

She'd spent her whole life in the town; few knew it as well. Here there had been joy and sorrow for her. The love of a long marriage. Time and the pestilence that had taken so many of her kin and friends. How does a life balance out, he wondered?

'Come in, come in,' she told him, guiding him to a stool. 'So the coroner has you looking into Timothy's death? Everyone said Nicholas did it and ran away.'

'Then everyone's wrong,' he said and saw her astonishment. Martha loved to be able to give fresh gossip to the other good-wives in the marketplace. Now he could offer her something tasty to pass on. 'Nicholas is dead, too. In the garden behind the house.'

'May God give him peace,' she said without thinking, then asked, 'What happened?'

Her eyes were full of curiosity and he told her what little he knew.

'What I really need is to know about Timothy,' John told her. 'And Nicholas.'

She poured ale for them both and sat, sifting through her memories.

'Timothy was very handsome when he was young,' she began. 'He was older than me, but I still noticed him. I think all the girls were in love with him.'

'Were you?' She blushed slightly, but didn't reply. 'Did he ever marry?' John asked.

She shook her head. 'No, he never seemed interested. He rode and hunted, that was what he enjoyed. There was talk that he had someone, but it was never more than that. No one knew a name, even if it was true. He grew up in that house on Saltergate. It became his when his father died.'

'So he had money.'

'That goes back a long way in the family,' she told him. 'That's what my mother always told me. Something to do with trading in wool. His father and grandfather before him. And Timothy carried it on.' She paused. 'Until his accident, anyway.'

'Accident?'

'His horse threw him,' Dame Martha explained. 'After that he couldn't walk much. He sold off his business and spent all his time in that house.' She chewed at her lower lip. 'I doubt I've seen him more than twice in the last ten years. He had to use two sticks to get around. I think he felt ashamed to be seen like that. After he'd always been so strong and active. I know he owned a few houses around Chesterfield but I'm not sure how much he had besides that.'

'No children anywhere?'

She shook her head again. 'Not that I ever heard of. Not around here, anyway. He hardly seemed to notice women. He had his friends and that was all. And the pestilence took most of them.'

He swirled the ale in the mug and took another long sip.

'How long has Nicholas been with him?'

'Oh, it must be years and years.' Martha brought a hand to her mouth, trying to think. 'Long before the plague, I'm certain of that. Timothy's parents died when he was about twenty. I suppose it was soon after that.' She turned to look at him. 'I'm sorry, I wish I could tell you more.'

'What was he like?' John asked. 'Timothy, I mean.'

'Pleasant enough when he was younger, I suppose. But he was always a little distant, as if he'd rather be somewhere else. He always rushed through his business to make time for his pleasure.'

'And then his pleasure was taken from him,' John said quietly.

'It was, God rest his soul.'

'Have you ever heard of a book of psalms in the family?'

'No,' she answered with a thoughtful glance. 'Nothing like that. Why?'

He ignored her question.

'What about Nicholas? Did you know him?'

'Not really. You should talk to Evelyn.'

'Evelyn? I don't think I know her.'

'Of course you do, John.' She swatted playfully at his arm. 'You repaired the hinge on her door back at the turn of the year. She's the one who lives over by West Bar. One of Timothy's tenants. Walks bent over. I often used to see them talking on market day.'

He remembered her now, one of Martha's friends. They stood together at the side of the church nave with the other goodwives during the Sunday service.

'You don't miss much,' he said in admiration.

'I like to know what's going on,' she sniffed. 'But since you're here, there's something I wanted to ask you. What are you going to do about Janette and Eleanor?'

'The girls?' He didn't understand. 'What do you mean?'

'They're very bright. They should learn to read and write.'

The thought took him aback. Reading? Writing? What would they need with that?

'But why?' he asked.

'Because everyone should,' she told him simply. 'I already talked to Katherine. She agrees.'

He smiled. Even if he objected he had no chance.

'Who'd teach them?' John asked.

'I would,' she told him as if it was obvious. 'Their numbers, too. I might as well be of some use in my old age.'

'You're not so old.'

'And you're not a good liar, John the Carpenter.' Dame Martha smiled and tapped him on the knee. 'It's settled then.'

• • •

'Yes, I know Nicholas,' Evelyn told him. She shook her head. 'I can't believe he could have killed Master Timothy.'

'He didn't,' John said.

She turned to look at him. Her face was lined with wrinkles, all her hair carefully tucked under her veil. Her wrists were like twigs, her fingers bent almost into claws by age. The years hadn't been kind to her. Her back had twisted so she could no longer straighten it, and she shuffled more than walked. But her mind appeared sharp enough.

'That's what everyone said.'

'Someone killed him, too.' He kept his voice low and gentle and put his hand over hers.

'But … why would anyone do that?'

'I don't know yet. Dame Martha says you knew Nicholas.'

'Knew?' She considered the word. 'We talked. I don't know if anyone *knew* him. Maybe Master Timothy did.'

'Anything you can tell me about him will help.'

'I don't know. He told me once that he was born in Dronfield. Nicholas never really said much about himself.' She looked around the small house. 'What will happen to this place?'

'What do you mean?' John asked.

'Timothy owned this house. That's the only reason I knew Nicholas, really. He came to collect the rent every quarter day.'

'I suppose the house will belong to whoever Timothy named in his will. Martha said he didn't have any children.'

'No, poor man. Not for want of offers when he was young.' Her eyes drifted into memories. 'We'd all have wed him if he'd asked. But all he wanted was horses and hunting. Hawking, too.'

'What about Nicholas? Did he go with his master?'

'I don't remember.' She gave a wan smile. 'I don't have a picture of it in my mind.'

'What other houses did Timothy own?'

'Where Richard the Cooper lives, close by the church. And one in the Middle Shambles. Edward the Butcher.'

The Shambles, John thought. The market for meat, but also home to most of the thieves and the whores of the town. Fine during the day, perhaps, but dangerous at night. A place for an honest man to take care of his purse and his life.

'Thank you,' he said. 'If you think of anything else, can you send word to me?'

She nodded her agreement.

'Martha says you're a good young man. Married now, she told me.'

'I am,' he agreed with a smile. 'To Katherine.'

'I know her. God wish she's chosen well.'

He gave a small bow. 'I hope so, too.'

• • •

The bell was striking the hour as he hurried through the streets. Ten o'clock in the morning and time for dinner. He greeted some of the people he passed, realising that he'd become a part of this place now. It was home; he'd become woven into the town's fabric. In its present and its future. Few chose to glance towards the past, and with good reason.

Back in the year of the pestilence it had seemed as if half the land was dying. In the towns where few were left alive, people seemed more ghost than human, silent and untrusting. There were villages where no one remained, the doors to the houses hanging open. In the fields the crops waited for the men who would never come to harvest them. Cattle lowed piteously, desperate to be milked. He was eight then. He could barely recall his mother, already long dead. Then his father took the sickness, going so quickly it seemed to pass in three breaths. And John was alone. All he had was the bag of tools that weighed heavy on his shoulder, and his skills with wood. The two things he'd inherited from his father. But his knowledge, his craft, was still unformed and untutored. He learned as he went. Not begging, but exchanging his services for food and a bed. Finally he became the master of it. The wood spoke to him. He could feel how it should be, what it wanted, the strengths and weaknesses of a length of timber. He travelled around the land.

And now he was here. Fourteen years after the Great Plague and Chesterfield was alive and bustling, as if nothing had ever happened. It was often kinder to forget all that had once been.

Katherine was dishing out the pottage as he walked into the hall. He'd fashioned wooden bowls for them all when he had an idle day. Simple enough work with a chisel and a few hours, but she'd been delighted by it.

He settled on the bench next to Walter, across from his wife, Janette and Eleanor on either side of her eating with the endless hunger of children.

'A busy day?' he asked the boy.

'It's been quiet, John.'

'Would you like to earn some money? Tuppence a day?'

Walter's eyes shone and he smiled. 'Does the coroner want me to work with you?'

'He does.' From the corner of his eye he saw Katherine frown. 'And I'd be glad to have you.'

'People are saying that Nicholas is dead, too.'

'He is, God rest him in peace.'

They said little more during the meal, but John could feel his wife's disapproval. She might reluctantly accept him working for de Harville, but she didn't want her younger brother doing it. It was too dangerous, too bloody.

As she collected the empty dishes she looked at him and inclined her head. He followed her into the buttery.

'Why are you involving Walter?' she hissed angrily.

'The coroner commanded it,' was the only answer he could offer. Not enough, he knew.

'Couldn't you have refused? I asked you.'

He shook his head. How could you say no to someone like that? She knew it well as he did. Her face was flushed, red with anger.

'I asked you, John,' she repeated.

He understood her feelings. The last time had seen them in danger of their lives.

'You know what he's like. I didn't have a choice. We'll be safe enough,' he promised. But they were blind words. Who knew what they'd find? He placed a hand on her belly and his voice softened. 'Honestly. I'm not going to take any risks. Not with this one waiting.'

She nodded. Her eyes were wet with tears that were ready to roll down her cheeks as he kissed her gently.

'Besides, I like coming home to my wife every night. I'll keep Walter safe.'

'Then who'll look after you, John?'

CHAPTER FOUR

'What do you know about Edward the Butcher?' John asked as they walked down Saltergate.

'People are scared of him,' Walter answered.

'Why?'

'He has a temper.'

'Are you scared of him?'

'No, John,' he replied with a shy smile.

'Fear isn't a bad thing,' he said. 'It keeps you alert.'

'Are you ever scared, John?'

'All the time.'

'You don't show it,' the lad said wonderingly.

'That doesn't mean it's not there. Sometimes it's best not to show what's inside.' An image of Katherine's face came into his mind. 'And sometimes you need to show what you feel.'

'Do you mean girls, John?' Walter asked with interest.

'I do.' The boy was growing up. Soon enough there'd be more questions, ones he'd need to answer. But not yet. He tousled the lad's hair. 'Come on, we have to go and see a cooper.'

• • •

The workshop had the warm smell of wood that always reminded him of summer. In the corner, water steamed in a long metal trough placed over burning coals. Richard the

Cooper was hard at work as they entered, while his apprentice adjusted a series of boards and tied them in place.

'God's grace on you,' John called out and the men both turned.

'God's peace,' the cooper replied, raising a hand. 'What can I do for you?'

'Just a word, if I might.'

Richard nodded at the apprentice to keep on working, then put down his saw. He was a large man, tall, with broad shoulders and heavy arms, a thick growth of beard covering his face.

'I know you,' he said after a moment. 'You're the carpenter. Not long here.'

'John.' He extended a hand and the cooper shook it. It was the firm grip of a man who worked hard.

'They say you do good work. But you'll be wasted here, if you're looking for a job.'

'Nothing like that.' His eyes were examining everything. Hammers, strips of iron, a bucket of nails. He understood how it all worked, the wood steamed and forced into shape for the bowed side of the barrels, the hoops fitted around to keep them in place. But seeing it here fascinated him, the way everything concerning wood did. 'You rent this place from Timothy?'

'Have done for years, may he rest in peace. I hope they catch that Nicholas soon.'

'They already have,' John told him. 'He was dead, too.'

'Dead?' Richard turned a sharp pair of blue eyes on him. 'How?'

'The same time as his master, probably.' He picked up a heavy pair of tongs, weighing them in his hands.

'I don't see why that would interest a carpenter.'

'The coroner asked me to look into the deaths.' He saw the man's quizzical look. 'I solved one last autumn.' John shrugged. 'Now the man thinks I should know every mystery.'

The cooper grinned. 'Come and have a mug of ale. I don't know about your business, but this is hot work.'

'Any work's hot on a day like this.'

The man dipped two chipped clay beakers into an open barrel and passed one over.

'You know I discovered him?' He waited as John raised his eyebrows. 'Paid a fine for my troubles, too,' Richard complained. 'Death's an expensive business.'

'And life is even more expensive for a poor man,' John agreed. 'What made you go to the house?'

'Some tiles had come off the roof.' He pointed with a thick hand towards the house next door. 'It was time to mend them so I went to remind them. The door was open. I called out and heard nothing.' He shrugged. 'So I looked around and Timothy was sitting up in bed. It was only when I touched him that I knew he was dead.' He shuddered.

'Did you move anything? Take anything?'

'Of course not,' Richard said dismissively. 'I'm not a thief.'

John nodded his apology. 'What do you know about Timothy and Nicholas?'

The cooper let out a long breath. 'Let's see. I moved here seven years ago. Nicholas comes every quarter day for the rent. I'd never seen Timothy before I found his corpse. Folk say he didn't walk well.'

'That's what I heard.' John took a long drink. It was good ale. Weak, but with a bite to the taste. 'What was Nicholas like?'

'I never had a problem with him.' The cooper shook his head. 'Not that we talked much, mind. I gave him my money and that was it. Just a few words. I never really thought about it.'

'He never told you anything about himself?'

'No. Like I said, it was business. The last time I saw him was Lady Day in March. Do you know who'll take over the properties now Timothy's dead?'

The same question as Evelyn. The dead were gone and the living looked to their futures.

'Not until his will's read. If he made one.'

Richard snorted. 'There'll be one. Men with money always make sure it's passed on.'

'Probably,' John agreed. 'Tell me, did you ever hear of Timothy owning a book of psalms?'

'No. Wouldn't mean anything to me, anyway. I couldn't read it if you put it right in front of me.' He placed a hand on a finished barrel. 'It's things that matter.'

John understood. 'Can you show me how you work?'

'Going to give me competition, Carpenter?' He asked the question with a grin.

'Not unless you become a joiner.'

'We're both safe, then.'

It was a good half-hour before he came back into the afternoon sun, Walter at his side. He'd learned a little of the trade, the way each stave had to be cut, so precise, wider at the middle. The way everything fitted together so perfectly. The crafting of a plug. He felt a small satisfaction in the knowledge.

'What did you think?' John asked.

'I don't think he did it,' Walter said.

'Nor do I.' Richard the Cooper had seemed honest and straightforward, a man happy to live with his labours. 'Let's see what this butcher has to say.'

'Please, John, be careful.' A worried look appeared in Walter's eye.

'I'll watch what I say.'

The shutters were still down on the shop in the Middle Shambles, forming a stall for the butcher to show off his cuts of meat. Flies buzzed heavily around, crawling on the flesh, so many that each piece seemed almost black and alive.

Edward stood in the shadows near the back of the shop, splitting open a carcass with a long, sharp knife. He reached a hand inside and pulled out the entrails, tossing them into a bucket and kicking at the dog that came around hungrily to sniff.

He was a large man, with a heavy, hawk-nosed face and dark eyes set deep. His belly strained against a stained leather apron over an old linen shirt and patched hose. Seeing the customers, he put down the knife and walked over, rubbing his hands on an ancient, bloody rag.

'Walter,' he said and the boy gave a wary nod in return.

'I'm John the Carpenter.'

'And what do you want, John the Carpenter?' There was a mocking smirk in his voice and he nodded at his display. 'I've got good meat for sale.'

'Just information.'

'About what?' He folded his thick arms across his chest with a forbidding expression.

'This place,' John answered with a smile. 'I understand Timothy owns it.'

'Did,' the man said with satisfaction. 'He's dead, or are you the only one in town who hasn't heard?'

'I know well enough. It was the coroner who asked me to look into his death.'

Edward cocked his head and John could feel his gaze.

'A carpenter who investigates death?' He sneered. 'What's it going to be next, a blacksmith healing the sick?'

'You didn't care for your landlord?'

'I never gave him a thought, and that's God's honest truth.'

'How often did you see Nicholas?'

'Rent days.' The man shrugged. 'Won't be seeing him again now he's run off.'

'Then there's news you haven't heard yet. He's dead.'

'Good riddance, too.' Edward hawked and spat.

A strange reaction, he thought. No one else had found Nicholas objectionable.

'You didn't like him?'

'Scared of his shadow, that one. I'm surprised he had the balls to kill anyone. Always brought a guard when he came down here.' He laughed. 'Afraid someone would rob him.'

He could hardly be faulted for that. A full purse down here was a heavy temptation.

'Who did he bring?'

'Roland. The big one from Hathersage, not the little one from Unstone,' he explained, not that John knew either of them. 'He'd get his money and be gone in a minute. No talk about him at all. Not when he was down here, anyway.'

'Thank you,' he said. There was nothing to learn from Edward. John left, Walter close on his heels as they hurried along to Low Pavement. The alehouse was open and he ordered for them both, sitting at a bench away from the other customers.

'Did you like him, John?'

'No. Not at all.' There was an edge of violence to the man, as if his mood could shift in a heartbeat. Much longer in there and it might have happened. 'Do you know the Roland he was talking about?'

'Yes,' Walter replied.

'We should go and talk to him.'

'Do you think Edward killed them, John?'

'No,' he answered after some thought. 'Do you?'

'I don't know,' Walter said after some thought, then added. 'I think he could.'

'So do I. But I don't think he did. Not this time. Do you see what I mean?'

'What are we going to do now?'

The carpenter drained his mug. 'We'd better talk to Roland. He's the only other name we have. Where does he live?'

'I don't know, but he works at the church.'

'The church?' John asked in surprise.

'He's a labourer.' Walter looked at him. 'He's very big and he has a scar here.' Walter ran a finger down his cheek.

He had a faint memory of the man now. But nothing more than that. He hadn't worked at the church long enough to know everyone. Just the carpenters and one or two of the masons. He smiled. 'Then let's see if we can find him.'

It felt strange to be in the churchyard doing nothing while all the workers moved busily around. Without even thinking, John raised his eyes to the steeple. The framework was almost done; already some of the joiners were fixing the cross-bracing in place. It was so tall that he needed to lean his head back to see to the top.

His hands itched a little, a lost wish that he could still be working on it. Those days were gone, he told himself. He liked the life he had now.

Roland was easy to spot as he emerged from the church porch. He stood a head taller than most of the others, his scar almost white in the sunlight. He'd stripped to just his hose and boots, sweat shining on the thick dark hair that covered his chest.

He made his way to the ale barrel, standing in the shade of an oak tree, dipped a cup and took a long drink.

'Are you Roland?' John asked, and the man turned sharply.

'I am.' He had a deep voice that seemed to start in his belly and resonate in his chest. Grave and slow, it commanded attention. But his face was open and cheerful, the type to break into a ready smile. There were the faint lines of laughter around his eyes, and he looked as if life amused him.

'I'm John the Carpenter.'

'I know who you are. You used to work up there.' He nodded towards the tower.

'That's right.'

'And everyone knows Walter.' He reached out, clapping a large hand on the boy's shoulder. 'What can I do for you, Master?'

'You did some work for Nicholas.'

'From time to time,' Roland agreed, his face darkening. 'I'd never have seen him as a murderer, though.'

'He wasn't.' He saw the surprise on the man's face. 'He was killed, too.'

Roland crossed himself quickly, muttering a few words under his breath.

'I've heard that you were his bodyguard when he went to the Shambles.' He waited for the man to nod, then continued, 'How did he come to ask you?'

'He saw me at the market and asked if I wanted to earn a few pennies.' He shrugged. 'Nothing more than that. I only went there twice with him.'

'Had he experienced any trouble?'

'I don't know. He was scared down there, though. You could see it on his face. Nervous.'

'Did anyone ever give you a problem?'

Roland grinned. 'No. It only took a few minutes. In and out. I went down with him on my dinner. Two pennies each time.'

'Did he say much to you?' John asked.

'Nothing more than a few words,' he answered, shaking his head slowly. 'He wasn't the talkative type. All business. But when we were in the Shambles his eyes kept moving around. He held himself very straight. Kept a hand on his knife, too. Like he was expecting something. So perhaps there'd been a problem before.' He shrugged once more. 'That's what I thought, anyway.'

'What happened when you left the Shambles?'

'I walked with him back to his house and he paid me before he went in. That was it. Thanked me polite enough and said he'd need me again on the next quarter day when he went back for the rent. I told him he'd be welcome. It was all done so fast there was still time for me to eat before I started work again. And now you're here and telling me he's dead.' The man looked down at John. 'I'm sorry, Master, that's all I know.'

The carpenter believed him. The big man seemed honest. As honest as anyone might be, anyway. Then a thought struck him.

'How many people did you tell about it?'

Roland frowned. 'A few, I suppose,' he answered eventually, his face reddening with embarrassment. 'It was a good story for the alehouse. Worth a laugh and a drink or two.'

'Did anyone seem especially interested in it? Can you recall?'

'Not really. No, wait,' he added after a moment. 'There was someone who kept asking me questions one night.'

'Who was he?'

'I've no idea. I was in that inn at the top of Soutergate with some of the lads from here.' He made a gesture back towards the labourers working around the church. 'Someone must have heard me talking. He bought me a mug of ale to hear it again, then another for a few questions.'

'What kind of questions?'

Roland shook his head. 'I don't remember.' He gave a rueful smile. 'We went out for a long night, if you know what I mean.'

'Do you remember anything about him?' John pressed.

Roland pursed his lips as he concentrated then said suddenly, 'Leather. He smelt of leather. And the crown of his head was bald like a monk.' He smiled, surprised by his memory.

It was something.

'Thank you,' John said and shook the man's hand, feeling the rough calluses on his palm.

As they walked away he looked back wistfully, seeing the carpenters climbing gracefully up the steeple to work. Another few weeks and the work would be complete, maybe even by St John's Day. A framework built over the wood and the oak tiles in place. A wonder for all the country around. Part of him wanted to be up there. It was dangerous work, but worthwhile for the satisfaction of creating something as remarkable as the steeple that stayed in place through its own weight.

Walter pulled him back to the present. 'What are we going to do now, John?'

'I'm going to see the coroner and tell him what we've learned.' He saw the hope in the boy's eyes and asked, 'Do you want to come with me?'

• • •

De Harville sat rubbing his temples. His face looked strained. The goblet of wine in front of him sat untouched.

'So you haven't found anything useful,' he said wearily after John had recounted the day.

'We've discovered a few things,' John objected.

'But not the killer.' He raised his head to stare at Walter. 'Have you, boy?'

'No, Master.'

'You could take lessons in politeness from him, Carpenter.' The coroner sighed. 'God's blood, why can't it be simple?'

The carpenter looked over at Robert. The monk gave a small shake of his head.

'Catch the killer,' de Harville ordered.

It was a dismissal. Outside the house, standing in the yard with the strong smell of horses from the stable, John looked up at the sky. Blue, not a cloud to be seen. A perfect day to be building something, not chasing a murderer. But he was in the hunt now and there was no turning back.

'John.' The monk had appeared silently beside him. 'Don't pay too much attention to him. His wife's no better and he went to visit his son at the wet nurse. He loves the boy, it always puts him in a temper when he has to leave.'

The carpenter nodded. 'I'll pray for him.'

'Pray for all of them.' He rested his gnarled hand on John's shoulder. 'He has too much on his mind at the moment. Everything's tearing him apart. Give him your forgiveness when he seems angry. He doesn't really mean it.'

'I will, Brother.'

The monk smiled. Like Martha, he seemed older, smaller. The habit hung loosely on his frame.

'And look after your wife, too. You know,' he added thoughtfully, 'if you talk to Will Durrant, he might be able to tell you more about Timothy.'

'Who?'

'Have you ever seen the blind man in town being led by a boy?'

'Yes.' The old man, as old as Timothy had been, stooped and shuffling with his hand on the lad's shoulder. 'Did they know each other well?'

'They grew up together.'

• • •

There was bread and cheese on the table. Walter chattered as they ate while John sat and looked at his family. He'd never imagined it would be this way. A wife, yes, and his own children to follow. But not a house already brimming with life and voices.

When he left York, running from a woman who'd been happy to betray his trust, he'd had few thoughts of settling. He'd tried that in the rich city and it had come to a bad end. He wanted the road, he wanted the freedom to practise his craft and go where he pleased. No ties, nothing to ground him.

Yet God had another plan in store, he thought. And he had no regrets. Katherine was more than a helpmeet, she was someone who made him brighten every time she smiled. And soon they'd have their son. Or daughter.

That brought its own fears, too. So many women died in childbirth, so many babies didn't reach their first birthday. A baby was an act of faith, of defiantly loving.

'You're very quiet,' Katherine said.

'I'm just thinking.' He reached across and squeezed her hand. 'The deaths?'

He shrugged, saying nothing. There was no need to tell her what was on his mind; it would only worry her.

'Just that I'll be glad when this is all over.'

'The coroner takes advantage of you,' she told him. 'Don't you be doing anything dangerous.'

'I won't,' he promised. She leant across and kissed him, the girls giggling to see the brazen affection.

'Hush, you two,' Katherine said, but her eyes twinkled and she was smiling.

'Yes,' John agreed. 'You're both going to be busy enough soon. Dame Martha's going to teach you to read and write.'

'Really?' Janette said. 'Really?'

'That's right,' Katherine agreed. 'Your numbers, too.'

With a giggle the girls slipped off the bench and out into the garden to trace imaginary letters in the dirt.

• • •

'Do you know Will Durrant?' John asked as he used his plane on the edge of the door, watching the thin curls of wood tumble to the floor. He tried it in the jamb again, seeing a spot where it still stuck.

'Of course I do,' Dame Martha said.

'Brother Robert told me he was a friend of Timothy's.'

'Long ago,' she said slowly. 'I remember them together when I was a girl. But that's years back.'

'I'll see him tomorrow.' He sighed and ran his thumb over the wood. It would fit now. A nothing job, but he was happy to do it for her. From taking him in as a lodger when he first arrived in Chesterfield, she'd become a good, trusted friend. 'I don't have anything else.'

Just the man with the bald crown and the smell of leather. He'd need to find him first.

'I don't know how much you'll get from him,' Martha warned. 'He suffered from the palsy a few years ago. Do you know where he lives?'

'No.'

'That old house next to the Guildhall on the market square.'

He could place it in his mind; he had a good memory for buildings and how they were constructed. Wood and limewash, with weathered oak shutters and a thick front door, the rivets on the hinges dark and heavy.

He rubbed his tools with an oiled rag before replacing them in the leather satchel, then swept up the shavings and the sawdust.

'You won't have any more problems with that.'

'You're a good man, John. If I was fifty years younger …'

'You'd just be a little girl, then.' He winked and she beamed.

'Get away with you.' She swatted his arm lightly. 'You're full of flattery. It's market day tomorrow. That means you'll see Will out and about. He never misses it. His servant's son leads him around.'

'I'll look for him there.'

The big Saturday market was always full. People came from the villages all around, some as far as Bakewell, to sell and buy. There was everything a man could want, not just food, but iron nails, horses, spices, bolts of silk and tiny bottles of sweet perfume. Jugglers and storytellers entertained the milling crowds.

He loved the place. Each market day felt new, like an adventure in a land touched with magic. He and Katherine would wander, the girls at their side hoping for a treat made from spun sugar or marchpane, knowing he'd give in and buy them one.

Tomorrow, though, would be a little different. He'd be searching for a man in the crowds. At least he should be easy to spot. There were other blind folk in Chesterfield, but none as old as Will Durrant.

. . .

They stood on the High Street, gazing down at the press of people. John took out a pair of coins then gave Katherine his purse. She looked at him and arched a brow, weighing it in her hand.

'It feels heavier than it really is,' he told her. 'Please, wife, be kind and leave something in it when you've finished.'

She giggled. 'Go and do your work,' she said with a grin. 'When you come home you can see how much you've earned my kindness.'

He gave an exaggerated bow and disappeared into the crowd. He was buffeted this way and that as he squeezed and elbowed his way through, stopping to glance around at faces.

Will Durrant was rubbing his fingers over a length of woven cloth when John found him.

'How much?' the old man asked in a cracked, shaky voice, shaking his head when the seller gave the price. 'Too rich for my blood.' He put a hand on the shoulder of the lad next to him and began to move away.

Like so many blind men, he walked with his head raised, as if he was looking up to the sky, with an old man's short steps. He sniffed a little, turned his head this way and that, using his other senses as his eyes failed him.

'Master?' John said, and Will stopped and turned to face him.

'Who are you?'

'John the Carpenter. I wish you a good day.'

'And to you.' Durrant smiled, showing a toothless mouth. His beard was white and patchy, thick round his chin and sparser as it grew up his cheeks. His hair had been cut so short it was little more than stubble. He could pick out a hesitant slur in the man's voice, the way his tongue slid over words as he tried to pronounce them. 'I've heard your name. You found a killer.'

'I did.' He had no sight and his speech might not be what it had been, but the man's wits were still clear.

'They said you're looking for whoever killed Timothy and Nicholas.' He moved his head so his eyes seemed to be staring into John's face. He knew Durrant couldn't see him but it was still disconcerting.

'I am, Master. You knew Timothy, I believe.'

'Once upon a time.' He gave a weary sigh. 'Old age takes men away from each other as it leads us to the grave.'

'I'm sorry.'

'Don't be. It's the way of the world and it always has been. So you want to know about Timothy?'

'Yes, I do.'

Durrant leaned towards the boy who was standing patiently. 'Go on home. The carpenter will look after me and make sure I get there. Won't you?'

'Of course,' John agreed, surprised by the trust.

'And now you can take me to the alehouse and buy me a mug or two.'

• • •

The man settled with his hands around the cup. His head moved, as if he was curious about everything around him. His fingernails were short, hands clean. His linen was neat.

It seemed that his servants cared for him. A leather jerkin was tied neatly over the top.

'You want to know about Timothy,' Durrant said. His hands shook a little as he picked up the cup, but not enough to spill the liquid.

'You knew him for a long time, I believe,' John said.

'I'm probably the last one here who remembers him as a boy.' The words seemed to come out reluctantly, as if he had to fight them to speak. But he smiled as he spoke. 'We used to hunt and hawk together.' He sighed. 'A long time ago.'

'You weren't always blind?'

'No.' Durrant gave a quick shake of his head. 'Not until I was thirty. One morning I was as fine as I'd ever been. Half a year later I couldn't see a thing.' He cocked his head to the side. 'You sound like a young man.'

'I am,' John told him.

'Are you married?'

John smiled. 'Yes, Master. Not long ago.'

'Treasure her,' Durrant said seriously. 'I miss my wife's face more than anything, even though she's long dead.'

'I'm sorry,' was the only answer he could give. After a pause, he asked, 'What was Timothy like?'

'Like a brother sometimes. Distant at other times.' The words arrived slowly, with difficulty. But it was a battle he endured many times a day. 'I never saw him lose his temper.'

'When did Nicholas become his servant?'

'Let me see.' His words vanished into thought. All around them, men who'd come for the market stood, talking as they drank. One, with a heavy beard, wearing torn hose and a patched shirt, told a joke, finishing in a bellow of laughter. Durrant didn't even seem to notice them. 'We must have been twenty-five. It was after his parents died, I know that. Nick was still a boy then.' He sighed.

'Did you visit Timothy?'

'A few times a year.' He ran a hand over his chin. 'Not that we ever had much to say. When you're old and can't do much, memories of when you were strong become embarrassing.'

'Did Timothy have any enemies?'

Durrant shook his head. 'If he ever did, he outlived them.' He gave a wan smile. 'But no, none I know of. Tell me, what was taken?'

'Money.' John paused. 'Did he ever mention a psalter to you?'

Durrant smiled.

'Yes. When my sight was going, he showed it to me. It was the last thing I ever saw, apart from my wife's face. Such a beautiful book.' His thoughts drifted away for a moment. 'Is that gone too?'

'Yes.'

'He told me he had plans for it when he died. Maybe he'd already done something with it?'

'He hadn't,' John said. Certainly not if he'd shown it to Father Geoffrey.

'So sad.' His words hung in the air. He lifted the mug and emptied it in a long draught. 'Take me home, please. I've had enough of the world for today.'

It felt strange to walk with a hand resting lightly on his shoulder. They talked haltingly, the weather, the way the crops were growing, until they stopped in front of Durrant's house.

'I've one favour to ask of you,' the man said.

'If I can, Master.'

'Please, come and tell me about your progress.'

'Gladly.' John smiled.

He watched as Durrant's hands moved on the door, opening it and stepping inside carefully, waiting until it closed before he walked away.

Trying to find out about Timothy was like grabbing smoke. The only one who'd really known him was Nicholas and he couldn't tell his tale.

But there was another road to follow. To find the man with the bald crown who smelt of leather, the one who'd asked Roland about Nicholas and the rent money.

CHAPTER FIVE

He weighed the purse in his hand when she gave it to him and raised an eyebrow.

'I've held feathers that weigh more than this,' he said in horror.

Katherine stared at him and folded her arms, drumming her fingers against her sleeve.

'You're not too old for a slap,' she told him, and he grinned.

'A joke.' He held up his hands. 'You're the best and most frugal of wives.' He kissed her lightly. 'And the most beautiful.'

She arched a brow. 'It'll take more than that to get back in my good graces.'

He studied her for a moment, then leaned close and whispered something in her ear. She blushed and tried to stifle a giggle.

'Will that help?'

'It might, as long as it's more than words.' She sighed contentedly. 'Did old Will tell you anything?'

'He confirmed that the psalter exists. But as far as he knew, Timothy had no enemies.'

'He must have had one,' Katherine observed.

He nodded. 'Or someone who saw an opportunity,' he said quietly. 'I need to go out tonight.'

'John …' she warned. He held up a hand.

'I'm only going to ask a few questions.' He saw her sceptical look. 'Nothing more than that, I promise.'

• • •

There were three taverns on Soutergate, all of them busy on a Saturday evening. In the first, John cradled a mug of ale and moved through the crowd. He saw a few men he knew, nodding his hellos, passing the time briefly with one of two of them. But his eyes were always searching. Plenty of men with the hair gone from the crown of their head, but none with the ripe smell of leather.

He waited a full half hour, watching and listening. Some mentioned the murders in passing, but no one lingered over the topic. No one seemed to stare at him. He asked a few questions, but none recognised the man from his description.

By the time he left and walked down the hill, full darkness had arrived, the stars bright in a clear sky. The scents of the fields and woods drifted in on a light breeze. He stood for a moment, breathing it in, before pushing open the door of the second alehouse into a fug of stale ale and sweat.

The old men had the benches, sitting and supping quietly. The young stood, louder, eager to drink themselves senseless and think of it as a good night. The stout alewife stood by the barrels, a heavy cudgel dangling from her wrist as a warning. Her veil was stained, the old dress shapeless on her body. She looked at him as he ordered.

'You're the carpenter,' she said. It came out like an accusation.

'I am, Mistress,' John admitted. Maybe she needed some work doing here.

'Investigating for the coroner.'

He nodded his reply.

'You'd better not be causing trouble here,' the woman ordered him.

'I won't.'

She kept her eyes on him. 'See you don't.'

Not that there was much chance of it. People were huddled in tight groups, not looking for strangers to join them. He moved around, squeezing between people. But there was nothing for him here, no one who seemed to fit what he sought.

People walked up and down the street. A pair of whores touted listlessly for business. Their time would come later, when the men emerged, reeling, not ready for their own beds yet.

The last of the alehouses stood at the bottom of the hill, close to the bridge over the River Hipper and the Derby Road. Downstream, he could see the fulling mill silhouetted in the moonlight, and he could hear the flow of the water as it passed close by.

The place was as packed as the other two, but it seemed different. There was nothing friendly about it. The man who took his order was surly, and the groups of folk seemed to talk in quiet voices, as if they didn't wish to be overheard.

No one resembled the man he was seeking, though. He moved around, asking his quiet questions. Someone believed he remembered the man, but couldn't give him a name. Others just shook their heads.

Finally, he emerged. He'd hoped for more, but life wasn't always generous. On Monday he'd go to the tannery; there hadn't been time today. He'd wager they'd know the man there.

The fresh air felt glorious against his face. Just cool enough. John stood on the bridge and stretched. Tomorrow, at least, he'd have some peace.

He heard the rush of footsteps and turned quickly, reaching for the knife in his belt. Before he could pull it the blow landed and the world became black.

• • •

He came to with the shock of cold water, blinking his eyes quickly, unsure where he was. He felt cold. Small waves rippled against his face, making him splutter.

The river.

The moon was strong enough to show the bank and he paddled towards it. Each stroke felt like an effort, but he knew he had to do it. It was that or drown. His left arm was weak, not even able to support him as he dragged himself out. He was close to the fulling mill. Two hundred yards he'd been carried.

On hands and knees, crouching on the grass, he began to retch, trying to get the water from his lungs. He was dizzy, he couldn't stand yet. His arm felt as if it was on fire.

He tried to look, but his clothes were sodden, stuck fast against his skin. He tried to crawl and gave up. He had to; he didn't even have the strength to move. If his attackers came to finish him off, he'd be simple enough to find. With his right hand he drew his knife. Perhaps he couldn't put up much of a fight, but he wouldn't die easy.

Time passed. He couldn't even begin to say how long. The cold seeped through to his bones and he started to shiver. John breathed slowly. Even the smallest movement made him dizzy and sent waves of pain through his arm.

Up at the top of the hill, the church bell tolled eleven.

Finally, gritting his teeth, he pushed himself to his feet. The world seemed to spin around him. He stood for a moment, then forced himself to take one step, then another. It seemed like the hardest thing he'd ever done. A pause, then a few more staggering paces. John closed his eyes until everything seemed even. Why did his arm hurt so much?

They'd hit him. He remembered that. Nothing more.

A few more steps, each one agony. His foot pushed against a heavy branch on the ground. Taking a deep breath, he squatted and picked it up, leaning heavily against it as he moved on. Five steps, six.

They must have thrown him in the river, thinking he was done for.

Another few steps. He wanted to scream from the pain in his arm.

The bridge was close now, just the slope up to the path and then the road. What if they were waiting?

No, John told himself. They'd gone. They must have gone. He prayed they'd gone.

The bell rang for midnight as he turned on to Saltergate. The walk should have taken no more than ten minutes. But he'd been forced to stop, to lean against the houses as he climbed the hill. Just long enough to regain his breath, to have enough strength to go a little further. Whenever he heard footsteps he hung back in the shadows. Just in case.

He was shaking with cold. Freezing. So stupid, he thought; it was a warm night. With his right hand he scrabbled for the key in his scrip, taking four attempts to force it in the lock then pushed the door open.

Inside was safety. Nothing could hurt him here. He hobbled into the hall and passed out on the floor.

CHAPTER SIX

The ringing of a bell seemed to hammer in his skull. He opened his eyes, no idea where he was. But everything seemed to swim in front of him, nothing clear. John tried to raise his head, but the pain was so sharp that he fell back.

He remembered a blow, the river, the long, hard walk home.

Home. He took in a shallow breath and tried to open his eyes again.

'John?'

He turned his head slowly, blinking against the pain it brought.

'I'm in bed?' he asked. His voice was a raw croak.

'You're at home,' Katherine told him softly. Her hand stroked his cheek. 'You scared me to death. What happened to you?'

'I was attacked. They dumped me in the river.' A sudden memory came. 'I need to see the coroner,' he said urgently. But as he tried to struggle up the pain overcame him.

'You're not going anywhere.' Her voice was firm. 'I'll send Walter and he can come here. For once it won't hurt him.'

Very carefully, John raised his right hand to his head. He could feel a bandage. But when he tried to raise his left hand, he barely managed an inch. The pain was too great.

'What's wrong with my arm?'

'You were stabbed.' She fussed with the blanket, pulling it up around his neck. He could see her properly now, just one of her, her face full of worry. 'And you had a blow to your head. You collapsed inside the door. Walter and I brought you up here, and I sent him for Mistress Wilhelmina.'

The wise woman.

'She made a poultice for your head and dressed your arm. She said you were lucky, but you'll be fine.'

Katherine put a hand behind his head and lifted it tenderly. She gave him a few sips of ale from a mug. The liquid felt like balm in his throat.

'Tell Walter to fetch de Harville,' John said. He lay back again, exhausted. He only meant to close his eyes for a moment.

$$\bullet \quad \bullet \quad \bullet$$

'Wake up, Carpenter. I don't have all day to stand here.'

He opened his eyes, waiting a little until the coroner came into focus.

'Master,' he said. He could make out Brother Robert standing in the corner, whispering with Katherine.

'You wanted to see me.' De Harville sat on the edge of the bed. He wore an elaborate leather jerkin over a heavily embroidered linen shirt. 'Well?'

'I know who attacked me.'

'Who?'

'Edward the Butcher from the Middle Shambles. He was with the man I was looking for last night. I don't know his name.'

'I'll send the bailiffs out for him.' He ran a hand through his hair.

'I don't understand it,' John said. 'When I talked to Edward he didn't seem to know Nicholas was dead. Why would he try to kill me?'

'Maybe he was helping this other man. Maybe he's a good play actor.' De Harville dismissed the concern. 'One way or another we'll find out when we catch him. When will you be working again?'

'When he's ready,' Katherine said in a tone that brooked no objection, her eyes fiery. 'Not until he's fit enough.'

The coroner stared at her, then finally shrugged and shook his head.

'Already under her thumb, Carpenter?' He stood up. By the door he gave an exaggerated bow, saying, 'Good day, Mistress.' The monk gave an apologetic glance as he trailed behind.

'I loathe that man,' Katherine said softly after they heard the men leave.

'It's just his way. And he'll have Edward arrested.'

'You didn't mention him to me.'

'It only came to me when we were talking. I could see his face ...' His voice trailed away as the bell began to ring again. 'You should go to service.'

Katherine shook her head. 'I'm not leaving you.' Her words had the tone of an order. 'When I saw you last night I thought you were dead.'

'I ...' he began. He hadn't expected anything like that. He tried to see a clear picture of it all through the fog in his mind. It had to mean that Edward and the other man had murdered Timothy and Nicholas. That was the only way the attack on him made sense. But when he talked to Edward the man had believed Nicholas was the killer and still alive. That was no play-acting, he'd swear an oath on it. But perhaps he was wrong, too trusting, and the butcher had been too clever for him. He raised a hand to his head, moving his fingertips gently over the bandage around his skull and wincing when he found the tender spot. Now the bailiffs would find them, they'd be tried for murder and hung. 'Did Wilhelmina say how long before I can be up?'

'Once you're ready,' she chided. 'She's coming back later to see how you are.'

He reached out with his good hand, taking hold of her fingers. 'I never thought anything would happen. Honestly.'

'It's too late now,' she told him stiffly.

'At least I know who did it. Let the bailiffs catch them.'

'I hope they do.'

He tried to smile. 'I'll be back to working with wood again. And Walter to his messages.'

'Pray God.' She gasped sharply and put a hand on her belly.

'What is it?' he asked, worried, but Katherine's face held a wondrous smile.

'The baby. It moved. It ... kicked.'

'Are you all right?' Was this how it should be? He had no idea, surprised by her laugh.

'John, it's natural. It means the child is healthy and alive. I'm going to leave you to rest. Wilhelmina said you'd need plenty of it.'

Her footsteps faded on the stair. The shutters were open, the sun shining warm on him. He wanted to sleep, his body ached for more of it, but his mind was tumbling. Who was the man with Edward? He'd only caught the smallest of glimpses before the blow stunned him. Small, with a feral face. Wild eyes, his mouth set in a snarl. He'd been the one with the knife; John remembered that now. He could recall the way the moon shone on the blade.

The pair of them had meant to kill, no doubt about that. It was just God's good grace that he hadn't died.

He could hear the muffled sounds of the house below. Katherine's voice, and the girls chattering away. The soft beauty of home. He tried to lift his left arm again, but it defeated him. The pain was too sharp.

He closed his eyes and tried to think.

• • •

'He has his colour back.'

John stirred as he heard the words, seeing a woman bent over him. Her fingertips were light against his arm. He turned his head to watch as she untied the bandage on his arm.

'You look better than the last time I saw you,' she said with a smile. He'd expected the wise woman to be old, but Wilhelmina still had an air of youth about her, with warm grey eyes, hair tucked into a crisp veil as white as January snow.

He realised his head wasn't pounding. There was a heavy ache, but he could move it, and his vision was clear.

'Rest helped,' he said with a thick voice.

'It always does,' she said gently. 'Nature's best physic.' With a soft touch she removed the rag and peered at the wound. For the first time he could see it, jagged and ugly at the top of his arm. Above the muscle, close to the pit of his arm.

'This should heal well,' the woman said. 'The cut's clean enough.' After a little thought she reached into her scrip and took out a small jar of ointment, spreading a little on the wound. It felt deliciously cool on his skin and he breathed in gratefully. 'That will help. It's going to ache and it will be a while before you can move it fully. But there's no great damage.' She bound the injury again.

'Thank you,' John said with relief. It wouldn't affect his work. His real work.

Very carefully she touched his eyelids, pulling them apart and studying what she saw. Her hands had the summer smell of herbs.

'Your eyes are clear,' she said slowly. 'How many of me do you see?'

'Just one,' he said with a smile.

'That's good. You should give thanks. I don't know what happened, but you took a heavy blow. You must have a thick skull.'

'That's what my wife tells me.' He smiled.

'She'd know,' Wilhelmina said with a bright laugh. 'Rest today, as much as you can,' she ordered. 'After that, if your head hurts, stop what you're doing. Lie down. Don't try to do too much. Our bodies talk to us. The trouble is that most people don't listen.'

'I will,' he promised.

'You have plenty of bruises and cuts, but they're nothing,' she assured him.

'The coroner will pay you,' John said and she raised an eyebrow. 'I was working for him.'

'I won't spare his purse, then.' She grinned impishly, then her face turned serious. 'Be careful. Next time God might not smile so kindly on you.'

. . .

He dozed and drifted, letting the day glide over him. Katherine came up, sitting silently with him for a few minutes and holding his hand.

Alone, his thoughts wandered hither and yon. Edward and the leather man. They likely believed he was dead, carried away by the Hipper, and they were safe. By now the bailiffs should have them, maybe the psalter, too. They'd be in jail, awaiting transportation to Derby to stand trial for murder.

Or they might have taken to the roads. A hue and cry might track them, but he knew how many were never found. A new town, a new name, and the past might never have happened.

Finally, as the afternoon was beginning to wane, birds calling on the breeze, Walter came up to the solar.

'Are you all right, John?' he asked nervously.

'The wise woman says I'll recover. What's the news? Have they arrested Edward?'

'No.' The boy looked worried. 'I saw the bailiffs go in to the Shambles, but they came out without him.'

So they'd fled, or they were hiding. John grimaced. He'd like to have seen them. He owed Edward and his friend a few blows. But that debt could gladly wait.

Even now, though, he could make neither head no tail of it. When he'd questioned Edward he'd paid close attention to the way the man reacted. He couldn't have misjudged the man so badly, could he? Perhaps he had.

'Last night … I thought you were going to die,' Walter's voice shook him from his thoughts.

'Don't worry, I'm not that easy to kill.' He grinned. 'They didn't know that.'

'What are you going to do, John?'

'I've been ordered to keep to my bed today. Tomorrow?' He tried to shrug, but the movement hurt his arm. 'Whatever happens, it's over for us. Coroner de Harville can deal with the hunt for them.'

He could see the disappointment on Walter's face. It was done so quickly, before he'd had a chance to show his value.

'Trust me, we're better out of it,' John assured him. 'It's not worth it. We're not fighting men.'

'If I'd been with you last night …'

'Then we might have both ended up in the river. Or worse,' he said.

'But, John …'

He shook his head. The sharp movement made him wince a little, a reminder that he'd hurt for a while yet.

'No. There's enough danger in life without going out to court it.'

The lad hadn't even been born when the pestilence came. He couldn't know what things had been like then. More death than life, everywhere in the country. There was no excitement or pleasure in hunting killers. Not when God had shown them the greatest killer of them all in a time when life had no value.

There wasn't even a need to go hunting for it. Insatiable, the plague took all the life it wanted.

'If you say so, John,' Walter said hesitantly.

He smiled. 'I do,' he answered. 'You did a good job. Maybe you'll have another chance.' But pray God not, he thought as the lad beamed in anticipation.

He must have slept right through the evening, struggling half-awake as Katherine came to bed. From the edge of his vision he saw the glow of a candle, the scent of tallow, and then darkness. The night was silent as he felt her curl up against him, the warmth of her body close to his.

CHAPTER SEVEN

As he opened his eyes he could smell the dawn. The freshness of it all, alive and new. He felt rested, all the tiredness purged from his body. Carefully, he eased himself out of bed. But he wasn't dizzy when he stood. His head throbbed, but he'd felt worse after a night of ale.

When he tried to put on his jerkin, though, he could barely raise his arm high enough to go through the hole. Tying his braies after going to the jakes, his fingers felt large and fumbling, like an old man.

With a bowl of bean and barley pottage in his belly, he left the house. People were already up and around, workers gathered round a fire outside the church. He passed in the shadows of first light, his boots light on the ground as he walked down Soutergate in his shirt and hose. By the time he reached the bottom he was out of breath.

He stopped at the bridge, hands resting on the cold stones of the parapet, and watched the flow of the River Hipper below, trying to piece together what had happened on Saturday night. They'd taken him by surprise.

'What are you doing, John?'

He turned to see Walter standing by his side; he'd been too lost in his musings to hear his approach. The boy smiled apologetically.

'What are you doing here?'

'I followed you. Do you mind?'

'No,' he replied. 'Not at all.' With his good right hand he pointed downstream. 'That's where I climbed out. I'm just trying to remember as much as I can.'

He stood silently for a little while. There were images, flashes, but nothing more. Maybe it would all return in time; maybe not. Finally he sighed and clapped Walter on the shoulder.

'Let's go and see the coroner. Maybe he's learned more about where Edward and his friend might be.'

'I thought we were finished with this.'

'We are,' John told him with a grin. 'But I'm like anyone else, I want to know the tale.'

●　●　●

As they walked into the yard on the High Street, they could hear raised voices, the coroner shouting somewhere inside the house. John put a finger to his lips, standing and waiting until there was silence.

'Should we go, John?' Walter asked.

'No.' He knew de Harville's temper; it was like quicksilver, always shifting from one mood to another. Another minute and his anger would have evaporated. He knocked on the door, and they were ushered in by a serving girl who was wiping the tears from her cheeks. The coroner was alone in the hall, sitting with his boots up on the table and peeling a dried apple from last autumn with his knife.

'Able to drag yourself out of bed today, Carpenter?' There was a hard edge to his voice.

'Yes, Master.'

'The dog and his pup together. Come to hear what happened?'

'I'd like to know.'

'It's simple enough. Your butcher has gone to ground. For all I know, he might have left Chesterfield altogether. He'd better, if he has a whit of sense.'

'Have you sent people out searching?'

De Harville took tight hold of the knife and plunged the point into the scarred wood. 'I'm not a fool. Don't go telling me my job.'

'What about the other man?' John persisted. 'Did you find a name for him?'

'We did,' he said with satisfaction. 'The monk wrote it down.'

He'd find Brother Robert later; he wanted to know.

'I still don't understand it—'

'You don't need to,' the coroner cut him off. 'They've already shown their guilt. But we still need to hoist them on the gallows. And I told you to find them.'

'Me?' he answered in astonishment. 'I can't if they've gone. Master.'

'Can't?' De Harville tilted his head. 'Didn't I give you a job, Carpenter? I expect you to finish it. Or have you become a poor workman?'

Inside, John bristled.

'I did what you asked,' he replied coldly.

The coroner pulled the knife out of the wood and pointed it at him. 'The job isn't finished yet.'

'I can't go chasing all over the county for them.' The man knew that just as well as he did.

'Then find out if they're still in Chesterfield.' His anger flashed briefly, then he smiled. 'I'm sure you could do that.' He selected another apple and began to peel it with fierce concentration. 'You have your orders, Carpenter.'

John looked at Walter. He left the room, the boy close behind.

Outside, he hunted for Brother Robert, and found him in the stable, feeding one of the apples to the roan horse. He turned at the footsteps.

'John.' A look of concern came into his eyes. 'How are you? Should you be up yet?'

'I'm better, praise God,' he answered, knowing how unlikely that sounded with a bandage wrapped around his skull. And he could feel the tiredness rising from the soles of his feet.

'When Katherine sent word, we were fearful for your life.'

'No need to worry, Brother, I'm not going to die that easily. And your master didn't seem concerned about my health this morning.'

'You picked a bad time to see him,' the monk said with a frown. 'The physician was here earlier. His wife is growing worse.'

'I didn't know.' It explained the ill temper; John felt guilty for his resentment.

'The child grows stronger, his mother grows weaker.' He sighed. 'The doctor says she might die.' He crossed himself. 'Pray for her, John. You too, Walter.'

'We will. He told me you have the name of Edward's companion.'

'He didn't remember?' Robert shook his head. 'Too much on his mind. It's Gilbert. He works for Edmund the Shoemaker on Soutergate.'

Of course. The man smelt of leather. He looked out through the gate.

'What do you think, Brother? Are they still here?'

The monk smile wanly.

'I don't know. Any wise man would run.' He paused a moment. 'But a truly wise man wouldn't have killed in the first place.'

'He wants us to find them if they're still here.'

'You know what he's like. Forgive him. He's not himself at the moment.'

'He doesn't make it easy. It's like he's filled with vinegar.'

'Some men thrive on conflict, John. He's always been that way, even when he was young.'

'So it would be a blessing if I helped him by finding Edward and Gilbert?'

The monk nodded. 'He won't show it but he'd be grateful.' He reached out a bony hand and grasped John's wrist. 'If you can.'

'I'll try,' he agreed.

'May God give you help.'

• • •

'What are we going to do, John?' Walter asked as they crossed the empty market square, walking towards Low Pavement. People were already at their work, the shutters coming down to display their wares, the tempting smell of food from the cookshops.

'I'm not sure,' he said. 'Why don't you go and see the shoe-maker and find out where Gilbert lives?'

'Gilbert won't be there, will he?' the lad asked nervously.

'No, he's gone. I'm sure of that. I'll be in the alehouse.'

He watched the boy run off on eager legs. Inside the build-ing, with the smell of ale and old rushes on the floor, he took a coin from his purse and sat with a mug. He wanted time to think, but he was weary. He simply needed to sit for a while.

The battering he'd taken on Saturday night had drained more from him than he cared to admit. A few minutes' rest and he'd be fine. He had to be now, with killers to seek.

He'd be willing to wager that Gilbert lived in the Shambles; maybe even lodged with Edward the Butcher. Wherever it was, he'd need to go there. They'd be gone, somewhere, but he might find some indication of where.

It wasn't a task he relished. Instinctively he touched the handle of his knife, just to check it was there. A small comfort for the Shambles.

He leaned back on the bench, closing his eyes. Just for a moment. He needed some rest.

Someone was shaking his arm. He opened his eyes, dragged away from a beautiful dream that vanished into the light.

'I've found out where Gilbert lives, John.' Walter sat down, beaming.

'Is it in the Shambles?' He drank some of the ale to wet his dusty throat. The lad looked disappointed.

'On Packers' Row. How did you know?'

'It was just a guess.' He smiled. 'Good work.' Slowly, he drained the cup, relishing the earthy taste. 'We'd better take a look at his room.'

The Shambles was made up of pinched little streets – Fisher Row, Potters' Row, many more. Runnels in every road over-flowed, filling the air with a stink the residents didn't even seem to notice. The buildings rose higgledy–piggledy, no order to them. Everything seemed to radiate out from the Royal Oak, the inn that stood at the centre of the area.

Conversations stopped as they passed. People stared at them. The folk in the Shambles had a look about them. Suspicious faces that seemed as if they'd never spent much time in the sun. Dirt was everywhere. A dead cat had been carelessly thrown against a wall. Walter stopped by a house that looked close to toppling over.

John brought his hand down on the wood. He waited, but no one came, and he tried again, pounding harder until someone inside drew back the bolt. She was a big woman, as tall as him, wearing a cheap dress layered in dirt and stains, a cudgel clutched in a thick hand. A wisp of grey hair escaped from her wimple, and her nose looked as if it had been broken at some time.

'What do you want?'

'Mistress.' He smiled and gave a small bow. 'I'm looking for Gilbert.'

'Why?' She didn't move an inch, filling the doorway, menac-ing with her size.

'The coroner's searching for him.'

She shook her head. 'He's gone. Left Saturday night. The bailiffs were here yesterday. I told them.'

'I'd like to see his room.'

She snorted. 'I daresay you would. But you can't. Someone else already has it.'

'Did he leave anything behind?'

The woman shrugged. Anything Gilbert hadn't taken was now hers, and he doubted there would be anything of value.

He could face her down, demand entry in the coroner's name. But from the corner of his eyes he could see a few people starting to gather. It wasn't worth the argument. John smiled and nodded.

'Of course, Mistress. May God go with you.'

Eyes watched them until they turned the corner. He stopped and let out a long breath, a mix of fear and relief.

'Were you scared, John?' Walter asked.

'Very.' He still had the wounds and the bruises from Saturday, and no desire for more of them. 'But I suppose we'd better check Edward's shop, too.'

In the tangle of lanes and streets he had no idea which way to turn. But the lad led him, right, then left, and left once more, until they were standing in front of the place. An apprentice, trying to look sure of himself, stood behind the counter.

'Good meat, gentlemen?' he asked. 'Fresh, cut how you like.'

'I'm looking for Edward,' John told him.

'He's not here.' The young man's eyes darted around nervously.

'Does he often leave you in charge?'

'Sometimes.' He lifted his head. 'Why, what business is it of yours?'

'That's between me and your master,' John told him, his face stern. 'When will he be back?' When there was no reply, he repeated, 'When?'

'He didn't say.' The apprentice tried to shrug it off. 'Soon.'

John kept staring, watching the man's face. 'How soon?' he asked finally.

'The 'prentice said soon,' came a voice behind them. John turned slowly, seeing a hefty man, his hose patched in many colours, his shirt faded, hidden by a vast leather apron covered in bloodstains. His face was covered with dark stubble but the hair on the top of his head was as short as bristles. A long knife hung from his belt, his right hand resting lightly on it. There was an air of violence about him.

'I heard him. I wanted to know how soon.'

'What is it to you, anyway?'

'I have business with Edward.'

The man looked him up and down and gave a grim smile that showed broken, brown teeth. 'It looks you like came off worse in the last business you transacted, friend. You might do well to think on that.'

John glanced back at the apprentice. He looked more confident now, cocksure in his gaze.

They left without a word, forced to squeeze by the large man in the doorway. He smelt of decay, dirt ingrained into his fingers.

Twice he'd been bested in the Shambles. But he'd been stupid to expect anything more. They looked after their own here. Edward and Gilbert could even have been tucked away, looking down at them from a second- or third-storey window.

'Come on,' he said, putting his arm around Walter's shoulder. 'Let's go home. Do you know who that man was?'

'Julian.' The lad stared at the ground. 'He owns the butcher's shop next to Edward.'

'He looked like more than a butcher to me.'

'They say he's killed people.'

From the man's face, it was easy to believe. He seemed cruel and arrogant. Someone used to being obeyed and making people fearful.

'Why haven't they hung him, then?'

'I don't know, John. Maybe they could never prove it.'
'Maybe so. Put him out of your mind. He won't hurt you.'
Walter gave a trusting smile.
'Yes, John.'

CHAPTER EIGHT

The noise persisted. He opened his eyes and it was still there. Someone banging hard on the door.

John eased himself out of bed. His arm hurt as he tried to dress quickly, dragging on his hose and tying them before pulling on his boots. Katherine stirred but didn't wake as he slipped down the stairs.

He had no idea what time it might be. Somewhere in the middle of the night. He turned the key and drew back the bolt, peering into the darkness.

'Master?'

He squinted, just able to make out the face of one of the bailiffs.

'What is it?' John asked. 'What time is it?'

'Not long rung two, Master,' the bailiff answered apologetically. 'The coroner sent me to fetch you.'

'What's happened?'

'We've found Edward and another man.'

'Alive?' he asked, knowing it was unlikely if the man was here at this hour.

'Bodies. On Tapton Lane.'

'Does he need me there?' John asked wearily.

'Yes, Master. He said you should come right away.'

Very carefully, biting his lip against the pain, he drew on his jerkin again the chill outside.

The town was silent, no lights burning in the houses. A dog was barking somewhere, and he heard a creature snuffling through a midden near St Mary's Gate. The bailiff had nothing to say, just moving with quick, sure steps along the road.

It wasn't too far, less than ten minutes. The moon appeared from behind some clouds, casting light and deep shadows over the land. Finally he heard low voices, and as they came close John could make out the silhouette of a body sprawled on the dusty road.

The coroner was leaning against the tree, Brother Robert sitting on the ground beside him.

'About time, Carpenter. You must like your bed too much. What do you make of this?' He gestured at the corpse.

John knelt. The moon was bright enough to make out the face of Edward the Butcher.

'Who found him?'

'A pedlar who was late on the road,' de Harville answered. 'When we arrived, this one wasn't alone.'

'What?' He started to rise, gazing around. All he saw was Edward. 'Who?'

The coroner shrugged. 'I don't know his name. But he was still alive. Two of the men took him back to town. He died on the way. Good riddance to him, too.'

Gilbert. He'd wager money on it.

'There was a pair of bloody knives by them.'

Both of them dead now.

Something about all this was wrong, he thought immediately. It was too convenient. Two wanted men fight and kill each other as they make their escape? He didn't believe it.

'Has anyone searched the area?'

'Why?' the coroner asked. 'We know what happened. We have the men who killed Timothy and Nicholas, the ones who attacked you. We don't even have the expense of a trial,' he said with satisfaction as he pushed himself away from the tree. 'I wanted you to see it. Everything's done.'

De Harville waved a hand and the monk struggled to his feet.

'I want to look around,' John told him.

'Do what you wish, Carpenter.' He shrugged and began to walk away. 'But you'll see better once it's day.'

'What do you want us to do with the body, sir?' one of the bailiffs asked.

'Leave him here and keep a guard on him,' he decided. 'I'll send a cart in the morning.'

Brother Robert started to limp after his master, the portable desk weighing heavy on one shoulder.

'Let me carry that for you,' John offered, hoisting the strap on to his good shoulder.

'Thank you, John.' The monk smiled with relief.

'What do you make of it, Brother?'

'It looks simple enough. They fell out and fought.' He gave a brief, tired smile. 'Thieves do that. They're with God now, ready to be judged. May He have mercy on their souls.'

'Do you think they deserve it?'

'I'm not the one who sees their sins.'

John let his thoughts wander as they trudged towards town.

'Where's the other body?'

'At the jail,' the monk told him. 'We'll see he's buried tomorrow. You should be glad it's over.'

'I'm not so sure it is.'

'Sometimes the obvious explanation is the real one, John,' Robert cautioned.

'Sometimes,' he agreed slowly. 'I'm just not sure it is here. Where's the psalter?' He stayed silent for a while, then asked, 'Do you know who Julian is? The butcher.'

'Don't mention his name around the master,' Robert warned quietly.

'Is he as bad as people say?'

'The talk is that he's murdered at least four.'

'Why not put him on trial for it?'

'No one will ever testify against him. And we've never been able to find any evidence. But we're certain it was him.'

'Who were the victims?'

Robert shook his head. 'Ask me in the morning, please, John. I'm too old to be sharp after a broken sleep.'

At the foot of Saltergate, close to the stone cross, they parted company.

• • •

The jailer was asleep at his desk, loud snores filling the room. John had to slam the door to make him stir.

'What do you want?' He was a heavy, jowly man who reeked of ale and sweat, not happy at having his rest disturbed.

'I want to see the body that was brought in tonight.'

'And who are you?' He turned his head and spat on the dirt floor.

'I'm looking into the killings for the coroner.' He paused. 'Go and ask him if you don't believe me. I'm sure he'll be glad to see you.'

They stared at each other until the jailer finally reached for his set of keys. Grumbling, he unlocked the door.

'I'll need some light down there.'

Slowly, the man took out his flint and tinder, striking the spark and blowing it into a flame. He picked up a torch coated with pitch and soon there was light. Without a word he handed it over.

It was Gilbert. The bald spot at the top of his head, The body which reeked of leather. The corpse had been thrown against the wall in an untidy tangle of limbs.

Wincing, he turned the man, holding up the smoking, stinking brand. Five wounds that he could see. One on the face, down the cheek, another three on the forearms, the last, the one that killed him, on his belly. It looked as if he'd been trying to defend himself. They could have come from a knife fight; it was impossible to be certain.

Gilbert's purse strings had been cut; just two small leather thongs dangled from his belt.

'Did you steal his purse?' John asked after he'd climbed from the cell.

The jailer spat again. 'No. I haven't even looked at him.'

He was telling the truth. It glittered in his hard eyes.

• • •

John unlocked the door to the house, moving lightly inside. Everyone still seemed to be asleep up in the solar. He found some bread and cheese in the buttery and half a mug of weak ale to drink with it.

Four dead now. Too many, far too many. And all for the contents of Timothy's house and a book the killers probably hadn't even known existed. One they very likely couldn't read.

Greed.

He sighed, feeling the weariness of a broken night climbing around him. His arm ached. There was a low throb at the back of his head. But there was no point in going back to his bed. His mind was working now; he'd never get to sleep.

In the morning he'd look at Edward's body. Very likely there was nothing to find, some cuts, a fatal blow. The tale – thieves falling out – could be a true one. It was certainly simple; it wrapped everything up.

But he just didn't believe it. No matter how much he wanted to, it wouldn't sit right in his mind.

The coroner was satisfied. Why couldn't he be, too?

He ate a little more, trying to think things through. Edward and Gilbert must have stayed in Chesterfield, not fled. They'd put their trust in someone. Had he betrayed them or killed them?

His mind moved to Julian, the brooding, threatening presence he'd met the afternoon before. It wasn't too difficult to imagine him behind all this. A man who'd murder without too many qualms. And people like that always had willing followers.

He ran his hands down his face, as if he could draw away the tiredness behind his eyes.

'John?'

He looked up to see Walter watching him. Sometimes the lad could move as silently as a ghost. At other times he clumped through the house like a herd of cattle.

'Do you want something to eat?' He gestured at the food.

'You left very early.'

'I know.' He sighed softly. 'The coroner needed me.'

'Has someone else died?'

'Edward and Gilbert.'

Walter's face turned pale.

'Don't worry. It's safe enough. They can't hurt anyone else now. I have to go back in a little while,' John continued. 'You can come with me, if you want.'

'I do, John,' he said firmly.

'Then get yourself something to eat first. It might be a long day. Are Katherine and the girls still asleep?'

'Yes.'

At least someone was, he thought wearily.

• • •

John knew that Walter was nervous. The lad seemed tense as he walked, eyes searching around in the early light. But he wanted to come along and see the dead. To be a part of this.

It was going to be another warm day. Dawn felt gentle, lulling, the sun appearing off to the east. The road was broad enough for two carts to pass, the verges wide, a King's highway that led all the way to Doncaster.

He breathed deep, taking in all the scents. In the woods there was a chorus of birdsong, the pretty music of the countryside. It was a morning for picking up his leather bag of tools and going to work. To make something that would last and feel the wood take shape under his hands. Not a morning for viewing the dead.

But the corpse was there, lying in the grass, exactly as it had been last night. The bailiff sat with his back against a tree, waving his hand in lazy greeting.

The flies had gathered on Edward's body; he had to keep brushing them away as he examined the corpse. The same type of wounds on the forearms. The fatal blow had been to the chest, a wide patch of blood dried rust-red on the man's shirt. He checked: the purse strings had been cut.

'Look all around,' he told Walter. 'Be as thorough as you can. I don't expect there'll be much to find, but we need to look.'

Half an hour later, with the heat of the day beginning to rise, he called an end to it. Nothing at all.

'What are the arrangements for the body?' he asked the bailiff.

The man shrugged a reply. 'They'll send a cart out soon enough. Are you finished, Master?'

He nodded. 'The pedlar who found him. Do you know where he's staying?'

'He'll be with old Gabriel out by West Bar. Always stays there. He's been coming round every few months for years now. Plenty of folk know him.'

Not to be suspected, in other words. He nodded and turned away, Walter beside him.

'What do we do now, John?'

'I think we'll start by finding out more about Julian the Butcher,' he said thoughtfully.

He rubbed his wounded arm. It would be several days before it was strong enough to finish work on the barn in Newbold. All of it empty time. He might as well do something to fill it. There was something here that just wasn't right, even if he didn't know what it was yet.

CHAPTER NINE

'Do you think he killed them?' Walter asked.

John stifled a yawn. Already it felt like a long day and it had barely begun.

'I don't know,' he said.

'But why would he do that?'

That was the question.

'Everyone seems happy with the idea that Edward and Gilbert fought and killed each other.' He watched as Walter nodded. 'Maybe they did. But it seems too simple to me, too easy. And both of them had their purses stolen.' He tried to put his thoughts into words but how could he describe what was nothing more than an instinct?

'It feels wrong. I can't even say why.' He let his thoughts turn and they came back to a single person. 'Who would know about Julian?'

The boy stayed quiet for a long time.

'I can think of someone,' he replied eventually. 'Christian of Dronfield.'

Dronfield. Where poor dead Nicholas had been born. Not even a handful of miles from Chesterfield.

'How do they know each other?'

Walter shook his head. 'I don't know. But they seem to talk a lot at every Saturday market.'

A friend, then, and one who might not want to say much.

'Anyone else?'

'Not that I know, John.'

'Then we'd better start walking. We can be in Dronfield before dinner.'

. . .

The road was dry, few carts around. Somewhere along the valley he heard a cow lowing. It was fertile land here, out towards Unstone, the grass and the growing shoots of wheat lush on the hillside. A few late blossoms remained on the apple trees, the sun catching the brilliance of a magpie's feathers as it flickered through the branches. A pair of crows were fighting over something, their caws briefly filling the air.

Everything was so peaceful, so placid, that it was hard to believe that just a few years before God had turned his back on the world. The sun was warm on his face, not too hot, as perfect a spring day as anyone could wish. Just right for a walk.

The village was clustered around a thin, gurgling stream that meandered through the bottom of the valley. The church stood halfway up the hillside, close to a long stone barn and an inn. At the peak, the manor house, staring down over everything. He'd passed through here once before, when he was first making his way to Chesterfield. The priest had shared his food and offered a bench in his house for sleeping.

It seemed like a contented place, one that might have looked exactly the same a hundred years before. A few of the cottages were abandoned, neglected and crumbling, but most were carefully tended, large gardens growing behind them.

John led the way to the alehouse, a cramped old building, its business shown by a green branch hanging over the door. Inside, the place was clean and airy, shutters thrown back to the sun, fresh rushes and lavender strewn on the floor.

A woman was bent over, tapping a barrel, filling a mug and holding it up before tasting it and giving a little smile of satisfaction at her work.

'A good brew, Mistress?'

She turned quickly, slopping a little of the drink over the rim. A tall woman, heavily built, past her middle years but still looking strong and smiling with pride.

'Indeed it is, Masters. Perhaps you should try it.'

'We will,' John told her. 'And two bowls of pottage.'

He paid and they sat at a bench, staring out through an unglazed window. In the distance men worked on their strips of land, tending the growing crops. A horse and cart moved lazily along the main street. It was like so many other villages he'd seen on his travels, where people lived and died surrounded by their joys and their sorrows.

'Do you know where we can find Christian?' he asked the woman as she brought the food. She jerked a thumb over her shoulder.

'The manor house, like as not. If he's not there he'll be going round the lord's fields. Have business with him, do you?' It was a natural villager's curiosity.

'Someone mentioned his name, and we're passing.' John shrugged. 'Did you ever know someone called Julian? Lives in Chesterfield now?'

'Him.' Her face turned hard. 'I wouldn't give you a farthing for him. You'd be hard pressed to find anyone here who would. Dronfield's a lot better since he left.'

'Why does everyone hate him?'

'He stole anything that wasn't locked up. Nothing anyone could prove, mind you. He was sly enough for that, but we all knew. Finally we decided to give him a warning: leave or pay the price. He went.'

'All the way to Chesterfield,' John said.

'It's far enough.' She shrugged. 'As long as he's not coming around here, I don't care.'

The food was good, heavily spiced and tasty. He finished the bowl, wiping it clean with a slice of bread, then washed everything down with the last of the ale. But even with the meal in him, Walter still looked hungry. He could wait for more; they had work to do.

The stone of the manor house was still bright, the windows glazed. Some lord's rich statement. The building looked no more than a few years old, but solid and ready to stand for the ages. Two men were working close by, turning over the soil. They stopped as they noticed the approach of two strangers.

'God go with you.' John raised a hand in greeting.

'And with you,' the older of the men said warily, a large hand resting on his shovel. 'Are you looking for someone?'

'Christian, if he's here.'

A shadow seemed to cross the man's face. It only lasted a moment then his expression was empty again.

'The steward's down in the bottoms, along the Sheffield Road.' He pointed north. 'They're draining a ditch.'

'Thank you.'

'Just follow the road by the stream and you'll find him.'

'What do you want with Christian?' the younger of the pair asked. He was thin, the hose baggy on his legs, arms no thicker than twigs.

John smiled. 'Just a little business. Good day to you, Masters.'

'Did you notice that?' he asked as they went back down the hill. 'The way that man's look changed when I mentioned Christian's name.'

'I don't think he likes him. You should have asked him why.'

'He wouldn't have told me.' It wasn't something to share with complete strangers. 'There's someone else I want to see while we're here.'

At the church he swung the door open. The air felt cooler, fragrant with the faint scent of incense. The priest was standing by the altar, lost in prayer. John put a finger to his lips as they entered.

As their soles rang out on the tile floor the man turned in alarm, his mouth still open. He peered with old eyes.

'I know you, don't I?'

'You do, Father.' John grinned. 'You gave me shelter for a night last summer.'

'You're a … carpenter?' He tried to remember.

'I am, Father. John the Carpenter. And settled in Chesterfield now, married with a child due.' The priest crossed himself with his hope for the baby. 'This is Walter, my wife's brother.'

'What brings you back here, my son?'

'Questions, Father. I'm doing work for the coroner.'

The priest raised an eyebrow.

'If you want to talk we should go outside,' he said after a small hesitation. 'There's a bench in the shade. It's a pleasant place to sit.'

Indeed it was. By the north wall of the church, in the shadow of the building, catching the small wisps of breeze that fluttered down the hill.

'Questions, you said?' the priest asked as he settled.

'That's right. I'd like to know about two people,' John told him. 'Christian the steward and someone who used to live here.'

The Father chuckled. 'If you're asking about Christian, then the other person must be Julian.'

'They were close?'

'They're cousins,' the priest told him. 'Their mothers are sisters.'

'That doesn't always mean much.'

'True enough,' he agreed with a nod. 'But the pair of them were closer than most brothers. Born the same year, grew up together.'

'And was Christian as bad as Julian?'

'Not as bad. You've heard the tale?'

'Only a little of it, Father.'

'Probably enough. Stories always grow bigger in the telling.' A flutter of wind ruffled his black cassock. 'Are you old enough to remember what things were like after the pestilence?'

'Yes,' John answered. Walter shook his head.

'Those were good days for lawless men,' the priest sad with a sigh. 'Or for those who wanted to be.'

'Julian and Christian wanted to be?'

'Julian did. He'd always been wild, the way some boys are, but his parents stopped the worst of it. After they died …' He shook his head.

'What about Christian?' John wondered.

'He was always easily led.' The priest sighed. 'But he was never as bad as his cousin. There are plenty of folk who still resent him for those times, though. And he's a hard man to work for.'

'But the villagers never demanded that Christian leave?'

'No. The lord had appointed him as steward by then, so there wasn't much we could do. Getting rid of Julian was enough. There's been no trouble here since then.'

'Christian and Julian often talk together at the Saturday market,' Walter said and the priest nodded.

'That doesn't surprise me. The kind of bond they had doesn't vanish.' The father turned to John. 'Why are you so interested in Julian?'

'Something he might have done. But even if he did it I don't think I'll ever be able to prove it. Tell me, do you remember someone called Nicholas? He was from here.'

'No. Perhaps it was before my time here.'

'Who owns the manor?'

'Sir Alexander de Sèvres. Not that we ever see him from year to year. He has most of the land from here to Doncaster. But it's the steward who takes care of it for him.'

Just like so many lords, who never saw their property. John stood.

'Thank you for your time, Father.'

'May God go with you and help you.'

They left him in the shade, staring into the distance.

'Are we going to see Christian now?' Walter asked as they strode back down the hill.

'No,' John answered. 'I doubt he'd be willing to tell us anything about Julian. Not if they're as close as people say. And we've already learned a lot.' He clapped the boy on the shoulder. 'Let's go home. You must have messages to deliver.'

'I like working with you.' The lad beamed.

'We've finished for today. You might as well make some use of it.'

• • •

After the peace of the countryside, Chesterfield seemed dirty and crowded. He watched Walter run off, then turned on to Saltergate. Later he'd go to find the pedlar and hear his story. For now, though, he needed rest. His arm ached and his head seemed heavy; the morning had started too early.

The girls were working, spinning wool as Katherine watched them and mended a pile of linen. Up in the solar, stripped to his shirt and braies, John lay on the bed and closed his eyes. The window was open, the air warm and lulling. A few minutes later he felt her settle next to him.

'The news is all over town,' she said. 'Martha came and told me.' She giggled. 'I think she was hoping you'd be here to get all the gossip.'

He smiled softly and felt sleep take him

He woke with a weight on his chest and the soft sound of purring. He opened his eyes to see a cat staring into his face, kneading his shirt softly with its paws. It was small, hardly more than a kitten, a tabby with dark stripes over the grey fur and a blaze of white on its nose. The rough little tongue licked his hand. Tenderly, he placed it on the blanket while he dressed, then went down to the hall with the animal cradled in his arm.

Martha and the girls were on the settle. They had their heads down as if they were concentrating on the slates in their laps. But their shoulders trembled a little, trying not to laugh.

'Have any of you ladies lost a cat?' he asked, smiling.

It was Eleanor who giggled first, darting out and stretching her arms up for the kitten.

'Oh, it's yours, is it?' John said.

'And mine,' Janette told him. 'Aunt Martha said we have to share it.'

'Did she now?'

The woman looked up, contrite but smiling. 'I thought it would be good for them to have something to look after.'

'We're going to call it John,' Eleanor declared proudly. 'Just like you.'

'Won't that be confusing?' he asked. 'You'll call him and I might come running.' He meowed and the girls began to laugh. 'What does your sister say about it?'

'Katherine says we can keep it if you say yes and we look after it.' The words gushed out from Eleanor.

He stroked his chin. 'Then it seems as if the cat lives here now. Why don't the two of you put a little milk in a bowl for him? I've heard that cats like milk.'

'I'm sorry,' Martha said over the noise from the buttery as the girls fed the kitten. 'I found it in my garden this morning. I thought it would be perfect for them.'

He laughed. 'Not to mention the mischief it'll cause?' He grinned as he sat next to her, moving the slates out of the way. Two of them had the first spidery attempts at letters made with tailor's chalk. On the third the alphabet was laid out in a neat, even hand, not that it meant anything to him. 'You started the lessons.'

'They're doing very well,' Martha said.

Who'd have thought it, that the girls would be able to read and write and count? And they'd pass on that learning to the child that was coming. Even if they never had the chance to use it, they'd still possess the skill.

'Thank you,' he said.

'Am I forgiven for the cat?' she asked, eyes twinkling.

'As long as it doesn't do too much damage. But I don't know how I can pay you for everything you do for us.'

She slapped him lightly on the thigh. 'Gossip is good currency. As if you didn't already know.' There was laughter in her eyes.

'Maybe some details about what happened last night?'

'That would be a good start.'

He told her what he'd learned, laying it all out as clearly as possible. It was for himself as much as for her. He wanted to see if there was any real reason for his suspicions, something he'd seen but not really noticed. But the only real mystery seemed to be the severed purse strings.

It was very little, but enough to gnaw away at him. Ample to send him to Dronfield and to carry on when the coroner said it was all over.

'That should give you a few things to tell them at the market tomorrow.'

'You know I never gossip,' Martha told him primly.

'Mistress, my apologies.' But they were already grinning at each other.

'This other man, Gilbert,' she began as he brought two mugs of ale.

'I'm going to find out more about him tomorrow.'

'Just be careful of Julian,' Martha warned. 'He's—'

Before she could say more, the girls came racing back into the hall, skirts flying round their ankles. Janette was carrying the mewling kitten, a pouting Eleanor right behind her.

'Elly says we have to call him John.'

He looked at Martha.

'Why don't you just call him Kit,' she said seriously after a little thought. 'That way everyone has their own name. Don't you think that would be better?'

Janette turned to her sister, sticking out her tongue and smirked as if she'd won some great victory. The cat slipped out of her arms and wandered away, stalking back into the buttery, the sisters in loud pursuit.

'We're going to have all sorts of arguments now.' He sighed.

'Just wait. It'll all be over by tomorrow,' Martha told him. 'Sisters squabble, it's the way of the world. Now, tell me about Dronfield. My husband and I used to walk out near there years ago.'

He started to describe the village, the church, the inn, watching her old face light up and make her young once more. He'd barely finished when the door opened and Katherine came in, struggling with a heavy basket. She was flushed by the heat.

He jumped up and took the load from her. She'd been down to the river to wash the clothes. Wet linen, and a good weight even to him.

Wearily, Katherine sat by Martha and wiped the sweat off her face. 'I swear someone's made that hill steeper.' She shook her head in amazement.

'Things will be easier once the baby's born,' Martha advised her. 'But harder still before that.'

'I'm not sure that's a comfort.' Katherine chuckled and shook her head. John handed her his mug of ale and she drank deep.

'It's worth it once they're here.' Martha squeezed her hand gently. 'You'll see.'

'That's what everyone keeps telling me,' Katherine said doubtfully.

'That's because they're right,' the old woman said with kind firmness. 'Come on, we'll lay this out so it can dry.'

• • •

The heat had built during the day, gathering close to the ground. Now it seemed to cling to him as he walked across the market square towards West Bar.

Gabriel's house stood just beyond the boundary marker, outside the town. It was a small place, carefully tended, with a large garden on the slope down towards the River Hipper. He looked like a capable man, strong and powerfully built, seeming younger then the lines that radiated out from his eyes. His head was completely bald, already brown from the sun. But a cloud of white beard covered his face, and a pair of intelligent blue eyes showed.

'Good day, Master,' John said. 'I'd like to see the pedlar if he's here.'

Gabriel studied him, then gave a brief nod. 'I've seen you around. You're the carpenter, aren't you?'

'I am, Master.'

'I've been meaning to talk to you. There's a hinge broken on the back door and I can't mend it.'

'I can look at it tomorrow,' he offered. Even with a bad arm he should be able to manage a small job like that.

'Come on in.'

The hall was small but neat; the man looked after his things carefully. Everything was old, but the wood was polished and cushions rested on the settle. Gabriel's clothes were clean, carefully mended.

'Luke!' the man called, his voice surprisingly loud. 'You have a customer.' He winked and said, 'He'll be out in a minute.'

It was no more than a few moments before a lanky young man strode in, rubbing at his eyes and yawning.

'I'm sorry, Master,' he said. 'I must have fallen asleep.' He grinned. 'I had a long night.'

'I heard about it.'

Luke was thin, but the legs in his hose were powerful from years of walking around the country, and his face was weatherbeaten. He was still young, looking innocent and hapless, with a ready smile, sturdy boots and an easy manner. But he'd need all that to wheedle his way into houses and sell his goods.

The man rubbed his hands together. 'Now, Master, what can I do for you? I've got ribbons for your wife, or your mistress if you don't want your wife to know. Thread, needles, even a pot or a pan if you need those.'

'I'm sorry. Gabriel misled you. I'm not here to buy,' John told him and saw the man's face fall. It couldn't be an easy life, always on the road, even during a good spring. It took a tongue like silver and a hide like leather. 'I work for the coroner.'

Luke looked up sharply. 'I've already paid my fine for finding the bodies.'

'This is nothing to do with that. I just have a few questions.'

The man nodded warily.

'One of the men was still alive when you found them?' John asked.

'Yes.' He chewed his lip. 'Barely. He was still breathing.'

'Did he say anything?'

'No.' Luke shook his head slowly. 'I tried talking to him but I don't think he even heard me. I'm not sure he knew I was there.'

'How closely did you look at them?'

'Enough to see if they were dead.' The man looked at him cautiously. 'Why?'

'Did you notice if their purse strings were cut?'

'No. As soon as I saw the smaller one was still breathing, I ran to town.'

John believed him. There was a sense of honesty about him. Maybe it was something he'd cultivated over the years, letting it grow like wheat. But this seemed genuine enough.

'Did you notice anything else?'

Luke was silent for a long time, moments finally turning to a minute.

'I don't think they'd been there long,' he said.

'Why?'

'When I touched the dead man he was still warm,' Luke answered, shuddering at the memory. 'Just like you and me.'

So they'd probably only been there a few minutes when the pedlar came by, he thought.

'Did you see anything else?' John asked. 'Hear anything or see anyone?'

The man pushed his lips together and shook his head. 'I hadn't seen a soul since I left Whittington.'

'Wasn't it late to be on the road?'

Luke shrugged. 'Not really. I've done it often enough before. There was a strong moon and I know the way. I thought it would give me more selling time here. I usually do good business in Chesterfield.'

'Did you recognise either of the bodies?'

'No. But, like I said, I didn't really look. I didn't think.'

'It doesn't matter.' John smiled. 'You said you had some ribbon?'

Katherine deserved a little something. He knew she was struggling with the pregnancy. She said nothing, but he could see the tiredness on her face, the fact that everything seemed like hard work. A little gift might raise her mood.

'John!' she said as he held it up. A small length of scarlet ribbon. 'It's lovely.' She looked at him and smiled. 'Thank you.'

He tied it round her neck, watching her blush with pleasure.

The girls were laughing and giggling, jumping up and down. Katherine stroked the soft material and began to cry. He put his arms around her, confused.

'What's wrong? I thought you'd be happy.'

'I am,' she told him, clumsily trying to wipe away her tears. 'I am.'

CHAPTER TEN

The sun was already over the horizon when he stirred. As he stood, his body felt easier. The bruises from his beating and time in the river were beginning to fade, the muscles moving more freely. Even lifting his left arm was easier. Another day and he'd probably be able to work again.

John heard Katherine moving around downstairs, small feet following her around. Walter's bed was empty. He'd never heard any of them wake. Lazily, he stretched and eased into his clothes, washing his face and hands in a basin.

She was still wearing the ribbon, pinned to her dress now so it fluttered and billowed as she walked. Janette and Eleanor were fussing over the cat, stroking it as it tried to eat some chopped offal. Walter had already gone. Another day.

There were plenty of shoemakers on Soutergate. Five of them on the street. He'd never understood how they could all stay in business. Surely the town was too small? But they all seemed to flourish. He started at the top of the hill, asking for Edmund's shop.

'Three doors down,' the man told him without raising his head.

'Did you know Gilbert?'

'The one who worked for him?' He didn't stop his labours as he talked, deftly sewing two piece of leather together with quick, even stitches. 'I did.' The shoemaker kept his eyes on the shoe and needle. 'Good at his job if he'd had any ambition.' He turned his head and spat. 'I'd not have had him here, though.'

As he finished an apprentice staggered in from the back, carrying an armful of skins and lowering them gently on to a table.

'Start cutting,' the shoemaker ordered him. The younger man rolled his eyes.

'Yes, Master.'

• • •

Edmund looked harried. He had a nervous face, hair cut short, the sleeves of his shirt pushed up to show hairy arms. An assortment of his wares was on display across the lowered front shutter. Fashionable shoes with long, pointed toes, lovingly worked in expensive leather. Sturdier, cheaper boots, made for men who laboured and needed something strong.

John looked down at his feet. He'd worn the same pair of boots for the last three years. New, they'd cost him a pretty penny, but they'd lasted well. Now, though, they looked scuffed and sad. Perhaps it was time to replace them.

'Good day, Master,' Edmund said with a smile. 'Looking for anything in particular?'

He could see the shoemaker assessing him, judging what type of footwear he'd need and how much might be in his purse.

'Perhaps.'

'What's your work, Master?'

'I'm a carpenter.'

'You need something that will last, then. But comfortable.' Edmund moved out from the counter. 'It looks like those have served you kindly. Doesn't look like the work of anyone local, though.' He smiled quickly. 'We all have our little touches. I don't recognise these.'

'I bought them in York.'

'York! They have good craftsmen up there. A wonderful place, people say.'

'It is.'

'I could make you a pair like these,' Edmund said, stroking his chin. 'Something to last you three years and better. They won't be cheap, but they'll still feel good after a day's labour.'

'How much?'

The shoemaker named his price. Half the cost of the boots in York.

'As long as they're strong.'

'The best, Master. I promise you that.'

'I'm surprised you don't have anyone working with you.'

Edmund's face turned sour. 'I did. A hard worker and he'd been with me a long time. Then he didn't turn up on Monday and the next thing I know he's dead out on Tapton Lane.'

'The men everyone's talking about?'

Edmund nodded. 'One of them. Gilbert, his name was. Fine with a needle, too; he could sew a pair of shoes as tight as anyone I'd ever met. But he had his ways.'

'His ways?' John asked.

'He liked to drink and wager. He could probably have had his own shop if he'd put his mind to it. But that wasn't Gilbert. You know how some people are. He thought that if he bet cleverly enough, he'd win and life would be easy.'

'Didn't they find another man out there, too?'

'Edward the Butcher. He was a bad sort. I daresay there won't be too many honest folk who'll miss him.' He looked around and leant closer, lowering his voice. 'The rumour is that they killed old Timothy and his servant. I wouldn't put that past Edward. There was something about him.'

'Were they good friends? Gilbert and Edward?'

'Drank together, gambled together.' Edmund shrugged. 'Must have been close enough, I suppose. Hand me your boots a minute, Master, so I can make some outlines.'

In a little while he was back on Soutergate. His purse was lighter, but a man needed stout boots for work. It was an investment, he told himself; they'd serve him for a long time. That was some consolation.

He spotted Walter at the top of the hill and quickened his pace to catch up. The lad vanished into a little jennel between two houses. John arrived in time to see the menacing presence of Julian at the end of the lane, blocking the way out. The boy stood, clutching a package to his side.

John drew his knife, walking along calmly. Walter turned in fright at the footsteps, then smiled with relief.

'I thought we could walk together,' John said.

Julian didn't move as they approached. He wore no expression on his face, eyes narrow, one hand resting lightly on the hilt of his dagger.

'Good day to you,' John said. 'You'll need to move so we can go past.'

But Julian stood his ground. 'You've been asking about me in Dronfield.'

'I have,' John admitted.

'Why?'

'I was on the coroner's business.' It was a flat statement. 'Maybe you'd like to talk to him about it.'

'You and the whelp ought to take care.'

'Should we?' He tightened his grip on the knife. 'Why's that?'

'Things might happen to people you love.'

In one swift movement John was on him. He planted a leg behind Julian then pushed hard so the man tumbled on to his back. He knelt on Julian's chest, pinning his arms with his knees and holding the knife at his throat.

'I'll say this once,' John hissed. 'And I'll only say it once. If anything happens to anyone I care about, if there's even a hint of it, I'll come for you. And next time I won't stop. Do you understand me?' He pressed the edge of the blade against the man's flesh, just hard enough for a thin line of blood to appear.

Julian stayed silent, a stare of pure hatred.

'If I need to ask questions, I'll do that without begging your leave,' John continued. 'We've had four men dead here. From all I've heard, another wouldn't be missed.' He reached down and lifted Julian's knife from its sheath, sending it skittering away. Then further, plucking another from the man's boot. It followed the first. 'Do I make myself clear, Master?' He spoke the title mockingly. 'You threaten people I love and there'll be no mercy for you. Do you understand?' He lent on the blade a little more. 'Do you?'

Cautiously, Julian gave a nod and John stood.

'I think we're done here, Walter.'

His heart seemed to beat so loud as he walked away he thought the whole town must be able to hear it. He pushed his hands into his belt so no one could see them shaking.

'How did you do that, John?' Walter asked in a voice filled with wonder.

'Do what?'

'Make him fall.'

'Something I was shown once.' He let out a breath. 'You'd better be careful. He's going to want his revenge.' The lad nodded. 'And not a word to your sister. I don't want her worried.'

'Yes, John,' Walter promised solemnly.

'No gossiping about it either,' he warned.

He watched the boy lope away. The day was as warm and sunny as it had been a few minutes before, but it felt different, as if there was danger in the air. He'd humiliated Julian, and the man wouldn't stand for that. He was the type who'd demand vengeance. Not a clean, fair fight, but at a time and place where he had the advantage.

But it also made him wonder just how deeply Julian was involved in all this. He wouldn't threaten unless he had something to hide. Could Edward and Gilbert have been working for him, and he'd killed them before they could be arrested and talked? That made sense, there was logic in the chain of it all.

Proving it would be another matter.

By the time he reached the weekday market on the north side of the church, he felt exhausted. The fear and anger had drained away, leaving a hole inside. All he wanted was to lie down somewhere quiet, to sleep and forget for a while. He might be recovering from his injuries, but he wasn't all the way back to himself yet.

The stalls were full of goodwives and servants shopping for milk, butter, eggs, and the produce on sale – young onions and wild garlic, the first fresh greens of the seasons, pulled from the ground before sunrise and carried into town.

He nodded good day to one or two he knew and raised his gaze to the spire. The oak tiles rose higher each day. Men climbed, held fast by harnesses, to nail them in place on the cross beams. It was a remarkable creation, tall enough to touch heaven. As impressive in its own way as the great minsters in York and Lincoln, the beautiful stone castles of God.

In the house, the girls were spinning with the type of playful concentration only children could manage. The kitten kept pawing at the thread, and they kept pulling it away. He paused to kiss them on the tops of their heads and stroke the cat. No one was going to hurt them, he promised himself. No one.

Katherine was working out in the garden, hoeing the weeds out from a line of crops. The first shoots of this and that, the soft fern tops of carrots, more he couldn't identify. He held her close for a moment and told her he needed some rest.

She eyed him doubtfully. 'Has something happened?' she asked him.

'I've bought new boots,' he answered with a grin, pointing to the ones on his feet. 'These have had their day. Spending money leaves a man weary. We're not like women.'

She swatted at him and he ducked back. With luck she'd never hear about the incident with Julian. Walter had been the only witness, he believed. And that was best for everyone.

The bed brought sweet comfort to his body. He'd rather have been working. Real work, with wood. But things were as they would be. Another day or two and he'd be ready. Before then he could indulge himself in dreams.

He woke in the middle of the afternoon, refreshed, his mind sharp and alert. He'd promised the man Gabriel that he'd come and mend his door. It was satisfying to put on the leather satchel of tools and feel the weight slapping against his thigh as he walked along Knifesmithgate and crossed the empty market square.

It was simple work. A moment to see the problem, no more than a quarter of an hour to repair it and see that the door opened and closed smoothly. As he was wiping the tools clean, Gabriel brought two mugs of ale.

'You could have done it yourself,' John told him.

The man shook his head ruefully. 'The last time I tried I only made it worse.'

'People have different skills.'

'I bought and sold.'

'A merchant?' he asked as he put the tools back in the bag.

'It's as good a word as any,' Gabriel said with a shrug. 'Bits of this and that.'

'A pedlar?' he guessed.

'No. I couldn't afford this place on a pedlar's income. I let Luke stay because he always has good stories and the gossip from all over.' He smiled. 'He brings the world to me. What do I owe you?'

'We'll say a penny. Is that fair?'

'Perfectly.' He took a coin from the purse on his belt.

'Were you born here?' John asked idly.

'Born here and this is where I'll die.' He stroked his white beard, a glint in his eyes. 'But I've seen plenty in between. As far north as York and all the way down to London.'

'Business?'

The man nodded. 'I had the chance to go to France but I didn't take it.' He sounded wistful. 'You're a young man. Always take your opportunities when they come. If you don't you'll only regret it later.'

'I'm a man with a wife and a child on the way.' He smiled. 'I've seen enough of the world for my tastes. I worked in York for two years.'

They fell into idle, easy conversation, whiling away the time. The warmth was lulling, the ale strong, and the company pleasant. They exchanged reminiscences and tall tales until John finally stood and picked up the leather bag.

'I knew your wife's mother,' Gabriel said. 'Long ago. She was just a lass then. It's funny. You see them grow and have children of their own. My sons are scattered now. The two who survived the plague, that is.'

'You must have known Timothy.'

'Never that well,' Gabriel said slowly. 'Not at all after his accident. It was a shock to hear he'd been killed, though. And his servant.'

'What was he like?'

'Quiet, I suppose,' Gabriel answered after some thought. 'When he wasn't working he was always off hunting and hawking.' He shrugged. 'That was a long time ago.'

'Did you ever hear any talk of him having a book?'

'A book? No–' He stopped himself. 'Maybe there was something. I don't know, it was so far back. Why?'

'He owned a psalter. He'd promised it to the church when he died.'

'And it was gone?'

'Yes,' John replied.

'It seems to me I remember something about a book, but I don't know what.'

'It doesn't matter.'

'I'll tell you when there's more work to do here.'

. . .

Outside the air was balmy. It had felt good to be using his hands again, to mend something that was broken. Another two days and he'd be back in Newbold, to see the barn take shape.

On an impulse he crossed over to the High Street, enjoying the satisfying weight of the tools as they banged against his leg. De Harville was in the yard outside his house, talking to his groom and preparing to mount a roan. When the servant looked and muttered a word, he turned. He was elaborately dressed in a black velvet jerkin over his linen, with hose the colour of dark red wine. His riding boots shone, and a shimmering peacock feather rose from his cap.

'Carpenter. And with your tools. Are you looking for business? There's nothing I need doing here.' He put a foot in the stirrup and pushed himself up into the saddle. 'What do you want? Be quick.'

'I don't think Edward and Gilbert killed each other. They might have murdered Timothy and Edward, but there's more going on.'

The coroner gave a weary sigh and patted the horse's neck. 'Why do you have to make trouble? We have them, they're dead.

That's an end to it. If you're trying to wheedle more money to continue, I won't pay it.'

'What was missing when they were found?'

'Their purses,' de Harville answered.

'And the book, if they were the killers.'

'What does it matter?' He dismissed it. 'It's over.'

Then he realised the thing he'd missed, the doubt that had gnawed at him since he'd seen the bodies.

'If they were leaving Chesterfield, where were their packs?'

It was enough to halt the coroner. Reluctantly he dismounted and threw the reins to the groom.

'Take her out and exercise her,' he ordered as he began to stride off to the stable. 'Maybe those were stolen, too.'

'It's possible, but I don't think anyone would dare walk around here in their clothes. People would recognise them.'

De Harville chewed at a thumbnail as he thought, a scowl on his face.

'I went to Dronfield and asked a few questions about Julian the Butcher,' John continued.

The coroner stared at him. 'And why would you want to do that?' he asked quietly.

'There's something about him. I hear you've had problems with him before.'

'For a carpenter you listen to a lot of gossip.'

'The people I talked to out there didn't have a good word to say about him. Someone told him; this morning he threatened me and my family.'

'What did you do?'

'I threw him on his back and held a knife to his throat.'

'There's still some fire about you, then,' the coroner chuckled. 'So you believe Julian's behind it all?'

'I don't know,' he admitted. 'Even if he is, I don't know how I can prove it.'

'The truth becomes very slippery around that man.' He flexed one hand into a fist and opened it again. 'I'd like to see Chesterfield rid of him.'

'I can't promise that.'

'No?' He raised an eyebrow. 'You disappoint me, Carpenter. You did so well last time.'

'He has a friend. Christian, the steward in Dronfield. They're cousins.'

'I've met him,' the coroner said. 'A surly sort. Yes,' he agreed thoughtfully, 'I could see the two of them as close. But what about it?'

'I'm not sure yet. I just want you to know in case Julian kills me,' John said plainly.

'Do you think he'll try?'

'He might. I humiliated him.' John shrugged. 'A man like him can't let that lie.'

'Then you'd better watch out for yourself.'

'I will,' he said with a grim smile. For all the threats and bluster, Julian would come after him, not his family. Even if John stopped investigating the murders. It was a matter of pride now. Julian needed to avenge what had been done. That was the way he'd think. It was a very personal matter, one to be settled man to man.

He'd make sure he was ready and alert. Julian had killed before, they said. Another death wouldn't trouble him too greatly.

'Do you need men to help you?' the coroner asked, his voice serious.

'No, they wouldn't do any good,' he answered. 'It would help me if you let people keep thinking you're satisfied that Edward and Gilbert were the killers.'

'Easily done.'

'Julian's arrogant. He'll make a mistake.'

'He hasn't yet,' de Harville said.

'How closely have you looked?'

'Perhaps not close enough,' he admitted. 'If he's guilty, I want him, Carpenter.'

'It might take time.'

'Make sure you're careful.' It was the first time he'd heard the coroner express any concern. He studied the man's face. His gaze was intense.

'Yes,' John replied and walked away. Now to pray God that Walter hadn't said a word. He didn't want Katherine to have worries on top of everything else.

But no one muttered when they saw him. No strange glances from folk as he walked along the street. In a town like this gossip passed like breathing. The lad had kept quiet. Much safer that way.

He was aware of everything as he moved. Faces, movement, sounds, taking it all in with a hand ready on the hilt of his knife. He'd need to be on his guard every single moment. And it would be better to stay clear of the Shambles.

How could he find any evidence? He didn't know where to begin. Even *how* he could begin. Julian must have friends, there must be a weak link in the chain around him. Finding it would be the problem.

By the time he reached the house on Saltergate he was none the wiser. The others were already seated at the table, eating a supper of bread and cheese, a jug of ale standing between them.

He glanced at Walter, but the lad was intent on his food.

'I'm sorry, I started talking to Gabriel after I finished the job.'

When they'd eaten, the girls wanted to show him what they'd learned from Martha. They scraped shapes on to their slates, explaining what they letters were and how they sounded. They were bright and so eager to learn.

He saw Walter crowd close, saying nothing but drinking it all in. Later, after Janette and Eleanor had gone up to the solar to sleep, John wandered out into the garden, relishing the evening air with its soft smells and quiet, contented sounds.

Walter was out there, scraping at the dust with a stick, concentrating on every movement. The same shapes he'd seen the girls make earlier. The boy's lips moved silently. John watched for a moment then gave a quiet cough. Walter turned quickly, scrubbing out his work.

'I didn't hear you, John,' he said.

'I'm sorry.' He drew close and said quietly, 'You remember what happened earlier.' The lad nodded quickly. 'You didn't tell anyone, did you?'

'No, John.' His eyes were guileless. He never lied.

'It's probably better if your sister never hears about it.' He was putting a weight on Walter, an obligation. He knew that. He knew it wasn't fair. But he didn't want Katherine fearful and fretting every time he left the house.

Women were hardy, even more than men. Martha had told him that. They'd been having babies for centuries. It was natural. But so was losing the infant or dying in childbed. He was the one who was scared – for her. A small lie now might make her life easier.

But the only way to be truly safe was to find evidence that would put Julian on the gibbet.

'I saw you go over to the coroner's house.'

He smiled. Walter might not say a great deal, but his eyes didn't miss much that happened.

'He wants us to look at Julian.' He almost whispered the words and saw the lad smile and nod. 'We'll talk about it in the morning.'

• • •

In the bed, Katherine cuddled against his back. Her breath was warm on his neck as she said, 'When are you back to work?'

'Another day,' he told her and cautiously moved his shoulder. 'Or the one after that.'

'There's nothing else, is there?'

'No. Why would there be?'

'It doesn't matter.' She kissed his skin.

He lay there, hearing the rhythm of her breathing gradually change. All around him the family was asleep. There was even the gentle night purr of the cat from the bed the girls shared. He wished it would come so easily to him.

CHAPTER ELEVEN

He was up early and on his way back to Dronfield before the sun had topped the horizon. He'd only managed to sleep in fits and starts, disturbed by wild dreams until rising was better than trying to rest more. He was outside, not even fully awake, letting his feet lead him wherever they would.

The sky was clear, stars bright over his head, the air light with the scents of dawn. It was past daylight when he arrived. He'd seen no one on the road, just the occasional distant figure of a woman trudging to the barn to milk the cows.

The River Drone was little more than a beck, lost in its trickle through the valley bottom. He continued through the village, past an inn to where the road curved up the hill. Three men were gathered, hoes and picks on the ground beside them. They watched him approach, standing silent. Labourers by the look of them, led by a bondman in old hose and muddy boots, shirtsleeves rolled up to show weatherbeaten arms.

'God be with you,' John said.

Warily, they nodded their greeting.

'I'm looking for Christian.'

'He'll be along when he's ready,' the man in the shirt answered. He had a thick growth of bristles on his cheeks and dark, suspicious eyes. 'What do you want with him?'

'Just some business.'

'He'll still be at the manor house,' the man said grudgingly. 'Top of the hill.' He looked at the others and they began work. It was slow, digging down and drawing the sludge from the stream. Two of them were stripped to their braies, standing in the water, hunched over and straining. The one still fully dressed spread what they dug up on to the field.

Backbreaking labour, and they moved slowly and methodically. This was some of the service they owed their lord, he guessed, so there was no rush to complete it. So many days each year. They ploughed and planted his land, harvested his crops and did whatever else was demanded. In return they had a house and strips of land for themselves. Their fathers and grandfathers had done it, their descendants would do it in the time to come.

He settled back on his haunches, watching and thinking. He couldn't have ordered anyone to do that. Just as well he never became steward of the coroner's manor. He didn't know country ways, all the tasks that needed to be done.

He was still musing when he heard the footsteps and a shadow fell over him.

'Who are you?'

'I'm John the Carpenter.' He stood, facing a broad man in good clothes. Expensive leather boots, a jacket of tight-woven wool and sturdy hose.

'What do you want?' The man had his hands on his hips, a sword hanging by his leg.

'If you're Christian, I'm looking for you.'

'Why?' He had a hard face with a long, thin nose, pale lips, and nervous blue eyes. His long hair lay lank on his shoulders.

'A few questions for the coroner in Chesterfield.'

'Is that right?' Christian gave a cruel smile. 'Then he can come and ask them himself.'

'I don't think you'd want that,' John said quietly. From the corner of his eyes he could see the men staring. 'He's not a good man to cross.'

'Neither is my lord.'

'Then better we take care of things ourselves,' John said with an easy smile. He held out a hand. 'What do you say?'

Christian ignored it, turning to the men. 'You have work to do.' His gaze came back to John. 'You were asking questions yesterday, too.'

'I was,' he admitted. 'But I didn't talk to you.'

The man stroked his chin. 'You might have had a wasted journey.'

'Then so be it.' He shrugged.

'Why do you want to know about Julian?'

'The coroner's business. People say you know him well.'

'All my life,' Christian told him. 'We're cousins. Did they tell you that?' John nodded. 'So you won't hear me say a bad word about him. Understand?'

'I do.' He smiled. 'But it's not going to stop the questions. If you don't answer them now, they'll be asked again later.'

The man snorted. 'Ask all you like. I'm still not going to answer.' He stalked away, back towards the village and the manor house. John stood and watched him leave. It was what he'd expected, but a man could always hope for more.

'You were lucky,' one of the labourers said.

'Why's that?' He turned to face the man.

'I've seen him beat people when he has a mood on him.'

'I'm safe enough. He wouldn't want to anger the coroner.'

'Don't be too sure, friend,' he said slowly. 'Christian has a powerful lord behind him. And you can guess whose side he'd take.'

'I appreciate the warning. You know,' he added after a moment, 'there's a way that job could be faster and easier.'

The man sneered. 'You know all about it, do you?'

'I've been watching you. Do you have an old bucket?'

'I daresay.'

'Put some holes in the bottom of that. Drag it along the stream then lift it up. The water will run out and the dirt will stay. You'll find it easier.'

The man considered the idea, working it through in his mind.

'That might work,' he admitted and nodded his head. 'Thank you. I'll warn you, though, watch out for Christian. He has an evil temper.'

'As bad as Julian?'

The man made the sign of the evil eye.

'You just met the only man here who misses him. It was a good day for Dronfield when he left.'

'And a bad day for Chesterfield when he arrived,' John said wryly. 'I'll bid you God speed. But try that idea.'

'We will,' the man assured him. 'A word to the wise, Master. A man should keep his eyes open just the far side of Unstone, where the wood comes down the hill, close to the road.'

'Is it dangerous there?'

'People have been robbed,' he answered and tapped the side of his nose. 'The roads can be dangerous.'

'Good advice.' He waved his farewell. 'Thank you.'

•   •   •

But there was no one lying in wait. For the first time he noticed that the stretch of wood was eerily quiet, though. There was no birdsong or scuffling of animals. Everything was hushed. Even the sunlight seemed to fade. It was as if something cut the place off from life. Many of the trees were dead, empty branches reaching to the sky. A dreadful place, as if something terrible had once happened here and the land was still in mourning.

He was past it soon enough, and the colours seemed even brighter than before, the scents in the air stronger. John strode out for Chesterfield, the spire tall in the distance.

He was home in time for dinner, everyone already at the table and eating. Even Martha was there; the slates she used for teaching were carefully stacked on the settle.

The walk had given him an appetite and he ate quickly, listening to the chatter but staying silent.

'You left early this morning,' Katherine said finally as she turned to him.

'I didn't want to wake you. I had to go to Dronfield.'

She looked at him sharply. 'I didn't know you had business out there.' Her voice was too low for the others to make out.'

'The coroner's business,' he admitted, and she arched a brow.

'I thought that was done,' Katherine hissed.

'I'm not sure it is. Not yet.'

For a moment she seemed ready to say more. Her eyes flashed. Then she gave a tight shake of her head and began to clear away the trenchers. The girls ran off to play with the cat and Walter left quickly, returning to work.

'What have you done wrong now, John?' Martha asked.

'I've been out to Dronfield again. Just to ask a few more questions.'

'Did you find any answers?'

'No.' Without thinking, he rubbed the wound on his arm. It was still sore, but it was healing quickly now and mending well.

'Maybe you need to get back to carpentry,' Martha said kindly. 'Idle hands are the devil's work, that's what they say.'

He smiled. 'Perhaps.' He stood. 'You're a very wise woman.'

'Me?' she answered in horror. 'God forbid it.' But her eyes were smiling as she spoke. She shifted her gaze towards the buttery. 'Go on,' she whispered, 'give her your apologies.'

'But–' he began.

'It doesn't matter. Sometimes it's better to give.'

He hefted the bag of tools on to his shoulder, feeling the familiar weight. Katherine kept her back to him as she worked.

'I'm sorry,' he said hesitantly. She stopped and turned to stare at him, her back against the table.

'I thought you were happy being a carpenter,' she said wearily. 'John … please.'

'I'm going out to Newbold now,' he told her with a hopeful smile.

'No more questions about all this for the coroner. I want you to promise.'

'Unless he demands it.'

'I heard what happened yesterday,' Katherine said sadly. He opened his mouth, but she continued. 'Did you think I wouldn't? It wasn't Walter, before you blame him,' she added quickly. 'Someone saw you. It's all over town. I felt embarrassed when I was told about it this morning. Everyone thought I must have known.'

'I didn't want to worry you.' It sounded like an empty excuse.

'Why, John?' she asked. 'Why did you do it?'

He didn't want to give her the real reason, didn't want her scared.

'He threatened me. And Walter.'

Katherine nodded and pursed her lips.

'No more.' She placed a hand on her belly. 'Please.'

He nodded and kissed her cheek. 'I'll be back for supper.' At the door he turned. 'Just carpentry.'

She nodded without looking at him.

· · ·

No more than a few days, but everything in the fields had grown. At the barn he put down the tools and examined the work he'd done before he'd had to leave. Everything looked solid as he tested it, pushing and pulling on the frame. Not a big building, just large enough to hold four cows and a pair of goats. It would last for years. He had pride in his work.

The farmer arrived, bringing a mug of ale, eager to know all the news from town. John gave it willingly, then lingered after the man left, fitting pieces here and there but nothing more. He dawdled, letting his mind wander. He'd disappointed Katherine. He felt guilty, even though he was trying to protect her. Maybe he should have blurted it all out. But with the child inside her …

Finally he picked up a piece of wood, measured by eye and cut it before nailing it to the frame. After that it all became easier. Within half an hour the natural rhythm took over and he was working up a fair sweat. He stripped off his shirt, feeling the sun warm on his skin. John grinned. It was good, it was *right*.

By the time he finished for the day he'd completed half of one wall. He rubbed himself down with a rag, flecks of saw-dust scraping against his flesh. Tomorrow everything should go faster. It was easy work. When everything was in place he'd daub pitch between the planks to make them watertight.

He sat in the shade of a beech, cleaning the tools with an oily rag. The saw needed to be sharpened; he'd take care of that tonight. Eventually he packed everything away, drew on his shirt, ready to walk home.

Katherine was right. Working like this was what made him happy. With a glance over his shoulder he started on the road.

As he turned the corner he saw a man in the distance, run-ning towards him and waving his hands. His hand drifted to the hilt of his knife; it was a natural reaction. You could never tell what trouble was coming.

Soon enough he was able to make out the man's face. One of the Chesterfield bailiffs. John picked up his pace.

'Master,' the man said breathlessly as he came close. 'The coroner wants you to come. I went to your house and they said you were out here.'

'What is it? What's happened?'

'It's Julian, Master. He's dead.'

CHAPTER TWELVE

They had to push their way through the crowd in the Shambles. Men parted grudgingly to let them by, the bailiff cursing and shoving, John following close behind. Two men guarded the shop. The shutters were closed but the door stood open.

Inside, he had to blink his eyes to adjust to the deep gloom. The smell of blood was thick and cloying, enough to bring the bile into his throat.

'Up the stairs, Master,' the bailiff said, leading the way. Carcasses lay on the bench, a cleaver next to them. Flies buzzed and gathered in clusters on the meat. A few landed on his face and he brushed them away quickly.

The room above the shop was spare. Just a table, a chair, and a bed of straw in the corner, covered with a sheet. A chest, the lid thrown back and contents strewn across the floor.

The shutters were open, late afternoon light pouring in through the unglazed window. De Harville stood there, gazing out at the street, hands resting on the sill. Brother Robert sat on a joint stool, the portable desk open on his lap, a quill in his hand.

'You took your time, Carpenter.' The coroner didn't even turn his head.

'I was in Newbold,' he answered. The room was fetid, stinking of decay. But there was no body. 'Where is he?'

De Harville waved a hand. 'I had him taken away. He looks worse dead than he did alive.'

'What happened?' Without a corpse it was impossible to tell. There was a dark stain on the floorboards that was most likely blood; the flies certainly crowded on it.

'The apprentice found him after dinner,' the monk said. 'Julian didn't go back to work after he came up here to eat. The apprentice started searching and found him dead.'

John looked around. No dishes laid out, no food. But no sign of a fight, either.

'Is there another way up here or is it only through the shop?'

'There's a door at the back, too,' de Harville answered lazily. 'The stairs there go out into the yard. No lock on the back gate.'

John looked around. 'Was the chest open when you arrived?'

'It was,' Robert told him. 'Whatever he owned has gone.'

But this hadn't been a fight and robbery. There hadn't been a struggle. It must have been someone that Julian knew, someone he trusted.

'How was he stabbed?'

'The wound was in his back,' the monk said. 'When we found him he was face down on the floor.'

'Was the weapon still in him?' He saw the monk shake his head, and continued, 'Had Julian drawn his dagger?'

'No.'

He paced around, stopping and staring for a moment then moving on, trying to picture it all in his mind. It would have been easier with the body still here. There might have been something; now he'd never know.

'What about his purse?' John asked suddenly. 'Had it been cut?'

'I don't care about a few pennies.' The coroner turned, his eyes empty, his voice like winter in the room. 'We have five bodies now. *Five* of them. Each time we have a suspect he ends up dead.'

'I thought you'd be happy to see the back of Julian.'

De Harville snorted. 'May he spend eternity in Purgatory for his sins. No one will miss him. But I still have to find his killer.'

'Where's the apprentice?'

'He has a room up in the eaves,' the Brother replied. 'There's a ladder. He's up there now.'

'Find me the murderer,' the coroner ordered. 'And make sure he's alive.'

The ladder was rickety, wobbling under his feet. At the top there was barely enough room to stand; the roof sloped away sharply to the sides. The young man sat in a crouch by the open window, staring down at the Shambles. It was high enough to catch a breeze, but that couldn't dispel the years of mustiness and sweat. A pallet had been roughly made up in one corner, and a tattered surcote hung on a nail.

John settled himself down, legs stretched out, his back against the wall. The boy hadn't even turned to glance at him. Caught in the light, his face showed an angry red welter of spots across the cheeks, greasy black hair tumbling on to his shoulders.

'You're the one who found him.'

The young man turned his head slowly, as if he was coming out of an enchantment. His eyes glistened, and he rubbed at them quickly with the back of a bony hand.

'Yes, Master,' he answered. His voice was husky.

'What's your name?'

'Piers, Master.' He ducked his head quickly.

'I'm John the Carpenter. Why don't you tell me what happened?'

The lad looked around nervously, biting his lip. 'I came back from my dinner at noon,' he began. 'The church bell was ringing. Julian left me to look after the shop. I heard him go up the stairs.' He paused.

'Carry on, Piers,' he encouraged softly.

'A long time passed and he didn't come back down.'

'Was that unusual?'

Piers nodded. 'He always liked to spend his time in the shop or going around. He had business to attend to, he said.' He reddened. The apprentice knew exactly what Julian did, he thought.

'Did you wait until you came up?'

'Just a short while. I tried shouting up to him but he didn't answer.'

'Tell me what you found. Was the door to his room closed?'

'No, Master.' He raised his eyes quickly. 'He always kept it closed, locked when he wasn't inside. I knocked and walked in and he was there … on the floor. Does the coroner think I killed him, Master?' His voice was trembling. 'Are they going to hang me?'

'No.' John smiled. 'No one thinks you're a murderer,' he said, and saw relief fill the boy's face. 'Did you hear anyone up here with Julian? Or anyone using the back stair?'

'No, Master.' He shook his head vigorously. 'But I was busy and there's always noise from the street.'

He considered that, framing his next question.

'Who used to come and visit your master?'

'I don't know.' Piers hung his head. 'The window doesn't look on to the yard.'

'You didn't see any of them in passing?'

'Only a few.'

'Do you remember their names?' He tried to keep his voice low and easy, hoping that the boy would be able to give him something.

'There was one called Stephen, I know that. I heard the Master address him. Two more who came a few times. But I never heard their names.'

'Can you describe these men?' John could feel his heart beating in his chest. Pray God that Piers had a good memory.

He did, and the lad possessed a sharp eye, too. He spoke haltingly, squeezing his eyes shut to recall details. By the time he finished, John could picture them as clearly as if Piers had drawn them in ink.

They were men of some standing, by the sound of it. Fur on their surcotes, even if it was just lamb. Velvet jackets and shoes with long points, in the style of the capital. One had six feathers in his cap, a gaudy display, while another wore parti-coloured hose in black and red.

The problem was that John couldn't remember seeing anyone like that in Chesterfield. With clothes like those they'd have stood out all too clearly and gossip would have flown around the town.

'How often were they here?' he asked.

'The two who came together I saw twice. Stephen three times.' His face reddened. 'They might have come more often. I didn't see everyone.'

'That's fine,' John assured him. 'When was the last time you saw any of them?'

'Stephen was here two days ago. It was in the evening. I was sitting up here and I heard the Master talking to him.'

'What about the others?'

'Not for a few weeks now,' Piers answered after a little thought, then shook his head.

'Do you know someone called Christian?'

'He's the Master's friend.' He stopped and corrected himself. 'Was. He often came into the shop on market day.'

'Never upstairs?'

'I didn't see him there.'

That was interesting, although he didn't know what it meant, if anything at all. John rose, moving to the middle of the room so he could stand upright.

'You've been very helpful. Thank you.'

He'd just start to climb down the ladder when Piers called out, 'Master!'

'What?'

'I just remembered. Stephen has a scar. On the back of his right hand. It goes from side to side, right across.'

'Good.'

That was distinctive; it should make him easy to spot. At least he could begin to ask questions. He looked through the open door into Julian's room. There was nothing else to see. De Harville and Robert had gone, leaving two frightened bailiffs to guard the shop.

Eyes followed him as he walked away. If looks were knives he'd have been dead five times over. He was an outsider, an interloper. In this area they liked to dispense their own justice.

•   •   •

He was late for supper. There was a trencher and a carved spoon waiting at his place on the table. The rest of the family must have eaten.

John walked through to the buttery. The back door stood open. The girls were playing with Kit. They had something tied to a string, tugging it around and delighting in the kitten jumping and running as it kept trying to pounce.

Katherine was on her knees, pulling up tiny weeds in the garden plot. There were still a few hours of evening. He could see the sheen of sweat on her face, just below the veil. Her fingers moved deftly, plucking stems and throwing them aside.

He knelt, placing his right hand lightly over hers.

'De Harville,' he said, as if it was all the explanation he needed. She sighed, staring into his eyes.

'But you still went.' Her voice was full of reproach, still so soft that Janette and Eleanor wouldn't hear.

'What choice did I have?' he hissed.

'I know,' Katherine said finally, letting out a long sigh and squeezing his wrist lightly. 'I'm sorry.'

'It doesn't matter.' Her moods had been up and down in recent weeks, changing in the space of a heartbeat. At first he hadn't known why, thinking he'd committed some grave sin. Now, though, he understood: the baby. He'd heard other men talking, saying the same about their wives.

She started to struggle to her feet and John put a hand under her arm.

'The pottage should still be warm. I'll dish it out for you.'

He ate hungrily; the work in Newbold had left him with an empty belly that even murder couldn't dampen. Katherine sat across from him. Finally curiosity got the better of her.

'Who was murdered?'

'Julian the Butcher.'

Her mouth formed an O of surprise and disbelief.

'But you were just fighting with him yesterday. Do they–?'

'No.' He smiled. Now the man was dead he could tell her the real reason behind the fight. 'Yesterday he threatened to hurt you or Walter or the girls. That's why I fought him.'

'And you didn't tell me?'

'I didn't want to scare you,' he told her gently. 'Julian can't do anything now.'

She stood up and left the room without saying another word. He felt as if he couldn't do right for doing wrong.

CHAPTER THIRTEEN

John knocked at the door on Knifesmithgate, waiting for Martha to answer. He'd spent a restless night, moving in and out of sleep, feeling guilt, anger, hopelessness. When he woke, Katherine was looking at him with sadness deep in her eyes. He stroked her face. She didn't pull away, but there was no joy in her expression, either.

'This is a lovely surprise.' Martha beamed. She glanced at him again. 'Is something wrong?'

'No,' he lied. 'Nothing like that. I'm just here for a little help.'

She arched an eyebrow in surprise. 'You'd best come in then.'

She busied herself arranging cushions on the settle for him, then bringing out two mugs of ale.

'Right,' Martha said briskly. 'What is it?'

'You know Chesterfield better than anyone I can think of. I'm looking for three men.' He told her about Stephen and the others. 'Does that mean anything?'

'No.' She pursed her lips. 'I don't think I've seen anyone like that. Would you like me to ask the other goodwives?'

'Please.' If one of them didn't recognise the men, no one would. They all had eyes as sharp as hawks on the wing and powerful memories.

'You know, there are plenty who think that anyone who killed Julian should be given a purse full of silver,' Martha said, sniffing as she tucked her twisted hands into her lap.

'He was still murdered.'

'There are some people who deserve rough justice, John. You've heard some of the tales about him?'

He nodded. 'But nobody has the right to do that outside the law,' he said.

'Julian did,' she pointed out. All he could do was shrug. 'He was the worst butcher in town, too,' Martha added. 'Cheap cuts of meat, half of it on the turn. I'm surprised he could make a living from it.'

Maybe he didn't, John thought. The man was a criminal. The butcher's shop could have been something respectable to hide everything else. He needed to talk to the apprentice again to discover how busy they were.

'Katherine wants me to stop all this,' he said after a lengthy pause.

'Are you surprised?' Martha took a small sip of the ale and stared coolly into his eyes. 'She's worried about you, especially with the baby coming. She wants the child to have a father.'

'But how can I refuse?'

'You're not de Harville's man, John. He doesn't have a hold over you. You have your carpentry. I've seen you work, you love it.'

He nodded. 'How can I say no?'

'Just say it,' she told him. 'It would do him good to hear it once in a while. He can't do anything to you.'

'Next time I will,' he said, hoping it was a vow.

'Think about it. Since you started this you've been beaten and left for dead. I heard you had a fight with Julian, knives drawn.'

All of Chesterfield must know.

'It wasn't—' he began, but she waved him down.

'And you wonder why Katherine's scared? Use your brain.' She gave a frustrated sigh. 'I know you have plenty of luck, John, but it has to run out eventually.'

He didn't even try to answer. There was nothing he could say. Every word she said was right. Maybe he could stand up to the coroner. But not now. He was in this, he had to see it through. His pride demanded it.

Finally he stood and ran a hand through his hair.

'I should go. If you learn anything …'

'I'll send word.' Martha smiled. 'God watch over you.'

'I hope He does.' He put a hand on her shoulder. 'And thank you.'

•   •   •

The coroner was in the solar with his wife. The wet nurse had brought the baby and he could hear the child mewling softly.

Brother Robert was working in the hall, documents laid out across the table, parchment and books in a kind of order only he understood. He sat with the quill poised over the bottle of ink, a short knife in his other hand, ready to sharpen the nib.

John settled into a chair, waiting until the monk finished his sentence and put down the pen. He related everything the apprentice had told him.

'There aren't many wealthy men around here,' Robert said thoughtfully. 'And Stephen …' He stroked his chin. 'There's someone of that name in Bakewell. He's a salt merchant. He has some money, I know that. But I can't see what he'd want with Julian.'

'What about the others?'

'Too vague. I'll ask the master later. What are you going to do?'

'I'll talk to the apprentice again. He might have remembered something else. After that I don't know. No one in the Shambles is likely to talk to me.'

'Watch yourself down there.'

He patted the knife and grinned. 'Don't worry about me, Brother.'

Upstairs, the baby began to wail.

'It won't be long before you hear much more of that, John.' The monk looked amused.

. . .

Heat seemed to cling to the stones in the Shambles. The air felt close, leaving him sweating as he walked. The runnels down the centre of each street stank of urine, mixing with the raw tang of blood from the butchers' shops.

A single bailiff kept his guard at Julian's door.

'Has anyone been in or out?' John asked.

'Plenty of them curious, Master,' the man replied. His grin showed a row of stained, broken teeth. 'I didn't let any of them take a look.'

'You haven't seen anyone leave?'

'No, Master.'

In the shop the carcasses swarmed with flies. He could make out a small mass of maggots writhing around on a cut of beef. He breathed through his mouth and climbed the stairs to the solar. Nothing had been disturbed in Julian's room.

John stood for a moment, listening. The only noise seemed to come from outside. The house had a hushed, empty quality. Quickly, he climbed the ladder to the eaves. The apprentice's room was empty, the coat missing from the nail. It was easy enough to leave by the back stair and out through the yard.

Maybe Piers had felt there was nothing more for him here besides trouble. Or maybe he had something to hide. He sighed. It was too late now. The boy had vanished and the chances of finding him were slim.

'Do you patrol around here?' he asked the bailiff. Even the stinking air in the street was better than the rank smell in the shop.

'Aye, for my sins.' The man grimaced. 'Worst part of town, you ask anyone.'

'Did you know the apprentice who works for Julian?'

'Piers?' He shrugged. 'By sight, not much more.'

'How long has he been here?'

'A year, more or less,' the man answered after a little thought. 'You could just ask him.'

'He's gone.'

He could read the bailiff's thoughts on his face. The mix of resignation and trepidation. The knowledge of the bollocking he'd receive for letting someone go when he was watching the place. Still, no one could blame the boy for leaving. If he stayed he'd just be tainted by an investigation into the murder. And there was little future for him in Chesterfield. Nobody would take on the apprentice of a man who'd been killed.

'It's not your fault,' John told him. 'He just left by the back stair. You can't be in two places at once.'

'Try telling the captain that.' He made a grim face and spat on the stones.

'I will, if needs be.' He paused. 'I'll make sure the coroner does, too.'

'Thank you,' the man mumbled.

'Do you know where Piers came from?'

'I never heard, but I can try and find out,' the bailiff said with a wry grin. 'There's one or two round here who'll still talk to me for a mug of ale.'

It couldn't be too far away, and the chances were that the boy would run back there to a place where he felt safe.

'That would be useful. Just send word to me.' He clapped the man lightly on the shoulder.

• • •

John caught the coroner striding across the empty market square, a look of determination on his face.

'Found me a killer yet, Carpenter?' he called. Heads turned to watch.

'No, Master.'

'Just as well, perhaps.' He gave a grim smile. 'As soon as you suspect someone, they die. What have you discovered?'

He fell into step with de Harville, walking along Low Pavement then past the churchyard. The line of oak tiles on the steeple was rising day by day. He saw two men sweating as they worked, nothing below except a long, deadly drop to the ground.

The smithy was close enough to the church to enjoy business from the construction, but far enough from the town to keep buildings safe if it caught on fire.

The heat seemed to draw the air from his lungs. It was hard to breathe. The forge roared and the blacksmith worked, concentrating on hammering the white-hot metal resting on his anvil. A coat of sweat covered his skin. He worked bare-chested, wearing only a heavy leather apron, powerful muscles on display. Sparks flew. An apprentice pumped the bellows to fan the flames.

Finally he was done, putting the piece into a barrel of cold water. There was a loud hiss as the steam rose. The blacksmith stood, rubbing a stained piece of cloth over his face.

'What can I do for you, Master?' he asked once he'd taken a long draught of ale. His head was shaved, his gaze intense.

'The bridle,' de Harville said. The man nodded and snapped his fingers. In a few moments the apprentice handed him the finished piece. The leather was beautifully worked, decorated with silver. The smith's thick fingers pointed out the repair.

'That should hold for years now, Master.'

The coroner nodded, reaching into his purse and passing over a coin.

In the light, away from the intense blaze where they could breathe again, de Harville examined the work.

'He costs, but it's worth every penny,' he said approvingly before crushing the bridle in his hands. 'You asked about Stephen.'

'Yes, Master.'

'The only one I know is the man Robert told you about. He has airs above his station, dresses like a lord.'

'It sounds like the same man,' John said. 'Do you know the others at all?'

'No.' The coroner's face looked drawn, the flesh tight over his bones. There were lines around his eyes and mouth. In the last few months he'd aged. All the worries in his life had taken their toll. 'Do you think they're involved?'

'I don't know. They all visited Julian.'

'Talk to the apprentice again,' the coroner ordered.

'He's gone.'

'Gone?' De Harville stopped. 'I told the bailiffs to guard the shop.'

'They have one man on the front, but there's a back stair.'

The coroner shook his head in anger.

'Do you think this Piers was involved in the murder?'

'I'm sure he wasn't,' John told him. 'But I think he probably has more to tell. If I can find out where he came from …'

'Yes, yes.' He waved his hand. 'This whole business has become too big, Carpenter. I need it taken care of quickly. If you don't think you can do that, say so now.'

'I don't know, Master,' he answered honestly. Katherine would be happy if he turned his back on the whole affair. He could return to what he loved, the thing he did well.

But if he didn't look into these killings, who would? Some innocent might end up dangling from the noose. Piers, perhaps. And the real killer would walk free, laughing behind his hand. Could he let that happen and still live with himself?

'I'll try.' It was all he could promise. 'But I'll need more authority than I have now. Who holds Bakewell for the King?' The town where Stephen lived.

'Sir Alexander de Sèvres.'

'The same man who has Dronfield?'

'He has plenty of land around here, more's the pity.' The coroner grimaced. 'He spends all his time in London trying to curry favour with the crown and his stewards milk the manors. Someone local should have them.'

'I'll need a letter from you giving me some power.'

'Fine,' de Harville agreed after a moment's thought. 'I'll have Robert write one. If anyone gives you a problem, remind them I'm the *King's* coroner.'

'Yes, Master.' He gave a quick smile.

When he arrived home there was a message waiting from the bailiff: Piers came from Bakewell.

The evening was warm enough to leave the shutters wide, sounds drifting in. The girls were both in bed, the cat curled on the blanket between them as they slept. He took one final look at them all, serene and innocent, then went quietly down the stairs.

'Walter, I could use your help tomorrow.'

The lad's face lit up at the request. 'Yes, John. What do you want me to do?

'I'll tell you in the morning.' He looked at Katherine. 'Would you mind if I had some time alone with your sister?'

He waited until he could hear Walter moving around quietly in the solar.

'More coroner's work?' she asked coldly.

'Yes,' he answered softly and reached for her hand. She pulled it away.

'I ask you to stop working for him and now you drag Walter back into it,' she hissed. There was fury in her eyes. 'What are you doing, John?'

'I have to.' He looked at her.

'De Harville can do his own work for once.'

'He's worried about his wife and son.' As soon as he spoke he knew he'd said the wrong thing.

'But you're not?'

'Of course I am,' he insisted. 'You know that.'

'I thought I did,' she replied slowly.

'If I don't do it, he'll use the bailiffs, and they can't see beyond the end of their noses. They'll just go for the obvious.' He told her about Piers, the apprentice who'd fled.

'Maybe he did it,' she said.

'No.' He shook his head. 'I'm sure he didn't. But there's a good chance he'll end up dead for it. I want the person who really did it all.'

'Why?' she asked. 'Why does it matter so much?'

'I don't know.' He tried to think, but there wasn't a reason he could pull out of the air. 'It just does. I want to find the truth.'

'Doing that put you in the river. Or have you forgotten that? It almost killed you.'

'I know.' It was still fresh in his mind. The wound in his arm had almost healed, the throbbing in his skull long past. But the memory was still raw. 'That's another reason. To find out who was behind that.'

'When you came home that night I thought you were going to die.' Katherine's voice was empty. 'Every time you leave now I'm scared that someone will come and tell me you've been killed.'

John reached for her hand again. This time she let him take it.

'Do you understand?' he asked. 'Why I need to do this?'

Very slowly and hesitantly, she nodded. 'But do you see how I feel, too?'

'Yes,' he answered, then tried to sound more cheerful. 'I'll make sure nothing bad happens.'

'John …' she began, then words failed her.

'I promise.'

'Please,' Katherine said. He could see the tears running down her cheeks and wiped them away gently with his thumb.

'I'll be very careful. But I feel I have to do it.' He tapped his chest. 'In there.'

She sniffled and gave a weak half-smile. 'I know. But I need to feel that we come first.'

'You do,' he assured her. 'But I'm involved in this now. I have to see it through. No one else will care enough.'

'You're a good man, John. Too good for the coroner.'

'There's nothing to be done about that.' He grinned. 'Come on, let's go to bed. I've a long day tomorrow.'

'Where do you have to go?'

'Bakewell. I'll probably have to stay overnight.'

'Just look out for yourself. Please.'

'I will.'

CHAPTER FOURTEEN

Bakewell looked smaller than Chesterfield, a neat little market town that stood on the far side of a new bridge.

John slipped down from the cart with thanks for the driver. He'd been lucky to find someone heading here after he'd only walked a couple of miles. The pace was little faster than walking, but he arrived fresh and with less wear on his boots.

He'd set off early, before dawn while the air was still cool. He'd given Walter his instructions – to find out all he could about Stephen the salt merchant and the two other mysterious men who'd visited Julian.

The boy had been disappointed not to come with him, but this was a job for one person. He had the coroner's letter of authority in his scrip. All he needed was to find the right people.

The market square was empty. A few shops lined the street, and a pair of alehouses were marked out by their signs. It seemed like a sleepy little place, one that probably only came alive on market day.

A few questions led him to the bailiff's house. The man who answered the door had a patchy beard, grey mixed with black, and hair receding from his forehead. His shirt bulged over a wide stomach, thick legs straining against a stout pair of hose.

John produced the letter. The bailiff looked at it quizzically. 'What is it?' he asked as he scratched an ear.

'It's from the coroner in Chesterfield. I need to ask some questions here.'

'Aye.'The man pursed his lips and handed back the piece of parchment. 'That's no good to me. I wouldn't be able to make head nor tail of it. You'd best come in.'

His name was Roger. He'd held the post for a year, since the old bailiff died. It didn't demand much, but it didn't pay well, either. At least he no longer had to give service to the lord of the manor and he had strips enough to grow what he needed.

'It's not a bad life,' he said as he poured another mug of ale for them both. 'We don't have much crime here. Just a few fights, really, or a dispute over boundaries. Now, what do you want?'

'I'm looking for two people. Stephen the salt merchant—' he saw Roger nod '—and a boy called Piers. He went to be an apprentice to a butcher in Chesterfield. I think he might have come back here.'

'Everyone knows Stephen,' the bailiff told him. 'He calls himself a salt merchant, but the amount of trade he does would hardly keep a chicken alive. Not that you'd know it to look at him.'

'A lordling?' John asked.

'He certainly dresses the part,' Roger agreed. 'What's he done? He's never given me any trouble here.'

'I don't know that he's done anything. It's who he visited in Chesterfield.'

He laid out the whole story for the bailiff, beginning with Timothy's murder and the theft of the psalter. As he finished, Roger rubbed a hand over the bristles on his chin.

'That's quite a tale,' he said in admiration. 'More like a puzzle.'

'You can see why I want to talk to Stephen. He might have been one of the last to see Julian alive.'

'I saw him first thing this morning, strutting around like a bantam cock. He should still be here.'

'What about Piers?'

Roger sighed. 'I knew he went off as an apprentice. I haven't seen him since. The boy has the devil's own bad luck. His father's first wife died in the pestilence. He married again and they had Piers and a brother. Then the plague came back three years ago. Took the mother and the other boy.' He shook his head. 'The father started drinking and he hasn't stopped yet. When Piers left I thought there was some hope for the lad.'

'Never much, given who was his master.'

'We can see if he's returned. Who do you want first – him or Stephen?'

• • •

In the end it was Piers. The cottage was no more than a stone's throw from the bailiff's house. Neglected, there were slates missing from the roof, a shutter hanging by a single hinge, the limewash faded and crumbling in place. Roger raised an eyebrow and knocked on the door.

Piers looked different in this place. His face was more open and he stood tall, not bowed. Then he saw the carpenter and all the bravado crumbled. He turned, then stopped, panic on his face.

'Don't worry,' John told him. 'I haven't come to arrest you. I just have a few more questions.'

Reluctantly, Piers nodded and stepped back into the house. It was a single room, forlorn and dirty, two pallets of straw in the corners, a single joint-stool and a battered table. A floor of bare, beaten earth, not even any rushes on the ground. Hardly a home at all. More a hovel.

The boy sat on one of the beds. He looked resigned, lost.

'You've grown since I saw you last,' Roger said with a smile. 'Shot up.'

Piers just nodded blankly.

'Why did you run away yesterday?' John asked kindly.

'You know,' the lad answered quietly.

'Nobody thought you killed him.'

'The coroner did,' Piers said. 'I saw the way he was looking at me.'

'I don't believe you did. And nor does he. But I think there are some things you saw and didn't tell me.'

The boy's head jerked up sharply. The spots on his face were bright red, as if they were burning. 'I didn't.'

'You're a very bad liar,' Roger said lazily.

'Who else did you see?' John asked.

'No one,' Piers muttered.

'He can take you back to Chesterfield and make you talk,' Roger said. Panic rose on the lad's face.

'Who else did you see?' he asked again.

'Christian.' The name came out as a whisper.

John squatted, looking directly at Piers. 'Why didn't you tell me before?'

'I'm scared of him … I thought you were going to let me hang.'

'No, I'm sure you're innocent.' He hoped the boy would believe him. 'When did you see Christian?'

'He came after the master had gone upstairs for his dinner. I didn't see him come down again.'

'Could you have missed him?'

'No,' Piers answered with certainty. 'Unless he went the back way.'

John let out a slow breath. Christian. That changed everything.

'You said you saw Stephen, too. When was that?'

'Just after the master went up. I had to take something out to the shed in the yard and he was leaving by the back gate.'

'You're sure it was him?'

The boy nodded. 'He didn't see me.'

'Was this before Christian arrived?'

'Yes.'

'Had you seen him arrive?'

'No.'

'I want you to stay in Bakewell,' John told him. 'I might need you to testify in court. Against someone else,' he added for comfort. 'You're not in trouble. Do you understand?'

'Yes.'

'Maybe it would be best if you came and saw me every day,' Roger added. 'Just so we can be sure.'

'I will,' Piers agreed.

Outside, the sun was hot and not even at its peak. The bailiff led the way to the riverbank and found a place in the shade.

'Who's Christian?' he asked.

'The steward of the manor in Dronfield. He and Julian have been friends since they were boys. Cousins.'

'What's he like?'

'The last time I talked to him, he threatened me.' He chuckled. 'The lord in Dronfield is the same one you have here.'

Roger snorted. 'The last time I saw the lord here, my son was ten. He's twenty now. The steward shows up four times a year for the rent. It's the reeve who looks after the moot court and everything else. Probably the same up there. Your Christian will have some power.'

'He seems to think so, anyway.' He plucked a blade of grass and put it in his mouth, chewing on it. 'We'd better have a talk with Stephen. Do you know him?'

'Not well,' the bailiff replied. 'He likes to think he has a higher status then me.'

'Haughty?'

'Very.'

John stood, dusting off the seat of his hose. 'Then the sooner we begin, the sooner I can start on my way home.'

'You're not staying?' Roger asked in surprise. 'It'll be long after dark when you reach Chesterfield. The roads are dangerous.'

'I have a pregnant wife waiting for me.'

'It won't help her if someone beats and robs you, will it? You can stay with me. Not as much room as an inn, but it's cheaper.'

'Are you sure?'

'It won't be luxury but you'll be warm and fed.'

'Then thank you.' He hadn't expected such a generous offer. 'Thank you,' he repeated.

'Right, let's see what Stephen has to say for himself.'

Stephen's wife met them at the door. A tiny woman with a shrewish face, wearing a gown of sarcenet. It had obviously been expensive once, well-cut and elaborately sewn, but its best days were long in the past, the colour faded and worn.

'He left this morning,' she said. There was a glint of triumph in her eyes. 'Gone over to Cheshire. He'll not be back before next week, probably after that.'

'How long ago did he go?' Roger asked.

'Two hours,' the woman told him. 'If you don't believe me, take a look in the stable. The pack horses are all gone.'

'I'll believe you, Sarah.' He held up his palms in surrender. 'He was in Chesterfield recently, wasn't he?'

'What about it?' she asked suspiciously.

'Was he?' the bailiff asked again.

'Yes,' she admitted.

'Did he visit someone called Julian?'

She lifted her head. 'He doesn't tell me his business,' Sarah said defiantly.

'Has he mentioned someone called Julian?' John interrupted.

She turned to stare at him. 'I wouldn't know.'

'When he comes back I'll need to talk to him,' Roger said. 'Make sure you tell him.'

'I will,' she promised reluctantly.

As soon as they turned away, she slammed the door.

'She's not much help,' John said.

'Sarah doesn't like me,' Roger explained. 'Years back we courted a little, then I met my wife, God rest her, and broke things off with Sarah. She married Stephen and she'll defend him to the death.' He shook his head. 'He had money when they wed. It's been going downhill ever since. It looks like this part of your journey is wasted.'

'Could we catch up with him? He can't be going fast.'

'There are two routes he could take. He has to go over the Pennines. We'd just be guessing. For what it's worth, I can't see Stephen killing anyone. It takes fire in someone to do that, and I've never known him have more than an ember. It's probably why he's never made much money.'

'Anyone can kill.'

'Maybe,' Roger agreed after a while, then his face brightened. 'How do you fancy some fishing this afternoon? There's a good spot on the river and we'd have it all to ourselves.'

'I've never fished,' John admitted.

'Never?' the bailiff asked in disbelief.

But there had never been the chance or the time. He'd always been working or travelling from one place to another and seeking a job. When he had some time, he slept.

'No,' he answered simply.

'Then you've missed one of life's great joys, Master.' Roger thought for a moment. 'You wait here. I have another pole, I'll show you. We can share a jug of ale. We might even catch our supper.' He grinned. 'And even if we don't, it doesn't matter.'

In the end they went home empty-handed. John came close twice, the fish wriggling off the hook before he could land it. But the bailiff was right. It was a satisfying way to make an afternoon stretch out. To spend an hour or two in the shade, talking about nothing, letting the cares of the world slide away and sipping ale, hoping something would bite.

The heat was slowly fading from the day by the time they left the river. He'd enjoyed the time doing nothing, forgetting all the strains and worries for a few hours. With no fish caught, they ate bread and cheese. Roger lit a tallow candle as darkness came, the fat, acrid stench filling the air.

'You look tired,' he said.

'I am,' John agreed with a smile. 'I had an early start.'

'Settle down then, lad. You've a long way back tomorrow.'

•   •   •

He was lucky on the trip back, too, finding a cart that was going to Baslow. From there, though, it was Shank's mare all the way. In the distance he could see the church spire, standing high and proud, like a beacon to the countryside all around.

It was far into the afternoon when he reached the market square. His feet ached and the stitching was beginning to come away on one of his boots. He wanted to be home, to see Katherine, to rest his weary legs. But if he did that, he'd stay there until the morning.

Instead, he walked across to the coroner's yard and knocked on the door. What he found in the hall made him stop in astonishment for a moment.

The coroner had his son on his knee, gently bouncing him up and down and making noises to keep the baby gurgling with pleasure. The wet nurse sat on a stool in the corner, ready to take the child when his father had had enough.

But de Harville showed no sign of tiring. He leaned forward, rubbing noses with the boy and grinning. He looked ten years younger, full of enthusiasm instead of boredom and worry.

'What do you need, Carpenter?' he asked. 'I'm busy.'

'I've just come back from Bakewell, Master.' He watched, finding the change in the man hard to believe. He was doting on the boy.

Would that be him in a few months? Softer, coming fully alive with his son or daughter? The idea made him smile a little.

'Well?' the coroner said, 'Get on with it.'

He recounted the little he'd learned. De Harville didn't seem to be listening, still playing with his son, tickling, smiling. But as John finished he turned his head sharply.

'So this Stephen left suddenly. It seems hasty. What do you make of it, Carpenter?'

'I don't know, Master.' He'd thought about it on the long walk back into Chesterfield. It could be a coincidence; after all, the man was a salt merchant. But he'd been one of the last to see Julian alive. He could even be the killer. 'When he returns we need to talk to him.'

'This Christian interests me.'

'He's Julian's oldest friend.'

'Friends have killed each other before,' de Harville said.

'He's the steward in Dronfield. I've tried to talk to him.'

'Then he'll need more persuasion. Leave that to me.'

'Yes, Master.'

'Is there anything else?'

'No.'

'Good. Go home, Carpenter.'

• • •

Home. He was glad to unlock the door and walk into a house full of sound. The girls laughing and screaming playfully, and Katherine trying to calm them down. As soon as he appeared past the screen, everything went quiet for a moment. Then Janette and Eleanor were dashing towards him, grabbing his legs as if he'd been gone for a year, not just a night. Katherine stood with her hands on her hips, looking amused as he was pinned to the spot. Even the kitten came to wind its way around his legs.

Slowly, he freed himself, hugging them both and grinning widely. They'd missed him; he was truly part of the family with them, like the father they'd never really known.

He held his wife, revelling in her warmth and softness.

'Was it worthwhile?' she asked softly.

'I think so,' he replied, letting out a weary breath.

'I'll bring you some ale.'

He sat at the table, the girls filling his ears with their chatter, the kitten rubbing around him and demanding attention. Drinking deep, he closed his eyes, waiting as Katherine shooed the girls outside to play.

'What's Bakewell like?' she asked eagerly.

'Small,' he said after a little consideration. 'Pretty enough, but there's no real life to it. I prefer it here. I saw something you wouldn't believe when I got back.'

'Oh?' Her fingers traced a pattern around his hand.

'The coroner cooing around his son. He looked so full of pride I thought he'd burst.'

Her mouth made an O of shock and surprise, then she began to laugh.

'I can't imagine that.'

'He kept doing it while I gave him my report.'

'So he's human after all,' she said as she shook her head. 'I'll never look at him the same way again.'

'I kept wondering if I'll be that way.'

She arched her brows. 'I hope you will.'

'It seemed to make everything real.' He gazed down at the ale left in the mug. 'I knew you were going to have a child, but ...' He couldn't find the words to say what he felt, everything churning in his head.

'We'll look after him. Or her.'

John nodded. It suddenly seemed such a big thing, like a mountain waiting in the future. Until now he'd felt some freedom, even with marriage and a family. But this truly was a new responsibility. Someone's life would belong to him. He had to keep them well, safe. Teach them. If it was a boy, pass on his skills.

It scared him. It terrified him.

'What are you thinking?' Katherine asked.

'Nothing,' he answered with a quiet smile. 'Everything. Does it all scare you?'

'Every minute,' she admitted. 'I thought you'd seen that.'

'Maybe I should have.'

He stretched, working out the knots in his back from the long walk.

'What happened in Bakewell?'

'I learned how to fish,' he began, then told her the whole story. 'De Harville said he'd take care of Christian,' he said as he finished.

'Better him than you. Just be careful, John. There's something about this that feels all wrong.'

'Nothing bad is going to happen to us,' he promised, and hoped he wasn't tempting fate with his words.

CHAPTER FIFTEEN

'What did you manage to find out about Stephen and the other men?' John asked. He leaned against the wall, staring out over the marketplace. It was still early, the light rising in the east as men moved around quickly, setting up their stalls.

'Stephen comes here often,' Walter replied. His voice was serious as he concentrated on what he'd learned. 'He sells salt to the bakers and the shops here.'

'How regularly does he come to Chesterfield?'

'About every fortnight. That's what I was told.'

A butcher might well need salt to keep his meat. His contact with Julian could be innocent. From the look of Stephen's house in Bakewell he didn't live extravagantly. Someone who once had money and lost it, Roger had said.

'What else?'

'He's done business with Julian for years. Edward the Butcher was a customer of his, too. Most of them in the Shambles seem to buy from him.'

'How did you hear all this?' John asked with a smile.

'I asked,' Walter answered with a shrug and blushed. 'It's easier down there now that Edward and Julian have gone.'

'Were you able to find anything about the other men?'

'No.' The boy lowered his head. 'I'm sorry, John, but no one seemed to know them.'

'That's fine. You tried.' He put a hand on the boy's shoulder. 'Come on, we'll get something from the cookshop.'

The two mystery men, he thought as he ate the warm oatcakes with butter. Nobody seemed to know anything about them, as if they hadn't really existed. Maybe they weren't even involved; coincidences did happen.

He sighed. This was all too complicated. Little trails that seemed to lead nowhere, or to dead bodies. Timothy, Nicholas, Edward, Gilbert, Julian. Why, he wondered? Did it all start with someone seeing Timothy as an easy victim? Or was there more behind it? And where did the psalter enter into it all?

John wiped his mouth with the sleeve of his jacket. The day had started off quite cool, refreshing, and hazy clouds filled the sky.

'I need to talk to the priest,' he said. 'Do you want to come with me?'

The indecision was plain on the lad's face.

'I can't, John. I need to run messages today. The horse traders are coming to the market. I'm sorry.'

'It's fine,' he assured Walter. 'Go and do your work. If I discover anything interesting I'll tell you later.'

'Yes, John.' The boy grinned broadly and scampered off, long legs raising dust.

The priest. But there was another place to visit first.

• • •

Edmund the Shoemaker was sitting on his stool, a shoe half-sewn in front of him. As John entered he looked up, his face breaking into a smile.

'Master! I was wondering when you'd come.' He turned, fumbling along the shelf for a pair of boots and rubbing the dust off the leather with his sleeve. 'Try them on and tell me if they're not the most comfortable you've ever worn.'

John slipped off the old, worn shoes, flexing his toes before pulling on the boots. They felt supple, snug without being tight. He took a few tentative steps. The sole was firm but bent freely. Sitting down again, he pulled them off, turning them in his hands and examining them.

'You won't find better boots anywhere, Master,' the shoemaker told him hopefully. 'You ask anyone in town, they'll tell you I'm the best.'

He put them on his feet again and paced around the shop. They'd need to be broken in, of course, but that should be easy enough. Finally he nodded his satisfaction.

'I'll take them,' he said and heard the man's sigh of relief. 'Can you mend these?' He put the old pair on the trestle. Edmund looked at them.

'I can, Master. They'll never be as strong as they were, but they'll hold for a long time yet.' He grinned. 'As second-best, of course.'

His feet felt light as he walked up Soutergate. Each step felt like a pleasure. The shoemaker was good at his craft. He kept glancing down to admire the boots. Maybe he'd have no regrets about spending the money, after all.

Men were working in the churchyard. The tiles on the spire reached almost to the peak now; the work would be finished very soon. Labourers were packing up, putting materials into piles and wooden boxes. All the chores that accompanied the end of a job. It was always the hardest time, knowing it would be over soon, then being paid off and wondering where to go next. He remembered that all too well, glad those days were all in the past.

Chesterfield would miss the men, too. The alehouses would do less business, landlords would have empty beds and no one coming to fill them.

In the church his heels clicked over the tiles as he made his way to the vestry, knocking on the door then opening it.

Father Geoffrey was there, his head bent in prayer, holding up a finger; wait until he was done.

His lips moved quickly and silently, then he crossed himself and sat back.

'Good morning, my son.' His face became quizzical. 'I saw you at Timothy's house, didn't I?'

'Yes, Father. I'm John the Carpenter. I work with the coroner.'

'I remember now. Sit down, sit down. What can I do for you, my son?'

'It's about the psalter that was stolen,' he asked as he settled on the low joint stool. 'You said Timothy had shown it to you.'

'Yes.' The priest nodded. 'And he promised it to the church as he had no heirs.'

'How valuable is it?'

'Valuable?' Geoffrey spoke the word as if it surprised him. 'Well, it's beautifully illuminated and carefully lettered. I don't know how old it is, but Timothy said it had belonged to his grandfather and maybe further back than that. So it might be worth a good sum if anyone was willing to pay.'

'And would people pay to own it?'

'Oh yes,' the priest replied without hesitation. 'It's beautiful and it's holy.'

'Who'd buy it, Father?'

'Rich families.' He paused, thinking, fingers stroking the stole around his neck. 'Maybe a church or an abbey, if they had money. But I hope they'd want to know where it came from.'

John nodded. But they both knew that many places would ask few questions if they truly wanted something, whether it was a relic or a book.

'Was there anything on the cover?'

'A cross in gilt. It was the loveliest thing I've ever seen.' He shook his head to clear the reverie. 'Do you read?'

'No.'

'I do.' Geoffrey smiled. 'Not very well. But the psalms were beautifully written, and the drawings looked just like life. When Timothy said he wanted us to have it I had to hold my breath and make sure I'd heard him properly. It would have been a very generous gift. Do you think you'll find it?' he asked bleakly.

'I'm trying, Father. But this is a very tangled web. And too many have died.'

'May God help you in your search.'

'I need all the aid I can get,' John told him and stood. 'I don't even know what's going on.'

It was the truth, he thought as he wandered out into the fresh air. The trees in the churchyard cast welcome shade. A group of labourers were gathered under an oak, drinking cups of ale. For a moment he wished he was one of them, enjoying the company. But there were no faces he recognised and they paid him no attention as he walked to the lych gate.

These murders made his head ache. Last time had been straightforward. This ... it was as if someone had set a puzzle, one that wound and twisted around itself until it was impossible to see ahead.

He'd barely started up Saltergate when someone called his name. Turning, he saw one of the bailiffs.

'What is it?'

'The coroner, Master,' he said breathlessly. 'He wants to see you.'

'Why?' Please God, not another murder. 'Where?'

The bailiff bent, hands resting on his knees, his face ruddy.

'At his house, Master. As soon as you can.'

He didn't wait for the other man but strode along Knifesmithgate to the High Street, his fist coming down heavily on de Harville's door. As soon as the servant saw him, she ushered him through to the hall.

The coroner was there, a thin surcote of brilliant blue over his shirt, one hand stroking his chin. Robert had his desk open, quill poised over a piece of parchment. And there was another man standing, his face set in determination.

He looked to be close to forty, the lines of age like a map on his face. His hair was short, the colour of iron, a beard cut close against his cheeks. He looked like a man used to being obeyed, his body relaxed, his hands resting on his belt. Expensively dressed, with good riding boots, fine woollen hose, and a nicely worked velvet jerkin.

'Well, Carpenter,' de Harville said with amusement, 'there's someone I want you to meet. Ralph of York.' The man gave a small bow. 'He arrived here an hour ago. He claims to be a relative of Timothy.'

CHAPTER SIXTEEN

'I don't claim to be a relative. I am a relative.' His voice was gruff, a man who didn't brook any argument.

'How are you related, Master?' John asked pleasantly.

'His mother was my grandmother's sister.'

A cousin of some sort, he thought.

'How did you hear he was dead?' York was a long way off.

'I was drinking in the York Tavern and I heard a carter talking about it.' He shrugged. 'I asked him some questions, then I came down here.'

John knew the York Tavern. In St Helen's Square, close enough to the Minster. He'd drunk in there a few times when he lived in the city.

But he wondered at Ralph's presence. No one had mentioned that Timothy had any relatives. Certainly they couldn't have been close.

'When did you last see Timothy?'

'I was a young man. I was remiss. I became busy with work and my own family.'

'What's your work, Master?' he asked genially.

'I'm a merchant. Goods to and from the Lowlands. Some wool, some cloth.'

'You haven't seen Timothy in many years but you still felt the need to dash down here?' the coroner asked.

'He's a relative. He deserves that.'

De Harville raised his eyebrows. 'And it wouldn't have anything to do with the fact that he had money you might inherit?'

'I have money!' Ralph protested.

'You have clothes and an arrogant manner. Were you hoping you'd be in his will?'

The man raised his head. 'I'm his only relative.'

The coroner turned to the monk.

'Does Lawyer Henry have the will?'

'No, Master,' Robert nodded. 'He says there's a will lodged in Derby, though.'

'Do we know what's in it? Is Ralph of York mentioned at all?'

'No, Master, no word on it yet.'

'If I'm not mentioned I'll challenge it in court,' Ralph said. There was anger in his eyes.

'You do that,' the coroner advised. 'Give the lawyers all your money and after five years get nothing in return.' He raised a goblet of wine in a toast. 'I wish you well of your adventure. If you want to pay your respects to Timothy, you'll find him in the graveyard.'

He stared at Ralph until the man had to look away, stalking out of the room and slamming the heavy wooden door behind him.

'A plague on him,' de Harville grunted. 'Well, Carpenter, what do you make of our claimant?'

John shrugged.

'He might be real enough,' he said. Who could tell?

'He made it up or just hoped it was that way,' the coroner said dismissively.

'It's possible.' He ran a hand through his hair. 'What are you doing about Christian, Master?'

'The monk told me I need to be diplomatic.' He shot Robert a dark look. 'I've sent a letter to the lord of his manor saying I need to question him.'

'I thought Sir Alexander spent all his time in London.'

'He does.'

'It could take weeks before you hear anything.'

The coroner smiled. 'I know, and justice won't wait that long. I'll bring Christian here on Monday.'

'Send three or four men. He won't want to come easily.' He thought a moment. 'But I doubt there's anyone in Dronfield who'll help him. He's not well-liked there.'

'I'll tell you when he's here.'

• • •

He was glad to be home. He hadn't gone far, hadn't even done much, but it seemed as if the day had disappeared around him in a welter of words. The only thing that seemed real from it all was the new pair of boots. He wriggled his toes. These would be worth the money.

Katherine was sitting on a stool in the garden, supervising the girls as they tugged weeds from the rows of plants.

'Not that one,' she told Eleanor. 'That's not a weed.'

They were making a game of it, seeing who could pull the most. He watched for a moment, then bent and kissed his wife's forehead. The kitten was asleep in her lap. Her face seemed drawn, her eyes weary.

'Is something wrong?' he asked.

'I'm just tired. These two have been running me ragged today.'

'Go and sleep. I'll look after them.'

She took his hand. 'There's too much to do.'

It was natural for a woman with child to be tired; Dame Martha had told him that. She'd given him so many instructions that his head reeled from them all. Treat her gently, but not like she might break. Make sure she rested. Comfort her.

'You're going to be good to her,' Martha told him, 'or you'll answer to me. I've seen too many men heedless of their wives. You're not going to be that way.'

Her eyes had flashed as she spoke. All he felt was fear of all the things that could happen. The way the baby could die, before or after the birth. How fragile life could be for mother and child.

Since she'd told him, the worry had never vanished. It lay there, at the bottom of his mind, peering up at times. Whenever she seemed tired the warnings all flooded back into his head.

'Rest,' he told Katherine. He was going to look after her, as well as he could.

After a small hesitation she nodded. He helped her up, watching until she was in the house. Then he turned to Eleanor and Janette.

'All the traders will be taking down their stalls at the market. Do you want to go and watch?'

'Yes!' Janette shouted.

'You have to promise not to run off.'

Solemnly they both agreed and holding them both by the hand, he led the way to the marketplace.

In the distance he spotted Walter, deep in conversation with a man putting his goods into packs while a donkey stood patiently waiting. The boy knew so many people. It still surprised him.

He took the girls around, pointing out this and that, buying each of them a pastry covered with marchpane. A little luxury. Let them feel spoilt for once; once the baby arrived they'd have less attention. They giggled as they ate, wrapping a few crumbs in a handkerchief to take home for the kitten.

The three of them wandered for an hour, walking out past West Bar, then up the hill and home along Saltergate. He glanced up at Timothy's house. Someone had closed the shutters; already the place looked uninhabited and neglected.

At home he cautioned them to be quiet, to find the cat and feed it. He walked lightly up the stairs, peering into the solar to see Katherine stretched out sleeping. There was a smile on her face, long hair spread over the pillow. She looked so gentle, so peaceful that the sight of her filled his heart. He could have stayed there for a long time, simply watching her.

• • •

The girls were in bed, the giggling growing more sporadic as they settled down. Every night it was the same. Katherine was preparing the dough for tomorrow's bread.

He sat at the table with Walter. The lad had been quiet for a long time, but he was fidgeting a lot. There was something he wanted to say, John could tell, and he waited patiently until the boy was ready to speak.

'John,' he said finally.

'What is it?' he asked kindly.

'The two men you were looking for …'

Julian's mystery visitors. 'Do you know who they are?' he asked with sudden urgency.

'I was talking to someone today who thinks he recognised them.'

'Go on.'

'He saw them the day Julian died.'

Now he was interested. 'The person you talked to, who is he?'

'He used to live in Lincoln. He'd seen the men down there. They work for the bishop.'

That was news worth knowing. But what would bishop's men be doing in Chesterfield?

'Is he sure?'

Walter nodded. 'Yes, John, he is.'

'Does he know their names?'

'No, John.'

'You've done well,' he said with a smile. 'Thank you.'

Walter had kept at it. He'd persisted, asking his questions and eventually discovering a few answers. It was more than he'd found himself.

But what did it mean? Why would a pair of bishop's men be visiting someone as unholy as Julian? There was only one reason he could imagine: to buy the psalter. Would they kill to have it, though?

He hoped not, but a part of him knew better than that. People could be ruthless to own the things they wanted. And the money saved could line their own pockets. Yet that still didn't explain Stephen the salt merchant.

Too many names. Too many people. Too much death.

There was a chain that linked them all. It began with Timothy, killed in his bed. Nicholas was not guilty of any crime, though. He was as much a victim as his master. Edward the Butcher and his friend Gilbert. They'd committed the first two murders. He was as certain of that as he could be. And now they were dead, too.

Everything pointed to Julian as their executioner. Maybe he really had been. But there were also parts of the picture still hidden from sight.

'What are you thinking, John?' Walter interrupted his flow.

'I'm trying to work out the puzzle.' He sighed. 'Have you ever watched people playing chess?'

The boy looked at him in confusion. 'Yes,' he replied slowly.

'If you watch them, they're always trying to think five or ten moves ahead. They're planning.' He looked at Walter, seeing him nod slightly. 'I think someone is behind all this, moving people around like the pawns.'

He'd always admired those who were good at chess. He didn't have a mind for the game and no one had ever offered to teach him. But he knew it needed a certain type of thinking, a person who planned well. And it seemed that whoever was behind this stayed two steps ahead of him, if not more.

'What do you mean, John?'

He tried to explain it, but the words eluded him and he tried to make sense of it all.

'I don't know,' he said finally, slapping his hand on the table in frustration. 'But you've done a good job there.'

Walter blushed at the praise.

'Thank you.'

• • •

He knocked on the door of the house on Knifesmithgate, the family behind him. The Sunday weather was fair, a light breeze to take the edge off the heat. Dame Martha stepped out, wearing her best clothes, the gown hung overnight to remove all the creases, her wimple as white as winter. She linked her arm through his, Katherine on his other side, and they processed to the church as the bell rang for the morning service.

The spire was complete now, the oak tiles glowing warmly in the sun. People stopped to admire it, pointing and smiling.

'What do you think of it now?' Martha asked him.

'It's magnificent.' His voice was full of awe. At one point it had seemed impossible, something just held on to the tower by its own weight. But here it was, finished.

'I never thought I'd see anything like it in my lifetime,' Martha agreed. Even the girls were silent, gazing up towards the top as it climbed to heaven. 'Come on, we'd better move. The service will be starting.'

She always stood with the other goodwives at the back, where they could exchange their comments and looks without anyone else noticing. He moved down the nave, the others besides him, standing and waiting. From the corner of his eye he could see the coroner over to the side with the other burghers of the town, the monk a pace behind him, head bowed in prayer.

Father Geoffrey appeared, resplendent in his robes and colourful stole, leading the prayers in Latin that hardly anyone understood. It was the rhythm of the words, the sense of devotion, the idea of coming together before God that mattered. The words droned by him, the way they always did, and his thoughts floated away.

Before the blessing he leaned down and whispered to Katherine to take everyone home; he had one small thing to do.

John waited as the church emptied. De Harville was talking to another man, nodding soberly as he listened before clasping hands and striding away.

'Master,' John called softly.

The coroner turned and waited, an impatient look on his face. 'What is it, Carpenter? News?'

'A little about those two men who were at Julian's. Someone recognised them from Lincoln.'

'Go on.'

'They work for the bishop.'

'Are you sure?' he asked quickly.

'That's what Walter was told.'

De Harville's eyes looked to the vestry. He smoothed down the silk sleeves of his surcote.

'You'd think the Father would know if people from My Lord Bishop were here, wouldn't you?'

'He never mentioned it to me.'

'That's food for thought.' He shook his head. 'What do you make of it?'

He explained his ideas as best he could, more clearly than the night before.

'You could be right,' the coroner acknowledged. 'For all we know the psalter might be in Lincoln Cathedral now, and that's the last we'll ever see of it. You know what these places are like, they love to collect treasures and relics. Especially if they can get them for very little.' He snorted. 'They're not likely to admit they possess it. Come and see me in the morning and I'll decide what to do.'

'Yes, Master. I thought you were arresting Christian tomorrow.'

'Arresting? I still have some questions for him to answer and I want to see his face when he lies to me.'

'Yes, Master. Have you heard any more from Ralph of York?'

'No, and I daresay we won't. See if that boy can find out anything more on those men from Lincoln. They must have stayed somewhere.' And with a curt nod, he was gone.

. . .

The house was bustling. Martha had the cat on her lap, stroking its fur as she told a story that kept the girls and Walter rapt.

John crept through to the buttery and put his arms around his wife's waist. It seemed thicker than just a week before, the life growing bigger inside her.

'What did he have to say?' she asked after she kissed him.

'Who?'

Katherine tapped his arm playfully.

'Who do you think? There's only one person you'd need to talk to.'

'Maybe we'll have a better idea tomorrow. Martha has everyone entertained. We could slip upstairs, they'd never miss us …'

'Shhh,' she said, but her eyes twinkled.

CHAPTER SEVENTEEN

Monday. He stretched in the bed, then rubbed his hands down his face before rising. John tied up his hose and pulled his leather jerkin over his shirt. No pain from his arm; the wound had fully healed. Downstairs, he put on the new boots, smiling with satisfaction as they seemed to mould themselves around his feet.

Chewing a hunk of bread he made his way to the High Street. There was a coolness to the morning, the air fresh and damp with dew. But before he reached the coroner's house, he turned away, walking out past the cottages beyond West Bar to the road that led to Brampton. There was no rush. It would be hours before they brought in Christian and there was nothing for him until that time.

He sat on the riverbank, listening to the song of the water as it burbled over the rocks. Things had preyed on his mind all night. His fears, Katherine and the baby, all mingled with the faces of the dead. Not just those from the last few weeks, but all the way back to his mother, her features blurred by memory.

John closed his eyes and let his head rest in the grass, feeling the gentle sun on his skin. But sleep wouldn't come. Instead, he just listened to the rhythm of his breathing, letting the day envelop him.

He wasn't sure when he first heard the sound. It crept around the edge of his hearing. Someone walking through the long grass, trying to be quiet. He half-opened his eyes and tried to locate the noise.

About ten yards away, he decided. Another cautious footstep. He strained and could make out ragged breathing. One more step.

With a single move, John sprang to his feet. One hand reached for his knife, drawing it so the blade glittered in the light. He turned, seeing the man.

Small and wiry, his hood pulled up over his head, leaving the face in shadow. He could only see the mouth, lips drawn back in a snarl to show rotting teeth. The man grasped a knife in his right hand, his knuckles white on the hilt. He was here to kill.

'Who sent you?' His voice was dry and rasping in his throat. The man didn't answer, circling slowly and intently, looking for an opening.

John feinted forward and the man calmly moved back a pace. He knew what he was doing. Not scared, taking his time. A hunter closing on his prey.

He could feel the sweat in the small of his back and on his palms. But he kept his eyes fixed on the man, forcing himself to pay attention to everything; the position of the feet, the way his hands shifted in the air.

John felt sure he didn't know this man from Chesterfield. There was nothing familiar in his appearance. It was impossible to see his eyes.

How much time had passed? It couldn't have been more than seconds but it felt like hours. The knife seemed heavy in his hand. He had to stay alert, aware of every tiny thing if he was going to stay alive.

He kept his breathing even. The assassin leapt forward a yard. John slashed down, finding only empty air as the arm moved quickly, the tip of the man's knife catching in his jerkin and slicing cleanly through the leather.

It was close. Too close. The man was skilled with his weapon. He was going to need luck to come out of this. He didn't want to die. There was far too much to live for yet.

The stone scudded off a tree with a dull noise. It was enough to break the man's concentration for a second as his head jerked around. The second stone caught him on the point of the shoulder. His fist opened and he dropped the blade.

John darted forward, cutting the man on the arm before his open hand caught him hard on the side of his head, sending him sprawling.

It was no more than a moment before he gathered himself. By then it was too late. The man had already gone and he didn't have the strength to pursue him.

He sat, taking a deep breath.

'You can come out now, Walter,' he said not even turning as the boy approached. He felt drained, as if he'd lived a whole year in the last minute.

'Did he hurt you, John?' The lad squatted in the grass, still holding the slingshot.

'No, God be praised,' he answered with a relieved smile. 'Thank you. It looks as if you saved my life again.'

'You could have beaten him.'

'Not that one. He was too used to fighting.' He reached out and picked up the man's knife. The hilt was bound with cloth so it wouldn't slip in his hand, and the blade had been lovingly honed to a deadly sharpness. 'Here,' he said, passing it to Walter, 'you might as well have that. It's better than the one you own.'

'Thank you, John,' the boy said in astonishment.

'Do you know who he was?'

'No. He didn't look like anyone I remember.'

'Nor me.'

A stranger. That was worrying. Had someone paid an outsider to murder him? Or was it simply a masterless man of the roads who saw an opportunity to take a few quick coins?
He scooped water into his palm and splashed it on to his face. The shock was good. Sudden, bracing.

'Come on,' he said finally, after his hands had stopped shaking. 'Let's go back to town. I think we'd better tell the coroner what happened.'

'Do you want me there, John?' Walter asked hopefully.

'Of course I do. If you hadn't come along I'd probably be dead now.' He cocked his head. 'What were you doing out here, anyway?'

The lad blushed. 'I followed you. I thought I might be able to help you.'

'You certainly did that.' He laughed, a mix of shock and disbelief. He could still see the man standing there, poised and ready. Only luck and God's good grace meant he was alive now. And Walter.

Another moment and it could have been so different. He looked over his shoulder but the assassin was long gone.

• • •

'Why would he want to kill you?' de Harville asked. He paced around the room, his cote billowing out behind him as he moved.

'I don't know, Master.'

Maybe he was imagining things, trying to connect the man by the river with all these killings. He didn't fit at all. Perhaps he was nothing more than a robber. He shook his head. It all seemed as complicated as being lost in a maze, unable to find the centre or the way out. There were too many people to suspect. What he needed was proof and that was precious hard to find.

'And it was no one you knew? No one local?'

'No,' John answered, looking at Walter. The lad shook his head.

'He was good, you said?'

'A fighter. The Bishop of Lincoln would have money to pay someone like that.'

'So would many others,' the monk said gently. He kept to his place at the table, quill moving rapidly across a piece of parchment as he took notes. 'And we know how many outlaws are around.'

'He's right,' the coroner agreed. He peered out through the glazed window at figures crossing the market square. 'Too many men on the roads seeking easy money.'

'When will Christian be here?'

'I'll send the bailiffs out once they've had their dinner. We'll have him by this afternoon. I have plans for the morning.'

With a curt nod he left, his boots making a sharp tattoo on the tiled floor.

'He's going hawking,' Robert said. 'He's been looking forward to it for days.' He sighed. 'Perhaps it will put him in a better humour.'

'How's his wife?'

Robert shook his head. 'No better. But no worse either, praise God.' He made the sign of the cross. 'Keep her in your prayers.'

'I will. And the baby?'

'He's blossoming like a weed. The master sees him three times every week. If only his wife would recover he'd finally be a happy man.'

'Do you think so?'

'I'm sure of it. Maybe then he'd let me return to the monastery.'

'I'll pray for that, too.'

The brother gave a weak smile. 'From your lips to God's ears, John. Walter, you did a good day's work. We're all grateful.'

The boy reddened quickly. 'Th-th-thank you,' he stuttered.

'What are we going to do now, John?' the lad asked as they left the coroner's house.

'Nothing yet,' he said. 'You have work and so do I. We should go and do it.' But he was speaking to himself as much as to Walter.

'Yes, John.' And the boy was off and running, a grin on his face.

The house was empty, only the kitten mewling around his feet as he gathered up the satchel of tools and hung it from his shoulder. In just a few minutes he was on the road out to Newbold, the dust rising around his feet.

A few hours of labour would do him good. It would stop him thinking about death and dying. Instead he could concentrate on the wood and listen to its voice telling him what it needed.

By noon he'd worked up a heavy sweat, drilling out holes in a beam to peg it for a doorway. Slowly, he brought another piece of wood into position and ran a hand over the end, feeling the grain before measuring and cutting to make the joint.

Two hours later he had the jambs and the lintel for the door fitted together and made secure with thick wooden pegs. He poured water on the pegs to let them expand in the holes. An old carpenter from Durham had taught him the trick. It created a bond that could last a lifetime.

John wiped the sweat and sawdust from his face and chest with an old piece of linen, then sluiced his flesh with water from the stream before putting his shirt back on. His skin was already brown from hours in the sun. All the scars from accidents stood out as thin white lines, a pattern of them on his body. He'd done all he could for today.

Christian should be in Chesterfield now, answering the coroner's questions. But he took his time cleaning the tools, giving a sharper edge to a chisel with his whetstone before packing it away.

There was no rush. The man would still be there when he arrived.

CHAPTER EIGHTEEN

'I told you, I didn't kill anyone.'

Christian spoke like a man weary of repeating the same thing. He sat on the chair, hands bound behind his back, his face red and shiny with sweat. The start of bruises showed where he'd resisted the bailiffs who tried to bring him here.

De Harville sat on the table, legs swinging. Brother Robert had his usual place in the corner, the quill poised as he waited. A broad bailiff stood guard inside the door, his hand ready on the hilt of his sword.

John leaned against the wall, the bag of tools at his feet. He'd been here for a quarter of an hour and heard nothing worthwhile yet. Christian simply denied everything. The only evidence against him was the testimony of Piers the apprentice. And that was precious thin.

'You were the last to see him alive,' John said.

Christian turned, eyes full of fury. 'And he was still alive when I left,' he roared. 'I've known him all my life. We're related. Why would I kill him?'

'You tell me,' the coroner said lazily. 'Maybe for the proceeds from the sale of the psalter. How much did it fetch?'

'I don't know what you're talking about.'

'No?' De Harville drew out his knife and carefully cleaned his nails with the point. 'Then what were two men from the Bishop of Lincoln doing visiting Julian?'

'I don't know anything about them.'

He sounded so honest, so confused by the idea that for a moment John could almost believe him. Then it passed; the mask of Christian's face seemed to drop.

'What happened the last time you saw Julian?' John asked.

'I had business in Chesterfield. I thought I'd see him.' He shrugged. 'I usually did when I was here.'

'Where was he?'

'In his room above the shop.'

'How long did you stay? What did you talk about?'

'I was only there a short while. We didn't talk about much. Nothing important.'

It had the ring of truth. But it was also vague. Too vague.

'Who were you in Chesterfield to see?'

Christian glanced at the faces waiting for his answer, eyes moving from one to the other.

'I had to arrange the sale of some fleeces when we shear our sheep. You can sometimes get a better price if you arrange it early.'

'On behalf of your lord, or on your own account?' de Harville asked sharply.

'My lord, of course,' the man replied, but the reddening on his cheeks showed the lie.

'I'm sure he'll be pleased to hear you're so diligent when I send him my report.'

Christian bowed his head, knowing he'd been caught.

'Who was the man you came to see?' John asked him.

'Thomas. He deals in wool. He'll tell you I was there.'

No doubt that part was true. The killing wouldn't have taken more than a minute. Easily done. John glanced at the coroner. He was still paring his nails.

'I know old Tom,' de Harville said finally. He beckoned the bailiff close and whispered something in his ear. The man left the room. 'If he confirms you visited him, you'll be able to go.'

'I was there,' Christian said, the relief plain on his face.

A heavy, brooding silence filled the hall. The only sound was the occasional scratching of Brother Robert's quill. Finally the bailiff returned, bending to speak quietly to the coroner.

'You can go,' de Harville said finally. As Christian stood, he added, 'I'll probably want to talk to you again. Next time come quietly, for your own sake.'

'Yes, Master,' the man agreed and hurried out of the room, glaring fire at John as he left.

'Well, Carpenter, is he guilty? Was I wrong to let him go?'

'Wrong?' he asked in surprise. 'I don't know. There was no proof to keep him. I think he was telling the truth – some of the time, anyway.'

De Harville cocked his head.

'And the rest of it?'

'I don't know. He could have killed, that's certain. He had the opportunity.'

'What do you think, monk?'

'I agree with John.' Robert said after some thought. 'We have nothing against him. But I can't say he's innocent. Not yet. There's something I don't trust about him.'

'Don't trust?' The coroner raised an eyebrows. 'You're always one to see the best in people.'

'I'm sorry, Master.' He lowered his head.

'Better an honest answer than piety.' He laughed. 'It makes a change for you, monk.'

• • •

He walked home slowly, lost in thought. Not about Christian; those answers might never come unless they had luck.

His mind was filled with the attempt on his life. If Walter hadn't come along he'd be dead; there was no doubt of that.

The man knew his trade, and was clever enough to flee once the odds turned against him.

Was it just someone seeing an opportunity or was there more behind it? How would he even know?

Yet why would anyone consider him so much of a threat? He'd discovered nothing damning, no evidence to convict. Everything was like a tangle of threads that he was slowly trying to unravel.

As soon as he walked into the house he knew Walter had told his sister the news. The place was hushed, no sound of children playing. Katherine stood at the entrance to the buttery. Her hair was carefully tucked under the veil, an apron covering the plain brown dress. She had her arms crossed over her breasts.

'You know,' he said and she nodded sadly.

'I …' he began and found he had no idea how to continue.

'Why?' Katherine asked.

'I don't know.' He lowered the satchel of tools to the floor and sighed. 'I can't make head nor tail of it.' He opened his arms but she didn't move. 'I can't even tell if it's connected to everything else. It might have been an outlaw.'

'And perhaps it wasn't. Is all this worth your life?' Her eyes were intent on his.

'No,' he answered without hesitation. Who killed who, what happened to the psalter, ought to be nothing to him. All that should matter was right in front of him. He'd plighted his troth to her, given her his hand and his heart. His future.

'You really don't know the reason?'

'No.' He sat on the bench, shaking his head. 'I don't.'

'John, you have to stop.'

'There's nowhere to go with it all, anyway. Nothing else I can do.'

'Promise me,' she told him.

'I swear it,' he said, and meant the words. His business with the coroner, with Timothy and the psalter, was done. He patted his bag. 'Tomorrow I'm back out to Newbold as if nothing had happened.'

'And if they still come looking for you?' Her expression had softened, he thought. That was something.

He tried to smile. 'I'll run.'

Katherine came to sit across the table, her hands reaching out to take his. 'What if de Harville comes back and wants more from you?' She spoke the name with anger.

'I'll refuse.'

'Will you?' It came out of her mouth like an accusation and he knew he deserved it.

'I will. I can make the same money doing what I love and I know I'll be home safe every night. With my wife.'

'The coroner will insist.'

'Let him,' John said. 'I don't owe him any service. I can stand my ground.'

'I pray you do,' Katherine said softly, but with little hope.

• • •

The days passed. He returned to the barn, taking Walter with him for the heavy work that needed two men. Two weeks and he was done, proud of what he'd built. All that remained was the thatching of the roof, and that was a skill beyond him.

The farmer paid him and he moved on to the next jobs. Small work that lasted two or three days, then on to another and another.

May ripened into June, the scent of wildflowers heady in the air when he walked outside Chesterfield. The stalks of wheat waved in the fields. The lambs flourished and the cattle grew fat on the grass.

It was as perfect a season as he could remember. When he held Katherine he believed he could feel her body thickening, almost day by day. Sometimes she placed his hand there and he could feel the baby moving and kicking inside her.

That was the miracle, he decided. Each time it took his breath away and brought a silent prayer for mother and child.

He almost forgot about Timothy and the other dead men. They slipped to the back of his mind, their faces only appearing if he walked back to the empty house at the top of Saltergate or saw the coroner from a distance.

De Harville hadn't sent for him. They'd exchanged little more than a nod in church of a Sunday or in the marketplace.

He slipped back into a familiar life and it fitted him well. For the first week he stayed wary, walking around with a hand on the hilt of his knife in case the killer returned. But there was nothing and he began to lower his guard.

His labours kept him busy. He felt content in his life, happy in his own skin, using the talent God have given him. Each day he returned home tired but satisfied. Walter had wondered when they'd look further into the deaths, but even he had stopped asking.

It was a small life. Yet he didn't want anything more. He had everything a man could desire.

• • •

The evening was long, warm enough to sit outside as the darkness gathered. He'd made a simple bench for Katherine, where they could enjoy the weather and the way the silence slowly grew around them. She had a rough shawl gathered around her shoulders. Her cheeks had grown plumper, rosy in the fading light.

His mouth was open, ready to say something, when he heard the hammering on the door. Worry flashed in her eyes. It was late for a caller. No good news ever arrived at this hour.

He heard Katherine behind him as he strode through the house and unlocked the door. One of the bailiffs stood there, looking apologetic.

'I'm sorry, Master,' he said, 'but the coroner sent me to fetch you.'

'Why?' John asked.

'I don't know, Master. He just sent me to tell you.'

He was silent for a few moments, composing the words.

'Please tell him that I'm flattered,' John began, 'but that I'm done with the business of death.'

'Yes, Master,' the bailiff replied. 'He won't be happy,' he added after a pause.

'I'm a free man,' he said kindly. 'I'm not beholden to anyone.'

'Yes, Master.' With a short bow, the man left.

The peace of the evening had been shattered. If there'd been a death he'd hear about it in the morning, along with the rest of the town. That was enough for him.

'Do you think he'll let it go?' Katherine asked.

'I hope so.' He put an arm around her. 'Come on, let's go to bed.'

But he'd barely settled when a fist was pounding on the door once more. If he didn't answer it, the neighbours would wake.

That was what the coroner wanted, of course.

He stepped into his hose and boots, glancing back at Katherine. In the moonlight her eyes looked fearful.

John drew back the bolts and turned the key. The coroner himself was there, face set.

'I sent a man for you.' He took a pace into the house.

'I'm done with all that. I told him.'

'He gave me your message.'

John smiled. 'Then I don't know what more to tell you.'

'People don't turn me down.' It sounded like a threat. 'You've done it twice. First when I offered you the manor and now this.'

'I have my business to look after.' He heard feet on the stairs and turned to see Katherine. She'd put on the simple brown dress, the veil roughly gathered over her hair.

'I need you for *my* business,' de Harville told him.

'Your business almost killed him twice,' Katherine said. 'Had you forgotten that?'

'The dam speaks.' The coroner's mouth twitched with amusement. 'Come now and we'll forget all this happened.'

'No,' John said.

De Harville sighed. 'What do you want?' he asked.

'We'd like you to leave us alone,' Katherine told him. She put her hand on John's arm. 'You're a father. How do you think your child would feel if you were dead?'

He acknowledged the statement with a nod of his head. 'What would you have me do, Mistress? Beg?'

'I'd rather you left,' she said.

'Carpenter, I need you.' He sounded sober, his tone serious. 'I've got nowhere since you left.'

'There was nowhere to go, the way things stood.'

'Maybe,' the coroner agreed.

'Why send for me in the middle of the night? What's so urgent?'

'Someone came and said they'd seen the two men who work for the Bishop of Lincoln again. They're here.'

'You can question them,' John said. 'You're good at that.'

'You do something more that that.' The coroner hesitated. 'You can see into their souls and judge whether they're lying or not. I don't have that gift.'

John shook his head. 'You're praising me too highly. I can't do that.'

'Don't forget I've seen you do it.' He smiled. 'I just want you there when I talk to them. Ask your own questions if you like, then tell me what you think.' He looked at Katherine. 'Nothing more than that, Mistress. I swear.'

John watched her face. She blinked and gave the merest hint of a nod.

'I'll be there in the morning,' he told de Harville.

'Thank you.' But the man said it to her, not him.

The door closed and locked, Katherine turned to him. 'Just talk,' she warned. 'Nothing more.'

'I promise,' he said, smiling. Most men would never let their wives dictate what they could and couldn't do. They'd say it went against the natural order. But their marriage was for love, not property or influence. He'd learnt a hard lesson, he didn't need to learn it again. 'We need our sleep,' he said, taking her hand and climbing the stairs.

• • •

It seemed strange to walk past the church and not hear the workmen. Without the sound of hammer and saw, the shouting up to the roof and the tower, the air was empty. Even the ale barrel had vanished from under the tree. Soon enough the grass in the churchyard would grow again and every memory of the workmen would fade.

The weekday market was busy, the goodwives up early, haggling over prices with beaten-down sellers. Men passed on the way to their labours, bareheaded in the balmy dawn.

John saw a face he knew here and there, then spotted Will Durrant. The young man was guiding him through the crowd.

'Good morning, Master.'

The blind man cocked his head, trying to place the voice. 'The carpenter,' he said, a grin of recognition growing on his face. 'Have you found your man yet?'

'No. I've been busy with other things.'

'Working with your hands. I can smell the sawdust on you.'

'Yes,' he admitted with a smile. 'You're well, I hope, Master?'

'Fair to middling.' He looked healthy, with just an old man's usual frailties and his blindness. 'But I hear the coroner has asked for your services again.'

He knew he shouldn't have been surprised. The town was small enough for gossip to fly on the wind. In a matter of moments it could be everywhere. But it still took him aback, to hear it said as if it was the most ordinary thing in the world.

'For today, maybe,' he allowed.

'Best not keep him waiting, John the Carpenter,' Durrant said. 'He has a temper. Not as bad as his father, mind, but still bad enough. I wish you peace of the day.'

'To you as well, Master,' he said as the young man led Durrant away.

• • •

Two chairs sat on one side of the table in de Harville's hall. A thickset man with a hook nose and a disdainful expression sat in one of them, a lanky fellow with greying hair and a long, lugubrious face next to him. They were plainly dressed, but the wool and linen of their clothes was expensive, well-cut and sewn. They wore their elegance lightly, boots of Spanish leather on their feet and velvet caps set on their heads.

'Your names, please, Masters,' the coroner asked. He was seated across from them, Brother Robert at his side, ready to make notes.

'I'm Richard d'Angers,' the heavier man replied in flowing French. 'This is Arthur of Warwick.'

'I'd prefer this in English,' the coroner said lightly. 'I assume that's no problem for you?'

'Of course not,' Arthur answered with a haughty nod. 'But we prefer French. An educated tongue.'

'And in Chesterfield we usually speak English.' He raised his gaze a little to look at John, standing in a corner behind the two strangers, his arms folded. 'I believe you work for the Bishop of Lincoln, Masters.'

'Who told you that?' D'Angers asked with amusement.

'Is it true?'

'We've helped the Bishop on a couple of matters,' Arthur acknowledged. 'But we don't *work* for him.' He spoke the word with disdain.

'Are you here on his behalf now?'

The pair glanced at each other. 'We are,' d'Angers answered reluctantly, then held up a hand before the coroner could ask his next question. The sunlight sparkled on a jewelled ring. 'But we're not at liberty to tell you why.'

'It's not your first visit here, I believe.'

'Oh?' D'Angers looked down his nose.

'You visited a man called Julian,' John said. Neither of the men turned to look at him.

'What evidence do you have for this?' Arthur said, staring at the coroner and the monk.

'You were seen,' John continued. 'What business did you have with him?'

'Does this man work for you?' Arthur asked de Harville.

'He works with me. Why do you ask?'

'He's a nobody. A nothing.'

'I'd value it if you treated his questions as if I'd asked them,' the coroner said.

'Very well.' D'Angers sighed. 'Yes, we visited him once. What of it?'

'What took you to his house?' John continued.

'We'd been told he'd be a good agent here for us. The Bishop is looking for fleeces to buy and sell on abroad.'

It seemed reasonable enough, he thought. Julian knew Christian, a man with fleeces to sell.

'And how did you find Julian?'

'He was a venal, grasping man,' Arthur told him. 'No more than you'd expect from a butcher.'

'Did you do business?'

'We did not,' he replied emphatically.

'How was he when you left?' John wondered.

'Disappointed,' d'Angers said with a heavy chuckle. 'Why, what does he say?'

'Nothing, Masters. He can't. He's dead.'

That made them turn, heads craning to see his face.

'When did this happen?'

'Shortly after you left.' He let the suggestion hang in the air.

'D'Angers stood, hand moving towards the hilt of his sword. 'Are you saying we killed him?'

'Sit down,' the coroner ordered. 'No one is accusing you of anything. You're easily upset, Master. You don't have anything to hide, do you?'

'I won't have someone like that insult my honour.'

'I didn't,' John said. 'I told you he was killed after you left. Do you know why anyone would want to kill Julian?'

'I would imagine there are many who would want to do that.' D'Angers smiled. 'Why? No reason beyond his manner. He believed he could behave beyond his station.'

'How?' the coroner asked, leaning back in his chair.

'No deference or politeness,' Arthur said. 'He seemed to believe we were equals.'

They were hiding something. He felt certain of that. They held themselves too still, John thought, and reasoned out their words too well before they spoke. Every sentence was calculated, and there was more than honour behind it all.

But if they'd bought or taken the psalter when they met Julian, why were they back in Chesterfield now? Revisiting the scene of a crime seemed to be a dangerous business. He felt the rasp of stubble as he ran a hand over his chin.

'Masters,' John said, 'it would be a great help if you could tell us your business here.'

'We can't tell you.' D'Angers bristled. 'Didn't you hear what I said earlier?'

'It would be useful.' The coroner gave a lazy smile. 'And we'll keep your confidence, I promise that.'

'No.' Arthur stood first, sword banging against his hose, then d'Angers. 'I think we've answered all your questions. I bid you God's peace.'

As the door closed behind them, de Harville raised an eyebrow.

'Haughty fellows, aren't they? What did you think, Brother?'

Robert shook his head. 'Nasty,' he said. 'Dangerous.'

'What about you, Carpenter? Did you see into their souls for me?'

'Not yet,' John said with a shake of his head. 'But I think it would be worth following them while they're here.'

'That boy of yours?'

'Yes.' They'd never notice Walter. He was so far beneath them as to be invisible. He'd be safe enough.

'Did they kill Julian?'

'Perhaps.' He couldn't say more than that. They were cold enough to murder without compunction; he was sure of that, especially if it was done in the service of the bishop, with a promise of absolution at the end. 'I'll see Walter and set him to work. Do you need anything more from me, Master?' He bent and hefted the leather satchel of tools on to his shoulder.

'A word of advice,' the coroner said. 'A man should never be ruled by his wife. It's not the natural order.'

He nodded his head in acknowledgement but said nothing. Outside, there was enough of a breeze to take the air from the heat of early June. If this continued, the farmers would complain. They needed warmth, but they needed rain, too.

Walter was where he spent his time when not delivering messages, squatting on his haunches with his back against a wall, gazing over the market square. He smiled as he saw John approach.

'I have a job for you.' He settled next to the boy. 'Coroner's work.'

'Yes John.' He smiled eagerly.

It was simple enough. And safe enough. He watched the lad pad away, then set off for Cutthorpe. The place was nothing more than a hamlet, a few miles away. But flax grew in abundance there, and looms stayed busy weaving it into linen.

CHAPTER NINETEEN

The job was small, a few repairs to one of the buildings where they stored the flax after it had been harvested. Yet it could lead to more. The other buildings around were all old and beginning to topple. He'd taken time to point it all out to the steward. Flax was the manor's wealth, it would be worth the money to keep it safe and dry.

He cut out the rotting boards, feeling the wood give under his fingertips, then adding a good six inches on either side. From there the work was simple enough. Measure and cut fresh boards of good oak that could stand the weather without warping.

There were three places around the building where the boards had to be replaced. The last one would take longest, down where the wood met the ground. He'd need to dig back the earth on both sides and put in rocks for drainage. That would wait for the morrow. He'd be able to complete all the rest today.

A servant from the hall brought him bread, cheese, and ale for his dinner. He rested in the shade of an old horse chestnut, surveying what he'd done and what he still needed to accomplish. He felt satisfied; this was the life he relished.

• • •

Dame Martha was busy setting out the trenchers of old bread when he returned to the house on Saltergate. Janette and Eleanor were kneeling on the floor, making their letters on the slates as the kitten tried to claim their attention. Already they seemed more confident, creating small words, comparing their work and laughing.

'They're coming along so quickly,' Martha told him with a gentle sigh. 'All they ever needed was someone to point them in the right direction.'

'You're doing that,' he said gratefully. 'Did you know Walter's trying, too?'

'Really?' It didn't seem to surprise her. Perhaps she really did see more in him than most.

'I've seen him trying to write with a stick in the dirt.'

She shook her head in wonder. 'He should just ask. I'd teach him.'

'He's too proud,' John said. 'Or perhaps he's afraid of failing.'

Martha sighed, wiping her hands on the spotless apron that covered her gown.

'Anyone can write, John. If you can speak, you can read and write. You know numbers, don't you?'

'In my head,' he replied.

'Then you could learn to write them down. It's not magic.'

But that was exactly how it had always seemed to him. A strange secret that the clergy and the rich held close, something not to be shared. The girls would know it, though, and the child that would scream its way into the world soon enough.

'Thank you.' He bent and kissed her cheek.

• • •

'Did you see them?'

Supper was done. Up in the solar the girls were in bed, Martha lulling them to sleep with a story. Katherine was in the buttery mixing the bread dough. John sat at the table, swirling the last of the ale at the bottom of his cup.

'Yes, John.' Walter smiled shyly. Richard d'Angers and Arthur of Warwick.

'Where did they go?'

'The alehouse and the cookshop. And into the church to pray this afternoon.'

That all seemed innocent enough.

'Who did they talk to?' he asked.

'A few people,' he lad replied. 'But just words in passing.'

'And they didn't see you?'

'No, John.' He smiled. 'They never knew I was there.'

'Will you have time to do the same again tomorrow?'

'I think so.'

'Good.'

• • •

He dreamed of noise, someone using a hammer, a pounding that seemed to make his head ring. Then Katherine was shaking him awake and whispering in his ear, 'Someone's at the door, John.'

He sat up, trying to clear the sleep from his head, and rubbing his eyes. Hurriedly, he slipped into his hose and boots, then took the knife from its sheath. It was always better to be safe in the night.

The bolts were well greased, slipping back noiselessly. He turned the key in the lock and pulled the door open, keeping a tight grip on the blade.

It was one of the bailiffs, holding up a brand, his face flickering in shadows from the flames. He looked very young and very frightened.

'Master,' he said nervously, 'the coroner needs you.'

'What?' he asked. 'Why?'

'A murder, Master.'

'Who? Where?' But he was already searching for his jacket as the night air brought goose pimples to his arms. 'What time is it?'

'Not long past two, Master. He wanted you to hurry.'

For a moment he considered going back up to the solar, to tell Katherine what was happening. But she'd know there was only one reason for someone calling in the middle of the night. Pray God she'd understand.

He hurried along, following the bailiff down Saltergate to the inn at the north end of the churchyard. Through gaps in the shutters he could see candles burning inside and the sound of voices talking in murmurs.

A group of people was gathered around the fire. The innkeeper and his wife, both looking glum and fearful, two men he didn't recognise, both looking as if they'd dressed in haste, along with Arthur of Warwick, his face unnaturally pale, the coroner, and Brother Robert. The only man missing was Richard d'Angers.

'There you are, Carpenter.' The coroner was smiling, a dark, knowing grin. 'It seems I need your services again. I trust your wife won't object too much.'

'Where is he?'

'You've spotted someone missing?' De Harville's eyes twinkled in the low light. 'He's upstairs in his bed. But he won't be rising again. Not on his own.'

John found the room easily enough, up on the second floor of the rickety building, close to the back stairway. The door was part open, a lantern burning inside. It was a typical room in an inn. A single large bed, hooks on the wall for cloaks, and a chest where travellers could keep their packs.

Only one thing was unusual in the room: the body of Richard d'Angers, his blood soaked into the sheet that covered his body, his eyes open and gazing towards Heaven. Holding his breath, John drew back the cover to examine the wound.

A single cut. It must have gone through into the heart. Murdered as he slept. At least death would have come in an instant. But there didn't seem to be any sign of a fight. The body was dressed only in his fine linen, the rest of his clothes neatly folded on top of the chest. He went through the scrip. A few faded notes on vellum. Coins in the purse, and plenty of them, the first thing any robber would have taken.

He replaced the sheet, drawing it up to cover the man's face. The flesh still had some warmth; this had happened within the last few hours. Nothing seemed to be disturbed in the room. A candle in its holder, extinguished, sat on the floor.

The door to the back stairs was unlocked. A precaution in case of fire, but it also allowed anyone to enter. Sighing, he returned to the room below.

'Were you sharing the room?' he asked Arthur of Warwick. The words seemed to pull the man from somewhere deep inside himself. All his disdain had vanished now.

'Yes,' he replied slowly. 'It was all they could offer.'

'Did you find him?'

Arthur nodded. 'Richard went up to bed early. Said he was weary.'

'What about you?'

'I stayed down here. I wasn't tired. I went up an hour or so ago and found …' He didn't need to complete the thought.

'Were you in here the whole time?'

'Except when I went to the jakes.'

John turned to the innkeeper. 'You saw him?'

'Right enough. It's like he said.'

'Who was in tonight?'

The man scratched his head. 'A fair few, on and off.'

'Any strangers?'

The innkeeper glanced at his wife. 'One or two faces I didn't know, but that's often the way in this business. No one causing trouble.'

'Anyone asking questions?

'No.'

'Are there any others staying here?'

'Not tonight, Master,' the goodwife answered in a croaking voice. 'We only have one room free. So there was just him and …' She raised her eyes towards the ceiling.

'When did your companion go upstairs?' John asked Arthur.

'I don't know. Not long after we ate, I remember that.' Several hours earlier, most likely. But Arthur hadn't committed this murder, he felt certain of that. He was too shaken and ashen-faced by the death. The man wasn't play-acting his horror.

'Do you know who might have done this?' he asked quietly. 'Have there been any threats?'

'Why would you think that?' Arthur turned quizzical eyes on him.

'I'm just asking questions.'

'No. There's been nothing of that kind.'

'Can I see your knife?'

'What?' The man looked astonished. 'Why?'

'To examine.' John smiled. 'Please, Master.'

Slowly, Arthur handed it over. John took it close to the candle, holding it near his face, searching for the slightest trace of blood. But there was nothing. The blade was as clean as if it had never been used. He passed it back and looked at the coroner. The man was standing half in the shadows, paying close attention.

'It would be helpful to know your business here. What brought you to Chesterfield?'

Arthur was silent for so long that he might have lost the power of speech.

'I'd need the permission of my Lord to tell you,' he answered finally.

'God's blood, this is a murder!' de Harville roared. 'Do you think we're here in the middle of the night for our pleasure? You were the finder. You'll pay your fine and you won't leave the town until we find the killer. If you try to go I'll have you arrested. You'd best think on that and tell us what we need.'

Arthur's stare was hard and angry but he didn't speak.

Finally the coroner clapped his hands together. 'Anything more you need here, Carpenter?'

'Not tonight.'

'Then we'll go.' He pointed at Arthur. 'Don't try to leave.'

John helped the monk pack his parchment, quills and ink in the desk, securing the catch. He could see the pain on Brother Robert's face and the awkward way he moved his hands, trying to rub some warmth into his fingers.

'Let me,' he said, hoisting the strap for the portable desk on to his shoulder.

'Thank you,' Robert said with a slow smile. 'That's a blessing.' He reached for an old woollen cloak and fastened it clumsily. 'Even the warm nights have a chill when you're old, John. Remember that for the years to come.'

They ambled back to the High Street. De Harville hadn't waited for them. He wasn't even in sight, striding ahead in his usual manner.

'What do you make of all this, Brother?'

'I don't know,' Robert replied, and there was worry in his voice. 'Six killings and no one caught. People were already growing scared before this happened.'

Were they? He'd seen no panic or heard any fearful words. But the monk could be right. The more the death toll mounted, the more people would begin to look at their neighbours with suspicion and wonder.

'I can't see any sense in it all,' John admitted. 'It's like walking in the dark without a light.'

'The Master's at his wits' end. With this many deaths, powerful people are going to take notice. Especially after this last one.'

That was true. The Bishop of Lincoln held large sway in England. He had the ear of archbishops and kings. The last thing de Harville wanted was some royal official arriving to take over the investigation. It would be a failure, a black mark against his name for the future. No more preferment.

'Do you have any idea why a pair of bishop's men should be here?'

'None,' the brother said with a sigh. 'I just wish he'd let me go back to the monastery.'

'He's still saying nothing?'

'No. He's too wrapped up in everything in his own life. He says he needs me here.' After a small cough he asked, 'How's Dame Martha? I haven't seen her to talk to since your wedding.'

'She's well. She's teaching the girls to read.' He thought a moment. 'Growing older, but we all are, Brother.' He clapped Robert very lightly on the shoulder.

'True enough, John, true enough.' He sounded resigned.

They parted at the gate to the coroner's house. He waited until the door closed behind the monk, the glow of a lantern spearing the night for a moment.

The town was silent as he walked home, his footsteps echoing off the buildings. What to make of this new death? It was linked to the others. It had to be. He didn't know how yet, but there could be no other reason. From Timothy and Nicholas to Edward the Butcher and Gilbert the Shoemaker, then Julian. And now Richard d'Angers. It was a twisted path. It had to be the psalter. For a book of psalms it was turning into a cursed document. And its tale hadn't finished yet. Not until the person behind all this was found.

He needed to know why the bishop's men had come here. Everything might revolve around that. But if they'd already bought the psalter, or if they'd killed to possess it, why would they return? It was tempting fate, and fate could be exceeding cruel.

He unlocked the door and crept in. Nobody else was up. There was no point in going back to bed. His mind was awake and working; he'd only toss and turn till dawn, waking Katherine and everyone else.

In the buttery he poured himself a mug of ale and tore a hunk off a loaf, chewing hungrily. At the moment he had no idea who might have killed d'Angers. The open back stairs and unlocked door made everything too easy. Still, the killer needed to know which room d'Angers occupied and that he'd be alone. Even then he must have been very quiet. Or it had been someone the man knew and trusted.

He stared out of the window at the night. Not even the first notes of dawn yet. A knife … He started, slamming down the cup and spilling some of the drink. D'Angers had worn a knife. It had been on his belt. But John had never looked at it.

As soon as morning arrived he'd return to the inn.

· · ·

The innkeeper kept yawning. He looked haggard, as if sleep had been short and hard-won.

'Is the body still upstairs?'

'Aye, Master, right enough it is. You know the way.'

'What did you do with the other man?'

'There's a room of sorts under the eaves. The servant usually has it.' He shrugged. 'It's nothing much but it's clean.' The man grimaced. 'Best I can do since I can't charge him for it.'

185

The corpse was already beginning to stink. Flies buzzed in the room and over the flesh. They'd have laid their eggs and the maggots would be wriggling.

He threw back the shutters, blinking as the sharp early light flooded in. He drew the sheet back to see the wound once more. But there was nothing he hadn't noticed during the night. Hardly daring to breathe, he drew the knife out of its sheath and held it up. John squinted, looking along the length of the blade.

Someone had tried to wipe it clean, but they'd done a poor, hasty job. In the light he could make out the small stains of blood dried on the metal. They looked like rust, but came away easily under his fingernail.

Another quick search, the body lying there like a sightless accusation, and he found where the blade had been wiped: along the hem of the man's cloak. At least he knew what had killed d'Angers. All he needed to learn now was the who and the why of it.

•   •   •

The house on Saltergate was bustling with life. Katherine looked harassed and gaunt as she laid out the food to break the fast. The girls were arguing. Kit twined itself around legs, mewling to be fed. Only Walter sat quietly, already eating, a mug of weak ale sitting next to him on the table.

He took the plate from his wife and carried it into the hall, calling the girls to eat.

'The coroner's business?' Katherine asked reproachfully when they were all seated.

'Yes. Another body.'

She crossed herself and Walter turned to him, eyes curious.

'Who was it, John?'

'One of the men you were following.'

Katherine pecked at her food, a nibble of this, a taste of that, pushing it around until she stood finally and stalked into the buttery. He followed.

'Why did you go?' she hissed. 'You could have said no. I thought we were done with all that.'

He knew what he'd promised and hung his head.

'Is this how it's going to be, John? De Harville whistles and you come running like a dog?' He started to speak but she waved him down. 'You made a vow to me.' Katherine placed a hand on her belly. 'You made *us* a vow. I know the husband is the head of the house but I want you here to help with your child. I want him to know his father.'

'Or her,' John said softly.

She shook her head. 'Him. I can feel it.'

'Him.' He put his hand over hers. For a moment he felt something move and looked at her.

'That's him,' Katherine told him. 'That's your son.'

He didn't know the words for what he felt. The life in her, growing. The life they'd made, that God had granted them. A fragile, fleeting existence on this earth.

'The man who was killed,' he tried to explain. 'It all goes back to Timothy and this psalter of his. I've been in this from the beginning. I *need* to know. Do you understand?'

Very slowly, she nodded. 'You always will, won't you? You can't refuse a mystery.'

He'd never thought of himself that way, but she was right. Each death was a challenge, a puzzle to try and solve, where he had to use his wits to find the answer. And she was right; he relished it, no matter how much he complained. That was the truth of the matter.

'Yes,' he admitted.

'I'll just have to accept it, won't I?' She took hold of his hand.

He breathed slowly. 'It won't happen often.'

'I pray not, John,' she said sadly. 'I truly do.'

.   .   .

The coroner was parading around his hall, a houpelande of grey silk over his shirt. The sleeves billowed so wide that they touched the floor. A pointless garment, John thought as he watched the man strut. Too thin to be any sort of coat. Just decoration for those with more money than sense.

'So we know he was murdered with his own knife,' de Harville said. 'That's useful, but what does it tell us?' He stood by the window, peering through the thick, clouded glass.

'Nothing too much.'

'Find out who used that knife, Carpenter.' It wasn't an order so much as a plea. The coroner was feeling crowded, he knew that. Too many deaths with no answers. Enough for his name to be spoken in London and for the authorities to wonder whether he should be replaced.

'Where's Brother Robert this morning?'

'I let him sleep after having him up in the night.'

It was the first time the man had shown any compassion for the monk.

'You should let him go back to the monastery,' John ventured.

'No.' De Harville shook his head firmly. 'I trust him. I need people around me that I can trust.'

'He's old, Master. He's served you well.'

'I said no, Carpenter.' The coroner dismissed the matter. 'Remember your place. Use your brain to discover the killer. Maybe then I can let him go.'

The hint of a bargain. Not that he believed a word of it.

'It would help if we knew why Arthur and d'Angers had come here. Not just this time, but when Julian was killed.'

'I'll see him again this morning.'

'I'd like to hear his answers.'

The coroner shook his head. 'Leave him to me.'

The words brooked no objection.

He left, out into the bright morning sun, and no idea how to start the task ahead. He'd learned all he could at the inn, he couldn't question Arthur of Warwick. What could he do? Nothing until he had more information.

• • •

The boards were a tight fit. Exactly the way he wanted. He took some of the iron nails and hammered the wood into place. Finally he heated a small pot of pitch over the fire until it would spread easily, then used it on the boards to make a seal. No damp would penetrate now. The cut flax at Cutthorpe would stay dry.

He'd stripped off his shirt, leaving it to hang in the shade. He took a piece of linen and wiped the sweat from his body.

Katherine had been surprised to see him return to the house for his tools. He'd kissed her before he left again, watching the girls sitting and spinning while the kitten attempted to play with the wool. Home, with all its pleasures and all its troubles. He was happy here.

John inspected the work once more then began to pack away his tools, making sure everything was clean and carefully coated with a thin film of oil to ward away rust. That was the secret, his father had said. The first thing he'd taught him in those summers before the pestilence arrived and tore England apart.

In his mind he could still see his father's hands. Large, the fingers long and supple, the skin hard from all the years of work. He held up his own. Perhaps he'd become his father. He'd have a difficult task to live up to the man he remembered.

Slowly, he walked back to Chesterfield. The spire stood tall in the sky, a beacon to everyone around, a marker, a guide. It was beautiful, the sun giving a warm glow to the oak tiles so that it seemed to invite everyone to come closer. God was there, it proclaimed.

At least he could say he'd had some small part in it. Not as much as he'd have liked, but a few little things. That alone would be a wonder to tell his children as they walked to church on a Sunday.

Bees droned in the air. A faint breeze whispered in the trees with a ripple of leaves. He'd hoped that a day away from the murders might have brought him some insight, a clue where to go, who to ask.

But there'd been nothing. Each way seemed blocked or led into an empty wilderness when he thought it through. He kicked out at a stone, watching it bounce down the track, kicked it again and followed it with his eye, then paused to watch a flock of starlings wheel and dart in the air.

There was no silence in the countryside. Sound was everywhere – the scuffling of animals, songs and calls, the men working in the fields. Not as loud as the town, but always there, a constant backdrop to the landscape.

By the time he reached home his throat was dry and hunger gnawed at his belly. He'd taken nothing for his dinner, working through to make up for his late start. And in the end he'd done a good day's work, although it was taking longer than he'd anticipated. God willing, he'd finish it tomorrow, then try to persuade the steward to spend money on the other buildings later in the year. For now, though, he had more jobs waiting. He'd have no chance to be idle during the summer.

The house was empty. No one in the garden at the back. The kitten came running for attention, mewling its welcome. He tore up a few scraps of bread and scattered them on the floor before he poured himself a mug of ale, drinking it down quickly then sipping at a second.

They'd probably gone to see Dame Martha, he decided. And Walter … he kept his own hours these days, never arriving until all the work was done for the day.

No matter.

He left the satchel of tools in the corner. The cat sniffed at it then stalked away, searching for something more interesting. John sat on the bench, resting his elbows on the table. A few minutes doing nothing, this was what he needed.

By the time Katherine and the girls bustled in he felt at peace with the world, ready for company. He grabbed Janette and Eleanor, tickling them until they giggled and screamed with laughter, wriggling away with innocent, happy smiles on their lips.

'You're in a good mood.' Katherine ran a hand through his hair.

'I'm content,' he told her, kissing her palm. 'And all thanks to you, wife.'

'Me?' she asked in surprise.

'Everything you've given me. Yourself, this place, a family.' He placed his hand over her belly, smiling. 'This.'

'And we need you here. All of us.'

He nodded. 'I know. But–'

'You've started something and you need to finish it.' He tried to identify her tone. Resignation? Or infinite sadness?

'Yes,' he admitted.

'I'm not a fool, John. I said it earlier. You love the mysteries. I can see it on your face. Just be careful, please. You want us, you have to take care of us.'

'I will.'

She smiled. 'Where's Walter? He should be back by now.'

He hadn't returned by the time they'd finished supper. Nor when they'd settled their girls on their pallet. The evenings stretched out longer, dusk lingered, slowly darkening the horizon. But at nightfall there was still no sign of him.

'I'm worried about him,' Katherine said. She'd tried to settle to needlework and darning, but after a few minutes she kept putting everything aside and pacing round the hall. 'He's never this late. Not without sending word.'

'I'll go and look for him.' He doubted that there was a problem; the lad was at that thoughtless age. He'd be off enjoying himself and not thinking of anyone else.

John slipped into his jacket, checking that the knife was in his belt. He wouldn't need it but better to be safe.

Somewhere in the distance the night birds were calling. As he walked towards the church his eyes adjusted to the darkness. His ears caught the whispers of a courting couple somewhere close by. Could Walter have found himself a girl? No, he decided. The boy would never have been able to hide that. It would have been all over his face.

The streets of Chesterfield were quiet. Most people were already in their beds, their lights extinguished. Groups of young men gathered on the edge of the market square, drinking and laughing, some arguing and on the edge of a fight. He walked by them all, trying to spot Walter's face in the moonlight.

Nothing.

He tried Low Pavement, along Knifesmithgate, then down the hill on Soutergate, all the way to the bridge over the Hipper. There were men around, the late stragglers.

But no Walter.

CHAPTER TWENTY

The cap lay atop the churchyard wall, close to the lych gate. He'd have missed it entirely in the darkness if the moonlight hadn't glinted on something metallic. The scallop shell pilgrim badge that someone had given Walter months before and that he'd pinned proudly to the hat.

The rough wool, the black raven feather. It was his. Could he have dropped it and still be out searching for it? That would be just like the lad, to become so caught up in what he was doing that he'd forget everything else.

John put the cap in his scrip and made his way back around the town. There were fewer people out now. Even the sots and wastrels had taken to their beds. His footsteps echoed off the cobbles as he walked, the only sound in the stillness.

Nothing.

Outside the Guildhall he spotted one of the bailiff's men. He hadn't seen Walter, but he'd tell the others and they'd keep watch for him.

He made his way back to Saltergate, muttering a prayer for God to keep the boy safe. He might have come home while John was searching.

But God wasn't listening tonight. Katherine was in the hall, starting hopefully as he came in. A lantern shone, casting long shadows around the room.

'I can't find him.'

She looked on the edge of tears. He held her close, letting her shake and shiver as he gently rubbed her back. Once she sat down again he drew out the cap and laid it on the table.

'It was by the church. I thought he might still be looking for it.'

She reached for him, her hand trembling in his. He squeezed it and gave her a smile he didn't feel. He was scared. But he needed to stay strong, to keep a brave, hopeful face. If he let his fear show, Katherine would know it.

'I'll go out again as soon as it's light. And the bailiffs are keeping their eyes open. We'll find him.'

'Please God,' she whispered. 'Not a word to the girls.'

'No,' he agreed.

The time seemed to crawl, one minute reluctant to become another. He'd open the shutters, see nothing and close them again. Then, finally, a band of blue low on the horizon. Soon it would be dawn. The first birds began their early calls; a few minutes later the air was a chorus of song.

They barely spoke, locked inside their own thoughts. The cat jumped on to Katherine's lap and she stroked it, hardly noticing its presence. John ate a little bread and finished the mug of ale.

'I'll go and look again,' he said, seeing her bleak, empty nod.

• • •

There was a freshness to the weather, the hint of a morning chill. Off to the west, clouds gathered over the hills. He fastened his jacket, eyes looking for any movement, anything unusual.

The market square was empty, the streets quiet. He glanced into yards as he passed, then went out beyond West Bar to search there.

John followed a winding track down to the river, peering through the undergrowth, eyes alert for places where the long grass had been rumpled. But there was nothing.

The water was undisturbed, nothing bobbing in the shallows, nothing carried by the current. The path showed no boot prints, no signs of a struggle. It was as if Walter had vanished.

He followed the river, searching all the way, and finished by the church, where he'd found the cap. Where was the lad? What had he done, where had he gone? He looked at the grave markers. Was that where Walter would be in a few days? Buried and consigned to the earth, left to God's mercy? He prayed not.

*   *   *

The head bailiff was seated behind his desk, still rubbing the sleep from his eyes. He knew John well enough to greet him with a nod and wave him to a chair.

'What can I do for you, Master? You look troubled.'

'Do you know Walter? The boy who runs messages for people?'

'Aye, of course.'

'My wife's brother. He's disappeared.'

'What did you do? Beat him?' As he looked up, the smile died on his lips. 'I'm sorry, Master.'

'He didn't come home last night. I found his cap by the churchyard. I'd like your men to search for him.' He paused. 'And no, there'd been no argument or cruel words at home. I talked to your night man. He said they'd look.'

'He said nothing to me. But we'll search, Master, I can promise you that. Everyone has time for Walter, he's a good lad.'

'Thank you. If you find …' He wasn't sure what to say. 'If you find anything at all, send word to my house. My wife is there.'

The coroner's house lay on the other side of the square. De Harville was breaking his fast, bread and a thick wedge of white cheese in front of him.

'What is it, Carpenter? Not good news from the look of you.'

'Walter's missing.' He told it all in a few quick sentences. 'The bailiffs are looking.'

'You've no idea why he's gone?' The coroner stroked his chin thoughtfully.

'None.'

'Are there any special places he likes to go? That boy's an odd one, he might have somewhere like that.'

Did he? Walter knew the countryside all around Chesterfield. The green lanes, the fairy roads that sprang up and seemed to lead nowhere. He'd discovered them all. But were any of them special to him? John didn't know. There didn't seem to be one in particular he went back to often.

He shook his head. 'I don't know.'

'The bailiffs will do their job. Was he on coroner's business?'

'I don't think so. I hadn't given him any instructions.'

'It's not a large town, Carpenter. Someone will spot him.'

As long as he was alive.

He returned to the house. Dame Martha was there, entertaining and distracting the girls. She looked up as he entered, her face falling as he gave a quick shake of his head. Katherine dashed through from the buttery, wiping her hands on a square of linen.

'I've looked everywhere,' he told her. 'The bailiffs are out searching and I've told de Harville.'

'The coroner?' she asked sharply. 'Why?'

She knew. He could see it in her eyes. She simply didn't want to be the one to admit the possibility that Walter was dead somewhere. And if he'd been killed, did it have something to do with the psalter and the string of murders?

'The more people who know, the better,' he offered as a defence. She nodded carefully.

'Katherine,' Martha said, 'would you take the girls outside for a while? I need to talk to John.'

'Of course.' She held out her hands. Janette and Eleanor scrambled to their feet and went to her, the cat hopping down to join them.

'Sit down,' Martha said when they were alone.

'What is it?' He settled on the bench.

'Tell me everything,' she commanded. He looked at her quizzically but did as she wanted, laying it all out from the very beginning. He made sure all the aid Walter had given him was in the tale.

'And you think all of this has something to do with this psalter that Timothy owned?' she asked when he'd finished.

'I don't see what else it can be,' he answered with a low sigh.

'I remembered something last night.'

He cocked his head. 'What?'

'I was young. Probably fifteen or sixteen.' She smiled. 'A long time ago now. Timothy was older. I suppose it wasn't too long before the accident stopped him walking. There was a rumour that he'd given the psalter to his mistress as proof of his devotion.'

'What?' He could hardly believe what she said. It was the first he'd heard of any mistress. 'But Father Geoffrey saw it a few weeks ago. That's what he told me. Timothy was going to leave it to the church here.'

'It was only a rumour,' Dame Martha said. She rubbed the back of her hand, as if she could wipe away the spots of age that marked her skin. 'You know how people love to talk. It seemed to die away soon enough.'

'He showed it to Will Durrant before he went blind, too.'

'Maybe they were just words.' She stared at him with her clear blue eyes.

He tried to think. 'His mistress. What was her name?'

She shook her head. 'I don't think anyone knew. Or even if it was true. It seemed strange to me, even then. Timothy never had any interest in women. He liked male company.'

'What are you suggesting?' He reached for a jug of ale and poured for them both.

'Nothing,' Martha said. 'Honestly. I don't even know why it came back to me. I haven't thought of it in years.'

'I don't see how it helps us find Walter.'

'No,' she agreed. 'It doesn't. But I wanted you to know. Maybe it's nothing, maybe …' She shrugged. 'Could Walter be hiding somewhere?'

'I hope so. But I've no idea where. Or why he'd need to. Do you?'

She was silent for a long time, turning the cup in her old, gnarled hands.

'There was a place,' Martha said finally. 'It must have been two or three years ago that he told me about it, before you came here. He dashed in, so excited.' She smiled at the memory.

'Where is it?' John asked quietly.

'Near the leper hospital. A big tree by a stream, that's what he told me. The water had washed away enough from the bank that he could crawl in among the roots. He might be too big for that now, though. He's grown so tall.'

'Yes.' He stood. 'Tell Katherine I've gone back to look for him.'

He didn't want to see the hopelessness on his wife's face. This was the first real possibility he'd had. He hurried, crossing the bridge at the bottom of Soutergate, heart beating fast. The lazar house stood in the distance, a wall surrounding the buildings to keep the lepers away from everyone else.

His eyes scanned the landscape, looking for tall trees and a stream. He spotted the water first, a little beck that meandered along, sluggish after so many dry weeks. As he moved along he could pick out the tree. It was an old oak, the trunk thick and ancient, leaning as if it was drunk. But the bank below it had been eaten away, leaving heavy roots that pushed down searching for earth and home.

'Walter!' he called, waiting. But no answer.

John scrambled down the bank, grabbing patches of grass to stop himself from tumbling. The only way to come close was by walking along the stream. The roots stood like bars on a jail. The space behind them was large enough for a man to hide.

Closer, he spoke Walter's name again. This time he heard something: a low, faint groan. He splashed through the stream, offering a prayer that it was the lad and he'd live.

He was there, curled in on himself like a child, his head tucked down.

'Walter,' he said urgently, reaching through to shake the boy. 'Walter.'

The lad moved his head like a man in a daze. His clothes were covered in dried mud, old blood on his hands.

'Can you hear me?'

Slowly, Walter nodded.

'I'll get you out of there. We're going home.' Praise God.

John tried to push the roots apart, using all his strength to move them. But they were too thick, too sturdy, and too close together for him to squeeze through. Walter was still thin enough to crawl inside. But he didn't look to have the strength to come back out.

John sawed at the roots with his knife, working desperately and keeping up constant chatter while he cut. Finally there was a space large enough for him to pass. Holding his breath and tugging himself free from the roots that caught and tugged on his jacket, he was inside.

God's breath, the boy looked bad. Bruises all over his face. Who'd done this to him? How long had he been here? Gently, John moved him, easing him over the dirt towards the entrance. No more than a few inches at a time, and each one bringing a moan of pain.

It took more than an hour to pull him out into the air. By the time it was done John was covered in sweat, boots soaked by the stream. He had to support Walter's weight; the lad still hadn't come to properly, caught on the cusp between sleeping and waking.

It was slow and tiring work. Walter was as heavy and awkward as a sack of stones. They went along the river, pace by pace, until the bank was low enough for him to haul the boy out.

John was panting, breathless. He needed to rest, his legs and shoulder aching, but there was no time. Walter needed to be at home with someone to tend to him. Too many hours had passed already.

He gathered his strength, seeing the distance to the dusty road slowly vanish. But even there it still seemed like a long way into Chesterfield. More than he could manage on his own. But he had to do it. There was no choice.

The rattle of a cart stirred him out of his great concentration. He turned his head, hailing the driver.

'My brother's been hurt.' Not the full truth but it would do for now. And it wouldn't frighten the man. 'Can you take us into Chesterfield, Master?'

The farmer looked at them, assessing the danger and the damage before giving a slow nod.

'In the back, on the hay,' he said.

It was a struggle to lift Walter, but finally he managed it, trying to make the lad comfortable before climbing in himself, exhausted.

'We live on Saltergate, Master. Do you know it?'

'Aye. What's happened to him?'

'A bad fall,' John lied and hoped the driver would believe him.

The journey seemed to drag along. The bullock pulling the cart was slow. By himself, John could have walked faster. But with Walter, this was better.

He studied the boy's face. He was breathing regularly and easily; that was something. The injuries were bad, but they'd probably look better once he was cleaned up. What worried him was the fact that the boy wouldn't surface into wakefulness. Perhaps the wise woman would be able to help.

The cart rumbled with aching slowness up Soutergate, turning by the church before stopping outside the house. John scrambled down, offering the driver a coin for his help. The man raised a calloused hand to refuse.

'It's a charity,' the farmer told him.

'Then God go with you.'

'And you. Even more with him.'

Supporting Walter, John kicked at the door until Katherine opened it, her eyes widening in horror when she saw her brother.

'Help me get him up to the solar.'

It took all his strength to support the boy on the way to his bed. Dame Martha took one look at Walter and dashed off to fetch Wilhelmina the wise woman. Katherine ordered the girls to bring a bowl of water and cloths.

John lowered the boy on to his pallet and started to strip him down to his braies, pulling off jacket, shirt, and hose. Bruises covered his body. Christ's blood, every part of him had suffered a beating. Katherine washed her brother with gentle strokes. The pain she was feeling showed on her face as she looked up at John.

'Where did you find him?' Her voice was steady.

He recounted the tale, from Martha's memory to the bullock cart dropping them at the door. By the time he'd finished Wilhelmina was climbing to the solar and shooing them away.

The woman's fingers examined Walter, his face, his body. She listened to his breathing, placing her hand over his heart to see how it was beating.

'Leave me with him,' she ordered. 'I'll do what I can.'

They went down to the hall, where Martha had gathered the girls close around her skirts. Everyone looked fearful, almost too scared to speak.

'Why?' Katherine asked finally.

'I don't know,' John answered. Had the coroner's work earned the boy his beating? Or was it something else? Walter talked so little about what he did. He turned to Martha. 'Thank you for the hint. I'd never have found him otherwise.'

'I just pray it wasn't too late,' the dame said.

'Be glad it was a warm night. He'd have frozen otherwise.'

'Is Walter going to be all right?' Janette asked. John looked to his wife, not sure how to answer.

'Let's all pray that he is,' she said gently and put her hands together.

• • •

'I've given him something to make him sleep,' the wise woman told them when she joined them in the hall. She saw Katherine opening her mouth and continued, 'I know, he's already asleep. But this will let the body begin to heal itself. There's nothing broken. More rest, proper rest, will help him. Make sure he has enough to drink, too.'

'Will he wake?' John asked.

'If God wills it,' Wilhelmina said after a while. 'There's no reason why not that I can see.'

'I'll sit with him,' Martha offered.

'We can take it in turns,' Katherine said.

At the door the woman turned, as if she was going to say more, then shook her head. He'd barely turned the key behind her when someone began to knock. Brother Robert.

'I heard you'd brought Walter back on a cart. The master said you came to see him this morning.'

'He's alive, thanks be to God.' He told the story once more as he poured ale for the monk.

'I'll pray for him, John.'

'It will all help.'

'But do you know why it happened? Or where?'

'No.' They sat at the table. The room felt warm and stuffy, even with the shutters wide open to the air. Where had Walter been attacked? And why had he gone out there, where no one might find him, rather than come home? It all troubled him. It made no sense at all, unless someone was pursuing him. And that brought the question back to who.

'I'd like to question Arthur of Warwick again. Is he still at the inn?'

'Yes,' Robert answered. 'Unless he's disobeyed the master.'

In truth he had very few questions for the man. He just wanted a look at him, to see if his fists were scraped or bloody. Whoever beat Walter would carry marks of his own.

'John,' Katherine warned. 'Please.'

'I'll be careful,' he told her. 'But I need to know.'

Her mouth became a thin line as she nodded her head. The monk put his arm around her and led her gently to the settle.

The innkeeper was fitting a fresh barrel of ale in place, ready to broach it, when he walked in.

'Master,' he said warily as he read John's face. 'How can I help you?'

'Is Arthur of Warwick here?'

The man shook his head. 'He went out early. Didn't even break his fast.'

'Did you see him this morning?'

'Aye. Why?'

'Did he have any cuts on bruises on his face or hands?'

'No,' the innkeeper answered in surprise. 'What's wrong?'

'Nothing.' He smiled to ease the man's thoughts. 'I was just wondering, nothing more.'

He left and leaned against the churchyard wall, trying to put his mind in order. He still needed to see Arthur for himself, to be certain. But it seemed he could put the possibility from his head.

Yet who did that leave?

Christian, perhaps. He had the size and strength. And the anger. He'd need to go to Dronfield to see, and this time he wouldn't go alone.

He started to walk along Knifesmithgate, past the large houses of the merchants and the rich men, then through to the marketplace. He stared at every man he saw, looking at their faces and hands for any sign they'd been in a fight.

But there was nothing. Nor on Beetwell Street, or any other place he went, out along Kalehalegate, Bishop Mill Lane, Tapton Lane, and in the other direction beyond West Bar. After an hour he gave up. To hope to spot someone was putting himself in the hands of chance.

He drifted home again. Brother Robert had gone. Katherine was trying to entertain her young sisters, but the strain showed on her face. One hand cupped her growing belly. He shook his head when she glanced up and went through to the buttery to pour himself some ale.

Walter should sleep for hours yet if the wise woman was right. He trudged up the stairs to the solar. Martha was still there, looking awkward on a low joint stool.

'Have you found anything?' she whispered.

'Not yet,' he answered, staring down at the boy's face. He'd taken a battering. Pray God he'd wake with all his wits about him and his memory intact. He reached down, stroking Walter's bare arm above the covers. No more than a few hours since he'd dragged the lad home and the solar already had the cloying stench of the sickroom. But not of death. That wasn't waiting here.

'Do you have any ideas who did it?' Martha asked.

'Nothing more than guesses.' Tomorrow he'd go out to Dronfield and take two of the bailiffs. If Christian was guilty, he wouldn't come easily.

CHAPTER TWENTY-ONE

He woke with a start, trying to recall what had made him open his eyes. A lantern burned softly on the other side of the solar where Katherine sat, anxiously watching Walter. The girls were asleep, making the soft, snuffling sounds of children at rest, the kitten settled between their bodies.

He slipped from the bed and put his arms around her shoulders.

'Any change?' he asked softly, lips next to her ear.

'Nothing.'

'Go and lie down,' he said. 'I'll watch him for a while.'

She seemed reluctant to agree, waiting a long time before nodding. He helped her up from the stool, then dressed in his hose, boots and leather jerkin as she settled on the mattress. Soon enough her breathing became gentle and regular as rest carried her away.

Walter twitched and jerked a few times and John was suddenly alert, ready in case he broke the surface of sleep. But he calmed again, eyes never opening, lips curled into a smile.

Time passed, carrying all the usual noises of the night. Quiet coughs, a snore, the hoot of an owl somewhere off in the distance. Eventually he could make out the first streaks of dawn beyond the shutters.

John stood and stretched. His joints felt stiff and he paced around to ease them. Down in the buttery he ate bread and cheese, staring out as the garden slowly became visible in the growing light.

He stopped suddenly, a piece of the loaf halfway to his mouth. He'd seen something from the corner of his eye. A deepening in the shadows as something moved. It could have been an animal – a fox, a badger – but it seemed larger.

John found his belt in the hall and took out the knife. Taking a breath, he unlocked the back door and slipped out, making sure no light showed behind him. Crouched by the corner of the house, he waited, listening intently for the smallest sound, eyes gazing around to try and spot what might be there.

A minute passed, then two. He kept his breathing quiet, holding himself still and ready. Then he heard it, the sound of a boot breaking a twig with a quick, sharp crack. He tensed, hand gripping the hilt of the knife.

The kitchen stood in the garden, built away from the house in case of fire. He saw a shift in the gloom behind it. Heard the noise as someone struck a flint. Without a thought, he was running.

The man had enough of a start to clear the low fence at the bottom of the garden. By the time John was there the footsteps were already fading. He stopped, walking back to the kitchen. The flint and steel lay in the grass by a small bundle of straw.

A fire in the kitchen. That would be enough to drag them outside, and all their neighbours along with them, but not kill anyone.

But why? What would it achieve?

He sat on the grass and pinched the bridge of his nose with his fingers. None of this made any sense. He stayed there for ten minutes or more, trying to work some reason out of it all. Finally he picked up the tools and returned to the house.

No mention of this to Katherine, he decided. She was scared enough as it was, not knowing when Walter would wake. By the time he'd finished the bread and a hunk of the cheese, daylight had grown.

The market square was already alive. Saturday. Market day. Men were setting up their stalls and unloading the items to sell. Out close to West Bar traders were lining up the horses and brushing them. Early summer; there'd be plenty of custom today. A bolt of silk hoisted on someone's shoulder caught the early sun, shimmering brilliantly for a moment.

He ducked between the crowds hard at work with their preparations and knocked on a door. The servant answered and escorted him in. Will Durrant sat at his table sipping a mug of ale.

'Who do we have here?' he asked, turning his blind eyes to stare at the doorway.

'John. The Carpenter.'

'It's early to call on someone so you must have a good reason.' He extended a hand. 'Sit yourself down. Bring him some ale,' he instructed the servant. 'What can I do for you, Master Carpenter?'

'Some more questions, if I might.'

Durrant smiled. 'I can't guarantee you any answers, but I'll try.'

'I've heard talk that Timothy had a mistress, and he promised her the psalter.'

The man gave a hearty laugh. 'That again? I thought that rumour was dead and buried years ago.'

'Is it true?' John asked and Durrant shrugged in reply.

'If it was, Timothy never said so to me. It was gossip, nothing more, something for the goodwives to discuss while they did their laundry down at the river.'

'Did he ever deny it?'

The blind man looked thoughtful for a while. 'Not that I recall. But he never admitted it, either.'

'What did he do?'

'Just let it all go by him until people grew tired of it and found something else to discuss. That was Timothy's manner.

Ignore things that didn't matter to him until they went away.'
He chuckled. 'I daresay it worked most of the time. And he
had enough money to do it.'

'Do you believe the talk?'

'No one ever managed to put a name to the woman that
I recall. Does that sound like truth to you, Master?'

It didn't. With a sigh he began to stand, but Durrant stayed
him.

'I count my life in two parts,' he continued. 'When I had my
sight and after. There's more of the after than before now,' he
said with a sad smile, 'but that's God's will. All the talk about
Timothy and the woman was when I could still see. And it was
after the chatter that he showed me the psalter. So he could
hardly have given it away, could he?'

'No,' John admitted. 'Thank you.'

'Was it a woman who remembered that tittle-tattle?'

'Yes.'

'Sometimes they let their imaginations run off with them.
I'm sorry I couldn't help you more.'

'I think you've stopped me going down the wrong path.'

'Good.' He paused. 'There was fresh gossip around yesterday.
Your brother-in-law.'

'He hasn't woken yet.'

'I'll say a prayer for him.'

'Thank you.' Maybe God would listen; it couldn't hurt.

• • •

The coroner was in the stable, supervising the groom as he
tended to the horses.

'News on the boy?' he asked, raising his head from inspecting a fetlock.

'Still the same.'

De Harville crossed himself quickly. 'Do you know who did it?'

'Not yet. But I want to go and talk to Christian.'

The coroner cocked his head. 'Why? Do you think he's responsible?'

'It's possible. I want to take two bailiffs with me.'

'Not until the market's done. I need them here to keep order. Keep your eyes open. Didn't you tell me that Christian used to come to the Saturday market?'

Of course. He'd forgotten that.

'I'll keep an eye open for him.'

There'd be time for that later, once the market began. For now, though, he had business elsewhere.

• • •

The girls were busy spinning wool. Katherine was seat at the table, half-watching them as she broke her fast.

'You were gone early.'

'Just some thoughts,' he told her. 'How's …?'

'He's still sleeping. Martha's up there with him. Have you eaten?'

'Hours ago,' he said with a smile, squeezing her shoulder lightly as he passed and climbed the stairs.

Martha raised her head at the footsteps. She was holding one of Walter's hands, lips moving in silent prayer.

'Have you found …?' she began, but he shook his head. It seemed so strange, not real to see the boy there. He was always the one out and about with his errands to run and his messages to deliver. Not here with his eyes closed, lost somewhere between life and somewhere else, his spirit trying to find its way back.

He stood for a moment, caught in the silence. Come home, he thought. We need you here. John reached down and patted the lad's leg through the sheet. It jerked in response even thought his eyes remained closed.

'Did you see that?'

'Pray God it means he'll surface soon. I've seen men do that before they come to,' Martha said.

He bounded down the stairs feeling hopeful, whispering in his wife's ear and seeing her smile before he left. His heart was lifted. There'd been a reaction. Walter could feel. Maybe nothing else yet, but it would come, he was certain of that now.

He scoured the market square, squeezing his way through the crowds. He kept one hand on his purse as he moved. But no sign of Christian.

At the cookshop he bought a hot pie, forcing himself to eat slowly, then washed it down with a mug of ale from the tavern on Low Pavement.

After an hour or more of looking he had to admit it: Christian wasn't there. But he still lingered, just in case. Nothing. In frustration he marched back to the house.

He found Katherine and the girls still sitting in hall. She was leading them in prayer. For a dark moment he believed that Walter had died and he felt breath being pulled from his body.

Then Janette was up and running towards him.

'Walter's awake,' she laughed. 'Walter's awake.'

He looked and saw his wife wiping tears from her eyes. Tears of joy.

'He woke just after you left.' She was smiling, sniffling as she tried to stop crying. 'He's fine, John. He's going to be fine.'

Silently, he thanked God as he drew her close, her head resting on his shoulder.

'Who's with him now?'

'Martha. She wanted to take Janette and Eleanor out, so they'd be away from the sickroom. He started to come to when he heard her voice.'

A miracle, he thought. He held her until the shaking stopped.

'I'll go and see him. Does he remember anything?'

'I don't know. I was just so happy to have him back …'

He understood.

Martha had eased herself on to a low joint stool by Walter's pallet. She sat, gazing tenderly at the boy. She put a finger to her lips to quiet him as he approached.

'He's sleeping again,' she whispered. 'But when he's awake, he makes sense.'

'Did he say anything about …?'

'I don't think he remembers. Give him time, John.'

'Is he in pain?'

She shook her head. 'The wise woman left some herbs we can steep for him to drink.' She looked at the boy. 'It's going to take him a long while to recover. Let him sleep as much as he can.'

'I know.' But at least he'd begun to mend. She reached out a hand and he helped her to her feet. Martha grimaced as she straightened her legs, then hid it again as she managed a step or two.

'Timothy's mistress,' he began.

'What about her?'

'Do you know anything about her?'

'It was years ago, John. More than half a century. I can't remember any more than I told you. I'm sorry.'

'Is there anyone who might?' he asked hopefully.

'After all this time? I doubt it. I don't think any of us knew her name. I don't even know where it all began.'

He escorted her down the stairs, feeling her lean into him. Once again he was surprised at how frail her body had become, the weightlessness of her bones.

CHAPTER TWENTY-TWO

The afternoon sun felt too hot. Sweat ran down his backbone as he walked and each step was an effort. Halfway to Dronfield he'd rested in the shade for a few minutes, the two bailiffs complaining loudly at trudging through a summer's day after a morning at the market.

He ignored them, splashing his face with water from the stream until he was cooled again. In the village they followed the road uphill to the manor house. No Christian. Nobody had seen him since morning; no one knew where he'd gone or when he might return.

A wasted journey.

'Does he have any recent cuts on his hands or face?' John asked the men who gave him the information. They shook their heads.

'I saw him last night and he didn't,' one answered. 'Why?'

'Just a question,' he replied with a smile.

They were going back with nothing. First, though, a small rest. The least he could do was buy the bailiffs a jug of ale after dragging them out this way.

Inside it was cool, some of the shutters closed against the day to leave the place shaded. While his companions wittered away, John wandered over to talk with the alewife.

'I hadn't thought to see you again,' she told him. 'I heard Christian sent you packing last time.'

He shrugged. 'Maybe he did.'

'Is that why you've brought them?' She nodded at the brawny bailiffs.

'Do you blame me?'

'Better to be safe when you're against someone with a temper.'

'That's what I thought.' He grinned and moved his mug around on the counter. 'What do you know about Christian's family?'

She snorted. 'His mother, as was. The father died years back. It was probably the best thing he could have done.'

'Why's that?' he asked sharply.

'He was a cuckold,' the woman said. 'Everyone knew it but him, poor soul.'

'So Christian's not his?'

'She's the only one who can tell you that. And she's been in her grave these ten years.'

'So whose bastard is Christian?'

'Ah.' Her eyes twinkled at the chance of gossip. 'That's what everyone asked when her belly started to grow. She'd been in someone's bed that wasn't her own, but she kept very quiet about it. Never a name, not even a hint.'

'Why couldn't it have been her husband?'

She laughed.

'His pizzle couldn't get hard. Everyone knew that. Couldn't satisfy a lass, never mind give her a child. That wife of his never let him forget it, either.'

'You don't look old enough to remember it.'

'Get on with you, Master,' she said but preened at the compliment. 'I was just little when it happened, but the way people went on about it, it was impossible to forget.'

'Is there someone who'd know more?'

'Try Goodwife Joan,' she suggested. 'The last house as you leave the village towards Chesterfield. She's the oldest around here. Can't move much any more but she's still sharp. Take her a jug of ale and she'll talk.'

. . .

The house was dirty. Cobwebs in the corners and the rushes on the floor hadn't been replaced in more than a year. He'd sent the bailiffs back to town when he stopped. For a minute he thought the alewife had played him for a fool. The hag looked ancient, a thick rheum on her eyes as she tried to peer at him. But with the first sip of drink she brightened.

'Christian?' she cackled. 'Thinking she'd save his soul with a name like that.'

'What do you mean?'

'He was someone's by-blow. Everyone here knew that.'

'Do you know whose?'

'Plenty of whispers at the time,' she remembered with a sniff. 'Not that she'd ever come out and admit it. Walked around like butter wouldn't melt in her mouth. But we knew, we knew.'

'Was there ever any talk of a rich man?' he asked. 'From Chesterfield?'

'Plenty of mouths flapping,' Joan told him. 'Lots of rumours. Rich man, poor man.' She turned her head and spat on the ancient, dry rushes covering the floor. 'Seems to me someone said she'd been seduced. A man promising her things.' She looked at him accusingly through the rheum. 'The way men do. Then vanished as soon as she was with child. She was married, she couldn't do anything except drag the child up.'

'What about the name Timothy? Was he ever mentioned?'

'Probably every name in Christendom at one time or another.' She said. 'Why?'

'I've heard he had a mistress and nobody knew who she was.'

'You'll not find out from her, not unless she can speak from the grave.' She gave another cackling laugh. 'Probably in hell for her sins now.'

He wasn't going to learn any more here. The most he'd come away with was a suspicion and that didn't help. Anyone could have been Christian's father.

'Thank you, Mistress,' he said as he rose. 'You've been generous with your memories.'

'She told me something once. Years later, when the boy was ten or so,' the woman recalled.

'What was that?' He stood by the door, one hand on the latch.

'That she'd seen a book once.' Joan shook her head.

'What kind of book?' he asked, holding his breath.

'What does it matter? She couldn't read. What use would she have for a book?' She poured the last of the ale into a cracked mug. 'She said it had jewels on the front. But she always liked to make things up.'

'Who showed her the book? Did she tell you?'

'Someone and no one, most like. She probably pulled the idea out of the air.'

'Did she say anything more about it?'

'Oh aye. The most beautiful thing she'd ever seen, she told me, with pictures and gold.'

It could have been the psalter, John thought. All too easily. Books were rare enough outside churches. Only the rich could afford them.

'What else?' he asked.

'Isn't that enough?' She tapped her skull. 'All in her head.'

'Thank you,' he said again as he left.

More than anything else he'd heard, the book pointed to Timothy. It all fitted. But he'd never know for certain. The man had been careful. He'd covered all the tracks he left.

He sighed as he walked back to Chesterfield. No marks on Christian, if everyone was to be believed. That ruled him out as Walter's attacker.

But Timothy as Christian's father? That was interesting. It offered up plenty of possibilities. There was even sense to it, a connection between him and the old man. And a reason for murder. Yet why would he wait so long for revenge on a father who'd cast him aside before he was born?

Too many questions that would never be answered. Christian wasn't going to tell him. Mysteries within mysteries and he was still none the wiser as he unlatched his front door on Saltergate.

He could hear voices from the solar. Katherine, Martha, and the girls gathered around Walter's bed. The lad had his eyes open but he looked stunned, surprised.

'It's good to see you back,' John said to him, taking his wife's hand and squeezing it lightly.

'You found me. That's what they've been telling me.' The words struggled out in stammers.

'And a right job it was getting you back here, too,' he answered with a smile. 'What happened to you, Walter?'

'I don't remember, John. My head's empty there.'

He understood. The boy couldn't summon it up. He'd seen it before when men woke from an accident; they had no recollection of what had happened. Sometimes it returned. Often it didn't, as if the mind was determined to forget the pain.

'It doesn't matter. We just have to make sure you're well again.'

'Listen to him,' Katherine told her brother. Her eyes glistened with tears and she bit her lip. She ushered the girls back down the stairs.

'Do you remember anything about the day it happened?' John asked. Dame Martha gave him a sharp look for the question.

'I went to work,' Walter replied brightly. 'I remember that.' His face clouded and he shook his head. Nothing more.

'Leave it, John,' Martha said quietly and he nodded. He couldn't force memory where there was none. 'I'll sit with him.'

'What would we do without you?'

She waved his words away into the air. 'You're family as much as any of my kin,' she said, smoothing down the front of her apron and easing herself slowly down on to the joint stool. 'Now go,' she said. 'Shoo.'

Katherine was in the garden, supervising Janette and Eleanor as they weeded between the plants. The kitten dashed after each stalk they tossed, pouncing and making a game of it all.

John squatted and looked at his wife. Her face was flushed with joy.

'He's going to be fine. It'll take time, that's all.'

'I know.' She gave a small, tight nod, as if she couldn't trust herself to do more.

'I'll be back soon.'

• • •

At the inn the owner looked fretful when he entered.

'Arthur of Warwick.' John said and the man shook his head.

'He hasn't come back yet, Master.'

He could feel a tingle at the back of his neck. 'Send word to the coroner as soon as he returns.' It was an order, not a request.

'Yes, Master.'

He found de Harville on a bench in the long garden behind his house. His wife was seated beside him, caught in the long shadows of evening. Her face was very pale, cheeks sunk, but she was carefully groomed, her veil a brilliant white, her gown simple but expensive.

'Carpenter,' the coroner said, but he was clearly annoyed at the disturbance. 'What do you want?'

'I was just at the inn to see Arthur.'

'And?'

'He's not there. Hasn't been all day.'

'I see.' De Harville frowned. 'I'll have the bailiffs scour the town for him. God help him if he's left.'

'If he went first thing this morning he could have covered plenty of ground.' Halfway back to Lincoln and the safety of the bishop's protection.

'I'm aware of that,' the coroner said brusquely. 'What else?'

'Walter's awake.' He waited for a reaction. Nothing. 'He's going to need a few weeks to recover but he'll be fine,' John told him. The man didn't even care. 'He just doesn't remember what happened.'

'Pity. We could solve this. Tell me the rest after church tomorrow.' He glanced at his wife with a look of concern.

Dismissed like a servant. He strode away from the house angrily, across the market square, to the alehouse on Low Pavement. He needed some time before he went home. A chance to let the anger fall away.

He drank the first mug quickly, trying to put everything out of his mind. Not that he managed it. Shards of this and that refused to leave. The way Walter looked, so helpless in his bed, face discoloured by bruises. The fact that Arthur was missing. All the questions about Christian. The other questions: who'd beaten Walter that way? Why had someone tried to set a fire by his kitchen? And who could have attacked him on the riverbank all that time ago?

The second cup lasted longer. He felt himself slowly calming, the flush of anger leaving his face, his breath slowing. Never mind the coroner. There was plenty to be thankful for this day. Walter would be well. That was the most important thing. Always.

CHAPTER TWENTY-THREE

Walter spent the evening falling in and out of sleep. Tiredness would suddenly overwhelm him and he'd turn his head away, closing his eyes. John sat by the bed, taking his turn with the others.

Wilhelmina, the wise woman, had come by to examine him, more than satisfied with his progress.

'Time,' she told them. 'That's all it takes now. His mind's sound, none of his limbs are broken, and there's no damage inside his body.'

He heard the words with relief. A full recovery. Katherine was smiling, close to tears again, Martha's arm around her shoulder.

And now he sat patiently, waiting for the boy to surface again. Maybe when he woke this time something would have changed and he'd be able to recall it all. He was going to discover who'd done it and make them pay. The beating had been brutal. Only God's mercy had stopped the damage being permanent.

Walter started to slowly move his head from side to side. A dream, with his eyelids moving rapidly.

Evening was slipping away. He went to the window and closed the shutters, watching in case the noise woke the boy. But sleep still held him fast. He'd spent another half-hour on the joint stool, watching and waiting, when a hand touched his shoulder.

'I must have drifted away,' he admitted.

'It doesn't matter,' Katherine said. 'I'll take over. It'll be time to put the girls to bed soon, anyway. I think Martha's ready to go home. Why don't you escort her.'

The goodwife clung to his arm as they walked along the road. The streets were empty, just noises in the distance to disrupt the peace.

'You know, don't you?' she said. When he glanced at her sharply, Martha continued, 'The killings. Who hurt Walter.'

'Not yet,' he sighed. 'But I will. I promise.'

He owed it to all those who'd died. It came down to two men. Christian and Arthur of Warwick. One of them was behind it all. How could it be anyone else? One of them had arranged the killings and then tried to hide their tracks. But which it was, he didn't know. Christian had a reason, if he was truly the bastard son of Timothy. And Arthur? That he didn't understand. He might never know, either; the man had the bishop's protection and he could do nothing against that.

'Do you want some advice?'

'I'd welcome it,' he said with a chuckle. 'Anything that can help.'

'When my husband was trying to sort a problem, he always thought the simple solution was to find out who'd profit most from something.' She glanced up at him. 'Does that make sense?'

It did. Whoever had the most to gain might be willing to take the greatest risks. But which one profited? Christian? Arthur?

'Thank you,' John said as they approached Martha's door.

'I haven't done anything,' she told him.

'Your friendship. That's beyond gold. Teaching the girls. Being here with us.'

It was impossible to be sure in the gloom, but she seemed to blush.

Walking back, he was concentrating on her words, trying to match them against the men he suspected. At first he didn't hear the footsteps behind him, then turned quickly, the knife in his hand.

'Peace be with you.' The man raised his hands as he approached. Father Geoffrey, wearing his surplice and stole.

'I'm sorry, Father.' He slid the dagger back into its sheath. 'You took me by surprise. What brings you out tonight?'

'Dame Gertrude is dying. They called me to hear her confession and give her the last rites.'

John crossed himself. 'May God grant her rest.'

'I heard what happened to Walter,' the priest continued.

'He's woken. He's going to be fine.'

'That's good news.' Geoffrey sounded relieved. 'I'll say a prayer for him.' He hurried by. 'I'll wish you a good night.'

'Thank you, Father.'

Another one dying. He'd met Gertrude a few times. She lived with her son and his family, a sharp-tongued woman who tried to rule the household. She was a woman with little kindness in her soul, it seemed to him. Always quick to find fault and slow to praise. In truth he doubted that many would miss her. She'd had a long life. But these days there seemed to be too much death and too little life.

At home everything was dark. Just a candle burning in the solar by Walter's bed. Katherine was sitting here in her shift, a shawl gathered around her shoulders.

'How is he?' John whispered.

'The same. I was just thinking what Walter was like when he was little. He was always running everywhere, even then.'

'He'll be doing that again soon.'

'I hope so.' He heard her sigh. 'Do you ever wonder what our child will be like?'

He had, right from the moment Katherine told him she was going to have a baby. He had his hopes, his dreams. A boy, someone to take on his trade, someone to carry his father's name.

And if it was a girl? He didn't know. Just someone as lovely as her mother. Finally he realised that he'd be happy with a child sound in mind and limb. That was all anyone could pray for. God might grant that; anything more was selfish.

'Come on,' he told her, 'let's go to bed.'

Light was edging the horizon when he woke. Dressing quickly, he checked Walter, hurried down the stairs and out into the world, pulling on the leather jerkin.

The inn was starting to come alive, a serving girl boiling water over the fire. The owner walked around, yawning wide.

'Arthur of Warwick?' John asked. 'Did he come back last night?'

'Right enough he did,' the man answered. 'Probably still sleeping.'

He took the stairs two at a time, then stood on the landing, fist raised to pound on the door. The back door leading to the outside stair stood ajar, a wedge at the bottom to keep it open. Odd, he thought. Why would anyone offer an invitation to thieves?

He knocked on the wood, watching it open before him. Taking a breath, he walked into the room. It was empty. He knew it would be. Arthur of Warwick hadn't slept in the bed. The lid of the chest lay open, nothing inside. John threw back the shutters to the early light. Nothing on the floorboards or hidden in the corners.

The stable boy was forking hay into the stalls, back bent and already sweating from the physical work.

'Is there a horse missing?'

'Aye, Master. One of the guests came with the dawn.'

'Arthur of Warwick?'

The lad nodded. At least he hadn't been gone too long.

'Did you get a good look at him?' John asked.

'Of course.' He answered as if the question was stupid.

'Did you see his hands?'

'No, Master. He was wearing leather gloves.'

'What about his face?' he persisted. 'Were there any marks on it?'

'His hood was up. I couldn't see.' The boy shrugged. It was nothing to him.

'Did he say where he was going?'

'Not to me.'

Of course. A stable lad would be beneath him, not worth his time or conversation.

'Thank you.'

In the Guildhall the bailiffs were preparing for work. A Sunday. The Lord's Day. But crime didn't stop for the Sabbath. A couple of them looked at John with faint interest before returning to their ale.

'Who was watching Arthur of Warwick?' he asked. The men glanced at each other, shaking their heads. The coroner hadn't ordered it. 'He was told to remain in Chesterfield. He left about an hour ago.'

The head bailiff shrugged. It wasn't his responsibility.

'Can you send men after him?'

'Was he on horseback?'

'Yes.'

'No point,' the man said. 'We'd never catch him.'

De Harville had gone to look at a corpse, a servant at his house said. John followed, finding him in a tumbledown cottage close to the river. A simple enough death. Hung from a beam in his own home, the joint stool kicked over. No food, no wood for a fire. A man with nothing left to lose, taking the only road he could see.

'Nothing for you here, Carpenter,' the coroner said when he noticed him.

'Straightforward enough,' John agreed. 'That's not why I'm here.'

'Then what?' de Harville asked wearily. Brother Robert righted the stool and settled, opening the portable desk and dipping his quill in a small bottle of ink.

'Arthur of Warwick.'

The words brought attention. 'What about him?'

'He left first thing this morning with his horse.'

The coroner kicked angrily at the packed dirt of the floor. This wasn't a home that had the luxury of rushes to cover the ground. There was nothing more than necessity here, and not even enough of that.

'No one was watching him?'

'The bailiffs said they hadn't been given any instructions.'

De Harville looked at the monk. 'Did I give the order?'

'No, Master,' Robert replied hesitantly, gazing down at the blank parchment. 'Not to me, anyway.'

The coroner slapped one of the beams in the house and stalked outside. Off in the distance the church bell began to ring, drawing the congregation close for service.

'You ought to go,' the monk said quietly. 'You'll be late if you don't.'

'He forgot, didn't he?'

'He has too much on his mind, John.'

'He might have let a killer get away.'

'Or perhaps Arthur is no murderer.'

'We'll never know now, will we?' John said sharply. 'He'll be on his way back to Lincoln and no one's going to catch him.'

'Forgiveness is a virtue, John.'

'He's the one who wanted me to investigate all this. Remember that, Brother. I've been thrown in the river and left for dead because of this. Walter was beaten badly because of this. He can't have it every way.'

'He's human. He makes mistakes.' The monk stared at him. 'Don't you?'

'Of course,' he admitted with a nod. 'You're right, I'd best get to the church.'

. . .

The girls were waiting outside the porch at St Mary's, safe in Martha's care; Katherine was at home, watching over her brother. John escorted them inside. The nave was full, more people than usual at the service. So many praying for a good summer and a strong harvest.

Outside, away from the press of sweaty, stinking bodies, there wasn't a cloud in the sky. Maybe the prayers would be answered. Some rain at night and warmth in the day, that was what they wanted.

He took the girls by the hand and walked back to Saltergate, Dame Martha at his side. She looked refreshed by the host, eyes bright, a little stronger, striding out briskly. She'd eat her dinner with them, as much part of the family as if she was a blood relation. But that was what he'd discovered over the years. Family had little to do with being blood and everything to do with trust.

'You look troubled,' Martha said when he let Janette and Eleanor run on ahead, skirts flying round their ankles, long hair flowing.

'Just answers I'll never know,' he replied. He explained about Arthur of Warwick.

'And he never said why they were here, even after his friend was murdered?'

'No.'

'Then breaking a coroner's order … it must have been important. Do you think they were on the bishop's business?'

'Very likely,' John said. But now he'd never be certain. From here he'd be venturing in the dark again. He sighed. 'Never mind. Let's forget it all for today.'

He wasn't sure if he was talking to her or himself.

•   •   •

Walter had been awake for an hour. Through all the bruises and the swelling he looked alert, carefully holding a wooden spoon and feeding himself pottage from a bowl. It was a good sign that he was recovering. His hand didn't shake as he ate and he had an appetite.

'How do you feel?'

'It hurts, John.' The words came out awkwardly, hindered by his injuries.

'That will pass.' He gave a smile. 'The pain will go. You'll be running to deliver messages again soon.'

'Have you found out …?'

'Who did it?' John asked. 'No. I wish I had. You still don't remember anything at all?'

The lad shook his head gently. Maybe it was for the best. Who'd want to recall a beating like the one he must have received, to relive the blows and the agony? God was being kind in granting forgetfulness.

'It doesn't matter. I'll find out one way or another.'

'What will you do then, John?'

'You'll have justice,' was all he said.

• • •

His eyes opened suddenly, as if something had disturbed his sleep. He lay silent for a few seconds, listening for any sound or scrape, but there was nothing. John eased himself out of bed, dressing quickly and quietly.

In the buttery he stared out of the window. Why had someone tried to set fire to the kitchen? What good would it have done? More questions with no answers. They seemed to pile, one on top of the other, taunting him.

Somewhere among them was the key to all this. Finding it, though, that was the trick.

• • •

He had many things to ask, but nobody to ask them of. There was nothing he could do to push things along, so he gathered up the satchel of tools and began the walk out to Cutthorpe to complete a final job they'd noticed. For once there was a hint of rain in the breeze, light clouds gathering over the hills to the west.

But the air was mild as balm as he strolled, and at the flax barn he set to work, cutting and planing the new boards for an exact fit. He lit a fire to warm the pitch that would seal any gaps, light shimmering and waving above the flames.

Soon enough he was lost in his work, caught in its rhythm and the tasks he knew by heart. There was sweetness in it, a chance to let his hands and his mind labour together. By the middle of the afternoon he'd finished the job. All his repairs were weathertight, he knew that.

At the house he received his pay, the coins jangling in his purse as he began the journey home. Once again he'd pointed out the work that needed to be done still, and what would be coming up in the next year or two. There'd been a promise to consider it; maybe more jobs for the future. He felt a sense of contentment as he walked.

The rain that had been a hint at dawn came through, but nothing more than a heavy shower that passed in a few minutes. Not enough for the farmers, he knew. They needed something that would linger and soak into the soil; this sharpness would simply run off.

Still, it was enough to drench his clothes. At home he stripped off in the solar, changing into his other shirt and hose. They were old, mended more times than he wished to count. But they were dry.

'You have scars,' Walter said.

It was true enough. Plenty of them. On his hands, his arms. One on his chest where a beam had slipped and sliced open his skin on a job in York. They were part of the job. It was no more dangerous than working in the fields. There a sickle or a hoe could take off a toe or a hand.

'I've earned them,' he replied. 'How are you feeling now?'

'Better.' The boy nodded and smiled. Two of his teeth had been knocked out, leaving the grin awkward and lopsided.

'You'll be up and around soon enough.' But would he ever be quite the same, as carefree as he'd been before. One more question without an answer – yet.

• • •

They'd eaten supper, the light just starting to fade, when he heard the knock on the door. He only opened it a crack, his free hand on his knife. These days it was better to be wary, he thought.

The coroner stood there, alone.

'Come in, Master. God be with you.'

De Harville stood in the hall, staring around awkwardly. He'd removed his velvet cap and was kneading it in his hands.

'Come on,' Katherine told the girls as they stared.

'No, Mistress, no need to leave on my account.' His voice was cracked and strained. He turned to John. 'I owe you an apology, Carpenter.' For the first time, he sounded humbled.

He could hardly believe what he'd heard. This wasn't like the man.

'Brother Robert took me to task,' de Harville continued. He stared down at the ground, feet rubbing at the rushes like a boy forced to say sorry. 'And he was right. I should have issued orders to keep a close watch on Arthur. I was distracted by my wife's illness.'

'I hope she's improving, Master.' It seemed to be the only possible response.

'Slowly, but pray God, yes she is. But it's not an excuse. I didn't do my job and we might have lost a killer. I know you've worked hard on this, that you were injured, and your brother-in-law …'

'He's mending.'

'Good.' He nodded his head slowly. 'I've treated you badly. Robert made me understand that. And I might have ruined the investigation. If you want to go back to … well, you've every right.'

John took his time to answer. He glanced at Katherine. She was staring in disbelief, the girls gathered close around her skirt.

'I'll see what there is to find,' he said eventually. 'But I can't give any guarantees.'

'Of course.' The coroner shifted his stance, holding himself square and upright. 'Do what you can, that's all I ask.' He bowed quickly to Katherine and her sisters, then left, silence in his wake.

'I never believed I'd live to see him apologise,' Katherine said after a minute.

'I wonder what Robert said to him.' He poured a mug of ale, surprised to see his hands shaking a little.

'Whatever it was, it worked.' She sent Janette and Eleanor out-side to play for a few minutes before bed. 'You agreed to continue.'

'What else could I do after that?' She'd heard the man. It was as close to begging as he was ever likely to come.

'You could have walked away from it, John. He gave you the chance.'

'He was hoping I wouldn't take it. After he came here like that, how could I refuse him?'

'That's what he wanted. Can't you see that?'

Maybe she was right and he'd fallen for de Harville's game. But he'd felt sorry for the man who'd swallowed his pride to come here. Even if it was no more than play-acting, he'd done it convincingly.

'I don't know. I believed him.'

Katherine held him close. 'You always believe the best in people. You have a good soul.'

'Does that mean I have your approval, wife?'

'As long as you take no risks, husband.'

'I won't,' he promised. 'Right now I don't even know which way to turn.'

. . .

Christian. With Arthur gone, he was the only card left in the deck, and much good it was likely to do him.

All he had was suspicion and hearsay. He'd known Julian, he could well have been Timothy's bastard son. He'd been one of the last to see Julian alive. He had an edge to his temper. It all weighed against him, but none of it was proof.

Dawn had cut the horizon into a shade of pale blue when John arrived at the Guildhall. Tuesday was the week-day market by the church. A quiet day, not one to tempt Christian into town.

'Dronfield again, Master?' the head bailiff said good-naturedly.

'If you've two big lads who fancy some exercise.'

'I think I can find a pair for you.'

Soon he was on the road, two brawny men at his side, armed with cudgels, knives and swords. This trip was becoming too familiar, he thought. A few folk were headed in the other direction, donkeys laden with early produce, milk, butter churned just that morning.

The valley rose sharply on either side as they passed through Unstone. The wheat was growing tall, but it would need more rain to ripen properly. He chuckled at himself. He was thinking like a farmer, not a carpenter. And he didn't have the faintest idea of how to raise a crop or even when to harvest it.

The village of Dronfield seemed strangely quiet as they passed through. Women had spread their linen over bushes to dry, stark white against the green. But there was no sign of any people, no voices to be heard, almost as if they'd all abandoned the place.

He walked up the hill to the manor house, following the twisting road out of the Bottoms, the tramp of the bailiffs' boots behind him.

The villagers were gathered outside the building, spread across the grass. Christian sat behind a table that had been carried from the house.

The manor court. It explained why everyone was gathered here, to settle disputes and pay small fines for their indiscretions. Christian was the steward here; he had the authority to run it. By his side, a tonsured monk sat and wrote down all that people said.

'We'll wait until he's finished,' John told the bailiffs quietly. But Christian raised his head and saw them.

'The court's ended for this week,' he announced suddenly, then people were complaining and arguing. He dismissed them with a sweeping gesture and strode off around the side of the house. John followed, the bailiffs on his heels.

Christian was standing by the well, drinking water from the dipper. He stood tall as John approached, pushing back his surcote to grab his knife easily. No scrapes or scabs on his hands.

'I told you not to come back here.'

'I have some more questions for you.'

'Do you?' He raised an eyebrow. 'What if I don't choose to answer them?'

'Then the bailiffs will take you back to Chesterfield and the coroner will make you answer.' He shrugged. 'Your choice.'

'Ask your questions,' Christian agreed after a short hesitation. 'But be quick. I don't have time for your accusations.'

'When did you last see Julian?'

'The day he died. I told you.' He kept his face stony and empty. 'He was still alive when I left him. And no, I don't know who could have killed him. What else?'

'Who's your father?'

The question took him by surprise. The mask on his face slipped for a moment. He recovered quickly, but not fast enough. Very briefly the fright showed.

'What do you mean?'

'The rumour is that you're the son of Timothy of Chesterfield.'

Christian's face reddened with anger. He took a step forward and the bailiffs reached for their swords.

'You've been listening to old women,' he scoffed. 'You're saying my father was a cuckold.'

'Was he?'

'I wouldn't ask a man that if I were you. It's a dangerous question.'

'Was he?' John repeated.

'No,' Christian answered firmly.

'How do you know?'

'He told me before he died. A man doesn't lie on his deathbed.'

He doubted that. It was the one time when a man's words might be believed. But that wasn't the same thing. Rumours fluttered on the wind, he knew that. They didn't always have substance. But the look that flickered across the man's face ... that spoke of truth.

'It would give you a reason to kill him.'

The laugh sounded surprisingly genuine. 'If I wanted to do that, wouldn't I have done it years ago?'

It was a fair question.

'Maybe. But I believe it was your friend Julian who committed the murder.'

Christian shook his head. 'Why would he?'

'Maybe acting for you. Claiming your inheritance.'

'What would that be?' He folded his arms, feet planted a little apart. He looked as solid as a church.

'Do you read?'

'What?' It was a question from nowhere, taking him by surprise.

'Can you read?'

'I'm a steward. What do you think?'

John shrugged. 'You tell me.'

'Yes, I can read. Does that satisfy you?'

'Timothy had a psalter. It had been in his family for generations. Very valuable. It would be natural for his son to want it.'

'If he had one.'

'If,' John agreed. The man was never going to admit he was Timothy's son. But his face had given him away briefly. There was nothing more to learn here, but he'd taken away food for thought. 'I'll bid you good day.'

'Don't come back,' Christian said. 'The warning still stands.'

'I'll go where I need.'

'Then you've been warned.' He gave a quick nod then walked away.

'Come on,' John told the bailiffs with a sigh. 'We might as well go home.'

• • •

'Do you think he's Timothy's by-blow?' de Harville asked. He was seated in his hall, feet up on the table, hand stroking his chin.

'Yes. His look gave him away. He knows it.'

'Where does that leave us?'

'I don't know, Master.'

'Monk?'

'If it's true, he has a reason,' Robert said. 'But Christian's right. Why would he wait so long for his revenge? And he'd be a cold man if he killed Julian, his oldest friend.'

The coroner nodded. There seemed to be a new seriousness about him, giving the killings his full attention.

'Revenge can do that,' John said.

'Perhaps.' De Harville sighed. 'What proof do we have?'

'None. The only way would be to find him with the psalter.'

That brought silence. Questioning Christian was one thing. Searching his quarters was another. His lord would object. Did the coroner's writ even run that far?

'What do you think, Carpenter? Is he guilty?'

'Of something,' John answered after a while. 'But I'm not sure what.'

CHAPTER TWENTY-FOUR

Janette pushed her slate under his nose, Eleanor crowding behind her. He could see words scrawled on them and smiled approvingly. They were learning so quickly.

'Martha's teaching us sums, too,' Eleanor said eagerly.

'You're going to know everything,' he said with a grin. Martha smiled at him. He leaned forward and whispered something in her ear. She nodded quickly. 'You girls are doing well,' he told them. 'I need to talk to Walter.'

'He looks better,' Katherine said from the door of the buttery. She was wearing a plain dress and an apron, a piece of linen over her left shoulder. John kissed his wife and went up to the solar.

The boy lay there, one hand behind his head. The bruising looked even worse today. But it would go down, he knew that. Soon enough his face would return to normal and he'd be able to move without pain.

'How do you feel?' He settled on the joint stool by the bed.

'I want to be up.'

'Give it another day. There are plenty who'd love to have this long in bed.' He could sense the boy's restlessness. He was improving. But better not to move too fast. 'Let me tell you what I've found.' Maybe he'd see something that John couldn't. A fresh mind, a new pair of eyes.

Walter listened attentively. Twice he asked for something to be explained. When all the words had been spoken he stayed silent for a while.

'You think it's Christian, don't you, John?'

'Who else could it be?'

'I don't know.' His eyes were open wide, his mouth pursed. 'But if you think it was one person, won't you try to make everything you find fit that? You told me that once.'

It was; he recalled the words all too well. And the lad was right. He seemed to have made up his mind that Christian was guilty. And from what? Rumour and a feeling that it had to be that way.

He'd forgotten Arthur, who'd run rather than answer questions. Who knew what else he'd ignored along the road?

'Thank you,' he said as he stood.

'What for?' Walter asked in surprise.

'You've made me think.'

• • •

The garden was quiet. He found a spot out of the way, on the far side of the kitchen. Settling with a mug of ale, John began to go over everything he knew, all he'd learned from the moment he first saw Nicholas dead in his bed.

He barely noticed the time passing, and when Katherine came to call him to supper he simply shook his head. Had he missed something? By the time evening arrived and the sun was falling behind the horizon he still wasn't sure.

He'd gone over everything, questioning himself each step of the way. Would things be different if he'd asked another question or tried a different path? For the most part he didn't believe it would change anything.

This was a story that seemed to start long before the first killings. Long before. But finding anything solid in the fog of history was almost impossible.

Eventually he felt satisfied that he'd done everything he could. Things were coming to a head, he felt, although he didn't really know why.

'John,' Walter whispered after he climbed to the solar, boots in his hand to make less noise.

'What?' He crouched by the boy's pallet.

'I think I've remembered something.'

'What is it?' he asked urgently.

'Something about the man who hurt me.'

Man, John thought. Just one.

'Go on,' he said softly. 'Tell me what you see.'

'His boots. The toe was coming away from the sole. I could see it when he kicked me.'

It was a sad, chilling memory.

'Do you recall his face? Anything else about him?'

'No, John,' Walter answered, disappointed. 'I'm sorry.'

'It doesn't matter.' He rested a hand on the lad's shoulder. 'What you've given me is a start. You rest now. Maybe tomorrow you can try getting up.'

'Do you think so?'

'Why not? We can see if you're ready. And Dame Martha thinks it would be a good time for you to learn to read and write.'

'Me?' He couldn't see the boy's face in the darkness but he could sense the smile.

'Yes,' he replied. 'You.'

Katherine was already asleep with her back to him. A boot that needed mending. What could he do with that?

• • •

He was waiting outside the shoemaker's shop when the man raised the shutters in the morning.

'Master,' the man said warily. 'Is there something wrong with the boots?'

'Nothing like that.' He saw relief cross the cobbler's face. 'Just a question, that's all.'

'What is it?'

'How many boots have you repaired in the last few days where the toe is coming away from the sole?'

The man laughed. 'Five or six of them a day, Master. It's the most common problem. Only take a few minutes to mend. But your new ones won't need that for years,' he added hastily. 'And I have your old ones ready. That's the problem they had.'

'Is it the same for all the shoemakers?'

'Always. It's been that way since I was an apprentice.'

He'd hoped this might lead somewhere. But it proved to be a path that would lead nowhere. There would be too many names, and people unknown. He shook his head.

'What's wrong, Master?'

'Nothing. I'd just hoped it might lead to something.'

He had nothing to lose by explaining it. The cobbler might have some helpful ideas. The man listened attentively but began to shake his head even before John had finished.

'It's not possible, Master. I've never seen half my customers before, and it's the same for all of us.' He gestured around. 'We spend our days in here. If we have an apprentice we can leave for a little while, but that's all. It's a solitary life, really. Why do you think I'm always happy to talk to my customers?'

'Thank you anyway.'

He'd been so hopeful when he left the house. Finally, it seemed, an idea that might lead somewhere. And now he had nothing, once again.

At the top of the hill he glanced at the church. A few

minutes of prayer and thought wouldn't hurt. Maybe God would grant him some insight.

The stone floor was cold against his knees; he could feel it through his hose. But today his supplications went unanswered and after a few minutes he stood again.

The door leading to the tower stood open. John looked around. There was no one else in the church. Quickly and quietly he climbed the winding stone steps that spiralled up inside the walls. Past the belfry, going higher and higher, all the way to the room at the base of the spire.

The last time he'd been here, everything had been different. It had still been open to the air then. He let his gaze drift upward, inspecting the frame of the spire. It was impressive, a testament to the skill of the carpenters who'd worked on it, and he felt a pang of regret that he hadn't been one of them. This was work that would last for centuries.

It still seemed impossible to believe that the only thing holding it in place was the spire's own weight, but as he looked around he saw that it was true.

The windlass used for bringing up materials still took up much of the floor, a heavy wooden wheel half as tall again as a man. They'd probably decided it wasn't worth the time or effort to dismantle once the building was complete. A low door led out to a small walkway around the base of the spire. He followed it, grateful for the breeze that caught his hair; there hadn't been a wisp of wind down on the ground.

Up here he could see for miles in every direction. Dronfield to the north and many more villages he couldn't even name scattered around the countryside. The fields looked green and lush, the sun was warm on his face. For just a moment he felt contentment.

Back inside, he traced a hand along the beam he'd been

putting in place when his arm was broken. He'd recovered fully, the injury not even a memory now. But it had been the end of his time here. Nobody needed a carpenter who could only use one hand.

He stopped as his hand touched something sitting on top of the beam. Even stretching himself he couldn't see what it was, but he felt around, curious, gasping and tugging and slowly pulling it towards him. His neck strained as he looked up. A small package, carefully wrapped in linen. Taking a breath, he pulled again, catching the object as it fell from the wood.

It was almost square, not too thick. John coughed away the dust that had been raised, heart thumping as he sat on the floor. His hand was shaking as he unwrapped the package.

A book. He could see the edges of the pages and the worn leather binding. Slowly he peeled away the last layer of linen to show the jewels on the front cover and the gilding in the shape of the cross.

His hands were shaking so much that could scarcely hold the book long enough to open it, holding his breath as he turned the pages. Each one was filled with brilliant, sharp colours and design, the words neatly, lovingly written in black ink.

He'd found the missing psalter.

But why was it here in the church tower?

CHAPTER TWENTY-FIVE

It was beautiful, no doubt of that. He wondered how long it had taken to make, every image so crowded, edged in vivid golds and greens. For several minutes he simply stood, trying to take it all in as his eyes moved from page to glorious page.

Finally he to force himself to snap it shut, bind it up in the linen once more and start down the staircase. It was the first book he'd ever touched and certainly the loveliest he'd ever seen. His mind was full of the images, reeling from the beauty and the sheer number of them. He'd seen the stained glass windows in York Minster, the pictures they formed, the vividness of them all. But this … to hold something like that. He'd never have believed it could happen.

In his hand the book felt like a living thing, warm. But it was dangerous, too. Men had died for this.

And he had no answer for why the psalter had ended up there, or who might have hidden it.

His footsteps echoed off the tile floor of the nave. At the far end a figure that had been bending over the font straightened.

'God be with you, Father,' John called.

'And with you, my son.' Father Geoffrey's face looked tight and worried. 'I didn't see you praying.'

'I was up in the tower. I wanted to see what it was like now it's finished.'

The priest's mouth curved into a smile. 'Was it worth the climb?'

'It was.' He held out the package, covered again. 'I found this.'

The priest cocked his head. 'What is it, my son?'

'Timothy's psalter. It was hidden in the tower room.'

The priest blanched. 'Here?' he asked quietly. 'Why would anyone do that?' He reached out a hand to touch it.

'I don't know,' John answered in frustration. 'Not yet, anyway.' For a moment he'd suspected Geoffrey, but he seemed shocked and surprised to see the book here.

'May I?' He took the book and unwrapped it with great reverence, drawing in his breath as he ran his fingertips over the jewels and leather of the binding. As he turned the pages, going slowly from one to the next, his lips moved in prayer and thanks. 'This is wonderful,' he said finally. 'Where was it?'

'On top of a beam. It was just luck that I found it.'

'What are you—' The priest coughed. 'What are you going to do with it?'

'Give it to the coroner for safekeeping. It's evidence, Father. Too many have given up their lives for this.' He reached out a hand to take the book back. Geoffrey was reluctant to pass it over.

'You could leave it here,' he offered. 'I'll hide it. No one will be able to find it.'

'Thank you, Father,' John replied with a smile. 'But I think it will be safer with the coroner.'

After a small hesitation, the priest nodded. 'Of course.'

•   •   •

'How did you find it, Carpenter?' de Harville asked. He was seated at his table, a thin silk surcote draped over the back of his chair. He'd unwrapped the book and was idly leafing from page to page. Brother Robert sat close, staring at the psalter with hungry eyes.

He explained it again. The third time. His throat was dry, but the coroner hadn't offered him any ale from the jug. Far from being contrite, today the man was back to his usual, arrogant self.

'The priest wanted to hold on to it,' he finished.

'I imagine he did,' the coroner said with a chuckle. He slapped the book closed and pushed it towards Brother Robert. The monk crossed himself before opening it. 'But I'll keep it here for now. Do you have any idea who hid it there?'

'No.' He'd questioned Geoffrey. The church was always open. It was God's house, available for prayer and contemplation. If the door to the stairs had been unlocked, anyone could have gone up to the tower.

But, John thought, it would probably need to be someone who already knew what was up there and had an idea where to secrete the psalter. That was the only way, otherwise it would have just been blundering around and hoping.

Still, many had been up there. Not just labourers working on the church, but those who wanted a view of the country-side all around. In the end, it didn't help.

'You don't think the priest did it?'

'No.' The way Geoffrey reacted seemed too honest.

'Is there anything that can help you?' the coroner asked.

John shook his head. It was the only answer he had.

'Now you've seen the book, do you think it's worth all those lives?'

'No,' he answered. 'Words aren't worth anyone's life. Even holy words.'

. . .

Walter was up and dressed, sitting at the table. He was holding himself very still, wincing each time he moved. But it was a start. He was recovering.

From the buttery, Katherine looked at him and gave a small nod of approval. John poured himself a cup of ale and drank thirstily.

'A little better?'

'Yes, John.' He smiled.

'Another few days and you'll be running again. You won't believe what I found today.'

'What is it?'

'The psalter.'

He had to tell it all again as the family crowded around, wanting to hear the tale. Janette and Eleanor wanted to know what a psalter was, and he tried to explain. When he finished, Katherine said, 'I wish you'd brought it here first.'

He looked at her, seeing the wishful, dreaming look on her face.

'Perhaps de Harville will let me show everyone.' He looked pointedly at the girls. 'But if I can, no touching with dirty or sticky fingers.'

He knew he'd have to go over the story at least once more; Martha would want all the details.

Not yet, though. He could still make something of the day. John gathered up his satchel of tools and walked to Beetwell Street. It wasn't a large job, just replacing a broken shutter for a family. He'd have the job done well before evening.

The house was no more than a cottage really, made of well-packed wattle and daub, with a covering of good limewash and a solid timber frame. But it was scrupulously clean, fresh rushes scattered on the floor inside. The goodwife put up her broom and brought him a cup of ale as he began work, measuring with a piece of twine and cutting the boards to size. One of the woman's children, a boy of maybe six, watched intently and silently.

'You want to be a carpenter?' John asked. The boy didn't answer, just nodded his head.

'You'll get nothing out of him,' the woman said cheerfully, tousling her son's hair. 'He's mute. Never said a word in his life.' She looked down at the lad with absolute love, as if speech meant nothing at all. The woman was short and round, with very pink cheeks and plump arms that stretched her old, patched dress.

'Would you like to help?' John asked the boy, seeing his eyes widen in excitement and nervousness.

'His name's Alan,' the woman added. 'He hears perfectly well, just doesn't speak.'

'Well, Alan.' He held out the length of twine. 'Hold this and you can work with me.'

It became a game, the boy doing exactly as he was ordered, moving quickly and easily, understanding everything with hardly an explanation.

It was good for the lad, and for him, too. Having to instruct meant he didn't have time to brood too long over the mystery of the psalter. Sooner or later the man who'd hidden it would find it gone. What would he do then?

He put it to the back of his mind, wrapping his hand around Alan's small one as he sawed, making sure the line was straight and the cut smooth. It took him back to his father doing exactly the same thing with him and a pang of loss rippled through him.

Would he be like this with his own son in just a few years? How would he feel, seeing his boy learn the trade?

By the time they'd sanded the edges of the wood, Alan was grinning, proud of what he'd done. John demonstrated how he was going to put the boards together to make the new shutter and the boy nodded eagerly; he'd already understood how it should be. He was a natural for this, with the vision. Maybe even the touch, if it ever had a chance to develop.

There was nothing the lad could do to help him hang the shutter on the window frame. He was too short for that, but he concentrated, taking in each action as John described what he was doing.

He let Alan help with the cleaning of the tools.

'Do this every day when you work,' he advised. 'That way your tools will last for years.' He drew out a whetstone. 'And make sure you always keep them sharp.'

When the goodwife paid him, reaching into the purse that hung from her girdle, he passed one of the coins to Alan and wrapped his small fist around it.

'You earned this,' he said solemnly as the boy stared in disbelief. Most likely he'd never earned anything before. He turned to the woman. 'If you want, he can work with me around town and learn what to do.'

'You think he has some skill?' she asked warily.

'He might,' John told her and saw the joy on Alan's face. 'There's only one way to find out. If he does, I'll teach him.'

'That's a generous offer, Master. I'll need to talk to my husband first.'

'Of course.'

'If he's willing, we'd be grateful.' She paused for a moment. 'How much do you want for his apprenticeship?'

He smiled. 'Nothing. It's not an apprenticeship. Nothing proper.'

'Then it's a grand gesture.' But she still sounded wary.

'I'll leave it with you.'

'Thank you.' She looked at the new shutter. 'You've done a good job. Both of you.'

• • •

He was in a good mood when he walked into the house on Saltergate, whistling as he walked, a song that had lodged in his head after hearing a minstrel play it at the market. But as soon as he entered he knew something was wrong. Katherine and Walter were sitting at the table, tension on their faces. He could hear the hushed voices of the girls out in the garden.

'What is it?'

'It's Martha.' Katherine turned her head slowly. 'She sent a message an hour ago. She wants you to go there as soon as you can.'

He didn't understand.

'What's happened? Why didn't she come herself if there's a problem?'

'She sent a boy. She told him that it has to be you, only you, that goes. I'm worried, John.'

It wasn't like Dame Martha. She'd always welcome any of them – all of them – in her house at any time.

'Right,' he decided as he put down the old bag of tools and took a breath. 'I'd better see what this is about.'

'Husband,' Katherine called as he left, 'take care, please.'

It was no more than a few hundred yards, just moments as he strode out. But long enough to loosen his dagger in its sheath and for all manner of thoughts to tumble through his mind. Something was wrong, it had to be. He closed his jerkin, making sure it was secure.

He paused outside the house on Knifesmithgate, wondering for a moment whether to knock or simply enter. He placed a hand on the door handle, feeling it turn silently in his grip; he'd always made sure the hinges were well lubricated. Then he was inside and past the screens.

The settle had been dragged away from the wall. She was sitting on it, looking up defiantly at him. A man stood behind her. Something glittered in the hand he held to her neck. He raised his head.

'I've been wondering how long it would take you to arrive.'

CHAPTER TWENTY-SIX

'I wish you God's grace again, Father.'

'And to you, my son.' Father Geoffrey smiled, but it was a dark grin, no warmth behind it. 'Has anyone told you that you're a lucky man?'

'At times.' He let his arms dangle by his side; still easy enough to reach for his blade if the chance arose. He moved his gaze to Martha. She kept her face resolute, sitting completely still and showing nothing. 'But you had me fooled. I never suspected you. What do you want?'

'I'm sure you can guess. Go and fetch the psalter from the coroner and bring it to me. Do that and the goodwife here will live.' He pulled her head back to expose her throat. 'Any kind of trap and I'll kill her.' He shrugged. 'After all, I've got nothing to lose now, have I?'

'And if I refuse?'

'The widow dies.'

Her eyes gave nothing away. No fear, no pain.

'That leaves you with nothing.'

'But you won't let that happen. I know you care about the old woman. I'm not a fool, Carpenter. You'd better go and fetch the book.'

'What do I tell the coroner?'

'That's your business. Come up with whatever lie you wish. Do it wrong and you'll be mourning her.'

'All right,' he agreed. 'But you'll need to give me a few minutes.'

'I've waited all afternoon for you,' the priest told him. 'I can last a little longer.'

He was sweating when he left the house, his hands shaking as he wrenched the door open. Moving along, he scarcely noticed anyone else as his mind raced. What could he say that would make de Harville part with the psalter?

None of this made sense. If Timothy was leaving the book to the church, why had Geoffrey needed to kill for it? And why so many? He'd left a long, bloody trail.

The coroner was sitting with the monk, hunched over his accounts, the glazed window opened to draw in some air. A thin silk coat in bright turquoise with vast belled sleeves had been idly thrown over a bench.

'What do you need, Carpenter? Do you have some news?'

'I do, Master.' He told it all in a few short sentences. When he finished there was just silence. 'What about Timothy's will?' John asked. 'Did he leave the book to the church?'

'It looks like he'd never intended to,' Brother Robert answered eventually. 'The lawyer in Derby had a copy of the will delivered here a few minutes ago. Timothy hadn't altered it in years.'

'Who gets the psalter?' His mouth was dry. He was scared to ask. Or to know the truth.

'Christian in Dronfield,' the monk told him. 'Timothy still didn't openly acknowledge him as his son, but this is as close as he's going to come.'

'I sent a bailiff out to give him the news,' de Harville added.

'I still need the book,' John said urgently. 'Dame Martha's life depends on it.'

'Geoffrey.' The coroner shook his head. 'He always seemed so reasonable. He can't believe he can escape with it, surely?'

'I don't know what he's thinking.' His voice became urgent. 'I need the book now, Master. He's waiting.'

'It's in the chest over there,' de Harville said after a moment's hesitation. 'I'll have bailiffs at the front and back of the house.'

'Just make sure nothing happens to Martha if he takes her with him.'

'You have my word, Carpenter.'

The psalter was still in its linen wrapping. He picked it up, hoisting it in his hand and started to leave.

'John,' Brother Robert said quietly, 'I'll be praying for Martha. We all will.'

. . .

He ran along the street, feet pounding on the ground. The psalter was clutched close to his chest, eyes scanning around for any trouble or obstacles. John turned the corner on to Knifesmithgate, twisted the knob on the door and tried to catch his breath as he entered the house.

Martha and the priest were in the same position, his knife at her neck. She wasn't going to let herself show any of the terror she had to be feeling.

'I'd expected you to be quicker,' Geoffrey said. There was no emotion in his voice. It was just words, empty.

'I had to persuade the coroner.'

'Then it's as well you have a silver tongue. Put it on the table.' The priest nodded in the direction. 'And your knife with it,' he added.

John did exactly as Geoffrey ordered, with slow, deliberate movements, keeping his hands in sight.

'Very good,' the man told him. He darted over, pulling the book towards him, on to Martha's lap. John's knife tumbled noisily to the floor. 'Open it,' Geoffrey told Martha.

She tried to hide the tremor in her hands as her fingers moved, but it was obvious. Yet as she saw the cover of the psalter, its jewels twinkling in the light, she couldn't stop a gasp of wonder. Martha ran her hand over the leather and stones, then opened the book.

He could see the longing and satisfaction in the priest's eyes as he gazed at the beautiful illustrations.

'Was it worthwhile?' John asked.

'Was what worthwhile?' Geoffrey's head jerked up, annoyed by the distraction.

'Killing all those people for this.'

'All?' He smiled. 'I killed two, that's all.'

'Does that excuse it? You persuaded others to kill for you. That makes you responsible for the other deaths.'

'Do you know what Timothy used to do? Whenever I went to visit him he showed me the psalter. And each time he'd taunt me and say he wasn't leaving it to the church.'

'Did he ever tell you who'd get it?'

'No.' The word came out curt and abrupt. 'He wouldn't say.'

'Tell me, Father. How did you persuade Edward the Butcher and Gilbert to kill Timothy and his servant?'

'I didn't have to.' Geoffrey smiled. 'Julian did that. I'd promised him, and anyone who helped him, absolution for it. I said he was helping the church by returning something that rightly belonged with God. He snatched at absolution for his sins, and he arranged everything. I told Timothy the men were coming to do some work he needed out of Christian charity.'

What would God think of that, he wondered? Precious little charity in a knife blade.

'And then you killed Julian.'

The priest shrugged. 'He'd become greedy. He thought a pardon for his sins wasn't payment enough. He wanted silver, too.'

'You beat Walter, too. My brother-in-law.'

'The boy was getting too close. He saw something he shouldn't. I'm surprised he survived.'

'Be grateful he did or I'd have killed you myself. Was it you who tried to set the fire in my kitchen, too?'

Geoffrey shrugged again. 'In the panic it might have been easy enough to go in and smother the lad. Just to be certain.'

'And when I was attacked out along the riverbank. A man on his own who wanted to kill me.'

'No,' the priest told him. 'Maybe you have more enemies than you know.'

'And the bishop's man? What about him?' He hadn't been able to understand how all these things fitted into the puzzle; there seemed to be no place for them.

'It muddied the waters,' Father Geoffrey told him. 'I knew who they were and why they were here.'

'And why was that?' It was something he wanted to know. Needed to know.

'There had been … complaints.'

'About you?'

'About my conduct with some of the women in the parish. The bishop sent them to investigate.'

'Were the complaints true?'

The priest shook his head. 'I've kept my vows. I'm celibate. But there's always tittle-tattle. Gossip has wings.'

'Those vows you took. Do they include killing, and coveting something that's not yours?'

The priest raised his head. His eyes were shining. 'Sometimes a thing is worth the world. You've seen it. Isn't it beautiful?'

'Very,' John agreed. 'But it's still just a book, a thing. How can it be worth *one* life, never mind so many?'

'Then you don't understand.' He reached down and took the book away from Martha, clasping it tight in one hand. The other still held the knife to her throat.

'What are you going to do now? You can't get far. As soon as you let her go the bailiffs will be on you.'

'We'll see. Change places with the woman.'

He did as he was ordered. Better him at risk that Martha. As they passed he took her hand for a moment and squeezed it lightly.

'Go outside,' Father Geoffrey told Martha. 'Tell them to clear a path from here to the church. If anyone tries to stop me, I'll kill your friend. Come back when it's ready.'

She fled. As the door opened he could hear a host of voices. Then it closed again and it was just the two of them.

'Going to claim sanctuary?' John asked.

'It's my right.'

'You can't stay there forever.'

'Forty days and nights. A great deal can happen. There's time to talk and agree. Plenty of chance for things to be forgotten.'

'The coroner won't forget murder. You can believe me on that.'

'We'll see, won't we? Right, they've had time to move people. Stand up.'

The priest stayed close enough for his dagger to touch the skin without piercing it.

'Don't take any fancy ideas,' he warned, his voice hissing in John's ear. 'Before I took to the priesthood, I was a soldier. I know how to use a knife.'

'You could give up. Claim benefit of clergy and they can't hang you.'

He should have felt terrified, but he didn't. The priest wasn't about to kill the man who could get him to the church. He was safe enough. And once Geoffrey reached sacred ground he'd let him go.

'Then spend my life in a monastery?'

'They have books there,' John said. He tried to think. What else could a man who'd claimed sanctuary do? Leave the country by the nearest port. 'Even if they let you abjure the realm, they'll never let you take the psalter.'

'Then I'll destroy it. Burn it.'

Would he, John wondered? Could he put the pages of something he loved so much, something he'd killed to own, in the flames? Probably not. But that was another argument, one that would never concern him, God willing.

One minute became five, then ten, time dragging out very slowly.

'Where is that woman?' Geoffrey said. 'Maybe she's left you to die with me.'

'No.' Martha wouldn't do that, he knew that. All he could do was wait. The time here was affecting Geoffrey more than him. The priest was nervous, scared. Twice the point of the knife had dug deep enough to pierce his neck, leaving a small trickle of blood.

The man's hands were sweating. He could see the discolouration on the linen as he clutched the book against his chest.

Finally the door swung open and Dame Martha appeared. She was breathless and red-faced, fanning herself with one gnarled hand. Her eyes looked at John and he could see the question in them. He gave a small nod: he was fine, no real damage done.

'They've cleared a path for you,' she said.

John heard the priest shift behind him.

'Come on then, Carpenter. It's time we took a short walk.'

The knife pricked the back of his neck as he walked across the tiled floor, his boots ringing out with each step. He paused at the doorway. The light seemed too bright. Unreal. He had to blink a few times before his eyes could take it all in.

People had crowded around. Word must have spread like a blaze. It looked as though half of Chesterfield had gathered to watch. The bailiffs held them back, forming a corridor. Men and women were shouting, their faces contorted by anger and curiosity, creating a sea of noise.

John took a breath and stepped out into the dust of the road. He could feel the priest behind him, the knife touching his skin lightly. The man was close enough for John to smell his sour breath.

As he walked, John gazed around. It wasn't far to the church. Just a few hundred yards. But it looked like miles. The steeple seemed to rise like a mountain in the distance. The coroner was standing by the porch, Brother Robert just behind him.

He could see the Holywell Cross, old worn stone catching the sunlight. Katherine stood there, holding on to the girls. Her eyes were begging. He smiled and winked at her. All would be well. This would be done soon.

No Walter, though. That was a shock. Maybe the lad was still too weak. It didn't matter. Everyone would be talking about this for days.

He kept walking, fixing his eyes on the church. Soon. Just a few seconds and he'd be there. John felt every step. Each one seemed like a great effort, as if his legs weighed more than he could lift. He had to force each one up then down again.

A bead of sweat trickled down his back, running along his spine, chilling him on a hot day. Geoffrey had to be scared. The people here would tear him apart if they had the chance.

Suddenly John halted in mid-stride. Just ten yards ahead Walter had appeared. He'd slipped past the bailiffs. Now he stood there, the bruises and cuts covering his flesh. The crowd shrank back from him. Maybe it was fear, maybe horror; there was nothing handsome about him in this state.

But the lad didn't move.

'Get out of the way, boy,' Geoffrey called. 'If you want your brother-in-law to live.' The knife jabbed against his neck.

It was now or never at all. Walter had all of Geoffrey's attention. John took a breath and let himself fall to the ground. As he tumbled, his hand reached into his boot and grabbed the knife he kept there. It was a lesson he'd learned years before. A weapon out of sight was often never found.

He pulled the blade out. As his shoulder hit the earth he reached around and sliced through the tendon at Geoffrey's heel, then rolled away before the man could collapse on top of him.

He heard a loud cry of pain, and the priest was down in the dirt. He'd dropped his knife and clutched at the wound with one hand. But the other kept a tight grip on the psalter.

It was over. Done. John kicked the man's weapon away. Geoffrey was writhing, screaming and bleeding. Safety was less than fifty yards away but he'd never reach it now. He'd probably never manage to walk properly again.

John wiped the knife on his jerkin, suddenly aware of the voices all around, as if he'd just emerged from a dream. But before he could say anything or do anything, someone pushed him roughly out of the way.

He stumbled, finding his balance after a moment, then turning, knife ready to strike again. Christian was kneeling heavily on the priest's chest. He had his thick hands around the man's neck, banging his head down and down against a rock.

A pair of stout bailiffs took hold and dragged Christian away, cursing and yelling as they pulled him off. The priest was dazed, gasping for breath. But he'd live.

John glanced and saw Walter still standing there, in the exact same position. He turned his head and picked out Katherine by the Cross. She was watching him, one hand clasped over her mouth in shock.

He left Geoffrey there and walked up to the boy, placing his hands on Walter's shoulders.

'Thank you.'

The lad was looking beyond him, at the figure still on the ground. 'It was him. As soon as I saw him I remembered.'

'I know,' John said quietly. 'He admitted it.'

'What's going to happen to him?'

It was the coroner who answered. He came, Brother Robert at his shoulder. Someone had handed him the psalter, still in its grubby linen wrapping.

'We'll keep him a while, then he'll go down to Derby,' de Harville said bitterly. 'When he's tried he'll plead benefit of clergy so we won't be able to hang him.'

'What's that?' Walter asked.

'All he has to do is read a verse from the Bible. Psalm fifty.' He kept his gaze firmly on the priest. Two of the bailiffs were lifting him to his feet. 'He'll just end up with a lifetime of penance.' He raised his voice. 'Take him away. Put him in the jail for now.'

Geoffrey hobbled away, supported by his guards, his useless leg raised off the ground.

'He'll always need a crutch,' John said. It didn't seem like much of a punishment.

'Good.' The coroner's voice was hard. 'He deserves to hang, if there was any real justice. You did well there, Carpenter. You took him by surprise.'

'If Walter hadn't been standing there I wouldn't have had the courage to stop.' He looked at the lad and smiled.

De Harville raised a questioning eyebrow. If the man didn't want to believe, so be it. But it was true.

'Do you always carry an extra knife?' he asked.

'I've done it for years. Geoffrey said he'd been a soldier. Unless he was lying, he should have thought about a second weapon.' He shook his head. 'Too late now.'

Two bailiffs brought Christian. He'd been stripped of his sword and dagger, but he was still struggling in their grasp. The coroner nodded to them to release him. They obeyed, still standing ready, untrusting.

'I didn't think my men had arrived soon enough for you to be here so quickly.'

'Your men?' Christian asked. 'I never saw them. I've been here since early morning. I had business to attend to.' Christian's eyes were blazing. 'Ask Adam the wool merchant if you don't believe me. I rode in this morning. I was about to leave when I heard the commotion. I saw the priest with that.' He nodded at the package. 'I wouldn't mourn if he killed the carpenter, but people were saying he'd murdered Julian. I couldn't let that lie. Not my friend.'

Rumour, John thought. It flew on the breeze here.

'What about the book?' de Harville asked. He held it up.

'What about it?' Christian snorted.

'Do you know who it belongs to?'

'No.'

'It's yours. Timothy left it to you in his will.'

'What?' he asked in disbelief. 'Why?'

'Because you're his son,' Brother Robert said quietly. 'It's his way of acknowledging you.'

The silence lasted a long time. Finally the coroner held out the book in its linen wrapping.

'This is yours.'

He didn't reach for it at first. Christian simply stood, staring at the psalter. Finally he extended a hand and took it, not even removing the covering.

'It's beautiful,' the monk told him. 'Keep it well.'

'I don't want it. I'll give it to the church in Dronfield.'

'Look at it first,' Robert counselled. 'Take your time before you decide.'

'I don't need time,' Christian answered. 'Timothy wouldn't call me his son while he was alive. Now he's dead I don't want his apology.' He nodded his head, said, 'Good day, Masters, may God go with you,' and walked away.

The coroner sighed. 'At least the priest there will gain something from it all.'

So many deaths, all for a book. God's words, every one of them tainted with blood now.

'Come and see me in the morning,' de Harville ordered, then left.

John turned. Katherine and the girls had gone. He put his arm around Walter's shoulders.

'There's someone we need to see.'

CHAPTER TWENTY-SEVEN

Brother Robert walked with them. The crowd had vanished, the road dusty under their feet. On Knifesmithgate John didn't pause to knock at the door, just entered.

Dame Martha had her head in her hands, sitting with her elbows on the table. Her body shuddered with the silent tears that were flowing. Katherine was next to her, comforting the older woman with an arm tight around her shoulders. Even the girls were sitting quietly.

John looked at his wife. She smiled briefly then whispered something in Martha's ear. The woman raised her gaze. Her wimple was askew, and the red eyes from crying made her look old and vulnerable.

'I'm sorry, John.' The words croaked out of her. 'Can you forgive me?'

'What for?' He squatted beside her and took hold of her hands. The joints were knotted, the skin covered with the brown spots of age. 'You did nothing wrong.'

'I almost got you killed.'

'He was never going to do that, Mistress.' He smiled at her. 'All he wanted was a safe passage to the church. I don't know what was on his mind, but it wasn't death. Not this time.'

'Is that the truth?' she asked him.

'Before God,' he replied solemnly.

She seemed to spy the monk for the first time.

'Is he right, Robert?'

'Yes.' The pair of them gazed at each other and all the years seemed to fall away from their faces. They were young again, the boy and girl who used to play together. Before the Church called him and marriage claimed her. Back when there was innocence in the world.

She nodded eventually.

'I'm sorry you were caught in this,' John said. 'I never expected that.'

'He couldn't hurt me.' There was iron in her voice. 'I'm old. I've had my life. Your time is just starting.'

'And yours isn't over yet.' He leaned close and kissed her lightly on the cheek.

'Tomorrow I'll get the girls back to their lessons.' Martha turned to look at Walter. 'And you, too. It's time you learned to read and write.'

• • •

By the time they left, Martha and Robert were sharing a jug of good wine, memories making them both laugh. Good medicine, he thought.

'Why do they have benefit of clergy, John?' Walter asked as they walked.

'I don't know. Maybe because they're men of God.'

'But he broke the commandments.'

'I know.' He paused. 'I didn't say they were all good men. But priests have power. These days maybe that's the same as having justice.' He shook his head. It was a country of two laws, it had been since long before he was born.

The girls were in bed, rushed whispers and stifled giggles coming from the solar. Kit had settled between them, already purring in his rest. Walter was asleep on his pallet. He was recovering, but not fully mended yet; the day had taken its toll on him. The slates were stacked on the table, one each for Janette and Eleanor, a third for Walter.

Katherine was sewing in the candlelight, delicate, tiny stitches on a piece of needlework. They'd talked over supper. Since then she'd been quiet, caught up in her thoughts.

He finished the dregs of ale and pushed his mug away.

'I was never in danger from Father Geoffrey,' he told her again.

'He had a knife to your neck, John,' she reminded him. 'He'd killed before.'

'He needed me. Without me he'd have never reached the church.' He stretched across and placed a hand on her belly, on the child inside. 'I wasn't taking a risk. I swear it.'

'How was I to know that? You've blundered your way through this as if we don't mean anything to you.'

'You know you mean more than anything. More than the world.'

'Do we?' She stared at him. 'Do I? Then please, show it in future. Prove it.'

'I will,' he promised.

The silence lasted a few long seconds, then she opened her mouth again. 'What would you think about asking Martha to come and live here?'

'What?' The question took him by surprise. 'Why?'

'She's on her own in that house. She doesn't need it all. And she spends half her time with us already.'

All of that was true. But …

'Where?'

'There's that good room by the buttery. Plenty of space for a bed and chests for her gowns.' She smiled. 'Janette and Eleanor would love it. And she's growing more frail. You've seen that.'

'Yes.' It was all true. But Martha was a woman who guarded her independence. She might not want to give it up.

'I'll talk to her,' Katherine said. 'Would you be happy with it, husband?' There was a gleam in her eye. She'd already made up her mind.

'You know I would.'

'Then I'll see her in the morning.'

• • •

The wet nurse sat quietly on the joint stool, tucked away in the corner, almost out of sight. De Harville bounced his son gently on his lap, the baby laughing and making joyful sounds.

'You did well yesterday, Carpenter.'

'Thank you, Master.'

'That was a clever move. Dangerous. Brave, too.'

He shrugged. He'd felt safe enough with the priest. He just didn't want him to escape the law.

'Not really.'

The coroner turned to stare at him. 'What can I do to repay you?'

It was a straightforward question, and he had a simple answer.

'Don't ask me to do this again. I have my trade and this isn't it.'

De Harville shook his head. 'No,' he replied. 'Ask me something I can grant.'

ABOUT THE AUTHOR

CHRIS NICKSON is the author of the Richard
Nottingham and Tom Harper series (Severn House),
as well as the Dan Markham mystery series, set in
1950s' Leeds (The Mystery Press). He lives in Leeds.

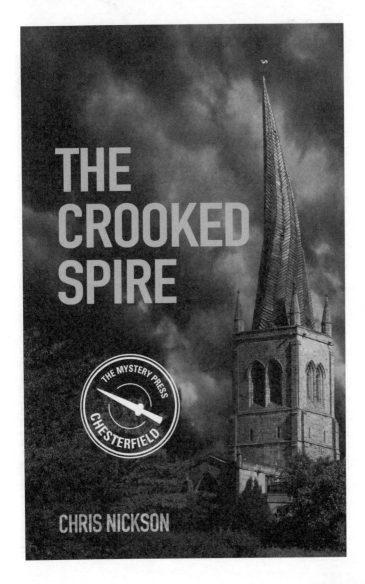

Also by Chris Nickson

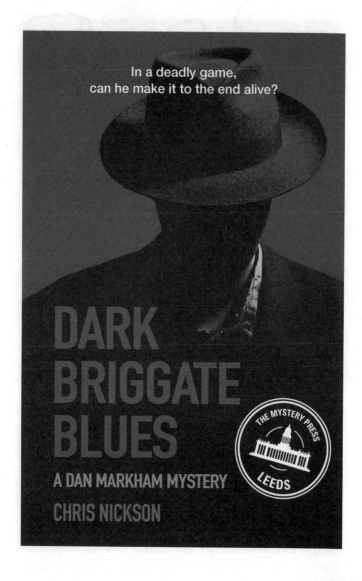

In a deadly game,
can he make it to the end alive?

DARK
BRIGGATE
BLUES

A DAN MARKHAM MYSTERY

CHRIS NICKSON

THE MYSTERY PRESS
LEEDS

Also by Chris Nickson

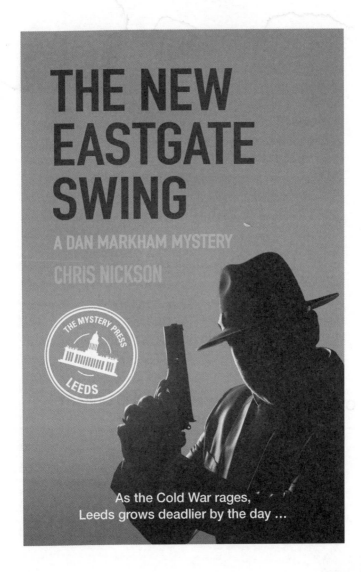

THE NEW
EASTGATE
SWING

A DAN MARKHAM MYSTERY

CHRIS NICKSON

THE MYSTERY PRESS
LEEDS

As the Cold War rages,
Leeds grows deadlier by the day ...

Find this title and more at
www.thehistorypress.co.uk

The
Mystery
Press